Last Lockdown

D. RAZOR BABB

Published by:

LWL Enterprises, Inc.
4475 Trinity Mills Road
PO Box 702862
Dallas, TX 75370

ISBN: 1-945484-00-4
ISBN-13: 978-1-945484-00-1

DEDICATION

This book is dedicated to all the locked down. May we all discover and attain our ultimate freedom, whether it be here or hereafter.

ACKNOWLEDGMENTS

I want to thank everyone who has contributed to bringing <u>Last Lockdown</u> to fruition, especially Leah Ward-Lee of LWL Publishing for efforts above and beyond; and V.W. Smith, a talented writer, poet, scholar and historian, who served as inspiration for Professor J. Bruno and contributed greatly to the early chapters. Although exigent circumstances prevented us from finishing the journey together, his presence, knowledge, humor and spirit are apparent throughout the story. I consider him one of the great literary talents of our time.

D. Razor Babb

Cover art by Tom Baus

CHILLIAST'S VISION: THE TIME OF THE BEAST

The prophets foretold it for ages.
   Their word went abroad and aloft;
It remained on the lips of the sages,
   Despite how the <u>clever</u> men scoffed.
Now the last golden age is ending.
   A sunset of blood palls the light ….
I see the Red Claw descending
   And the start of a thousand-year night.

How futile the search for the Grail!
   Mine, the Fisher King's wounds go unhealed.
The State shows contempt and betrayal;
   The perfidious wife is revealed;
And the ruin of the house is impending
   From her avarice, malice, and spite.…
I see the Red Claw descending
   And the start of a thousand-year night.

Injustice, intolerance, violence
   Take forms not allowed years ago.
And where protest was raised, now there's silence
   Is the court process merely for show?
Will the iron boot, unyielding, unbending,
   Now trample on each human right?
I see the Red Claw descending
   And the start of a thousand-year night.

I hope and I pray for redemption,
   Though I'm still towards the precipice hurled.
And why expect any exemption?
     As my fate, goes the fate of the World!
My soul remains pleading, attending
     The Lord of all goodness and light - -
But my eyes seen the Red Claw descending
   And the start of a thousand-year night ….

                       – V.W. Smith

D. Razor Babb

Contents

PREFACE

This story is narrated in alternate chapters by Frankie V. and Professor Jordan Bruno. Frankie V. is a typical, yet, thoughtful convict with a very distinct set of personal issues. The professor is an eminent scholar, and was a Stanford University Professor … until convicted of a capital crime. The characters find themselves in rather difficult circumstances, in unique and unusual times. The story is set in the not so distant (or improbable) future.

As the sun begins to set on the tranquil waters of the Pacific Ocean, Frankie finds himself stranded along Highway 101 in Northern California ….

PROLOGUE

(Frankie V.)

The bleeding had let up a bit, but the arrow was still embedded in my gut. I knew I'd never be able to withstand the pain required to extract it. I read the look on the girl's face as she examined the wound. I'd seen that look before – I knew what it meant. Six months ago I didn't even know these people; now, Valerie and the Professor were closer to me than anyone in my own family had ever been. There was much that needed to be said and not much time left to say it.

"Valerie, there's something I need to tell you … something you need to know."

Her face clouded over and her eyes flashed lightning. She couldn't speak, but her expression said everything. She didn't want to hear it.

"Val, I …." She turned away, shaking her head violently, refusing to listen and not letting me see her face. The sky was turning dark and it began to get cooler, almost cold. I wrapped my jacket around her shoulders and held her. I could feel her shiver in my arms. Whether it was from the biting wind or fear, I wasn't sure.

Finally, the professor appeared on the horizon. He

was limping badly and exhausted from the trek. His face was ash-gray and the look in his eyes foretold that the news wasn't good. I had to ask anyway.

"Well, Professor, what happened? What did you find?"

Several seconds elapsed before he spoke. The words were a whisper, "It's gone. It's all gone."

"What? What do you mean, it's gone?"

I tried to read the expression on his face. What was it I saw there? Fear? Distress? Concern? No, something worse … hopelessness.

"The city, the whole damn city. San Francisco is gone!"

The earth was spinning beneath me. I didn't want to believe what he was telling me, but I knew the professor had no reason to lie. Of course, it had to be true.

What had begun as a hellish nightmare six months ago, had deteriorated into an all-out catastrophe. It appeared that our arduous journey toward, at least some semblance of understanding, had ended abruptly, leaving us all in limbo. Where were we to go? What was left to be done? And how long might we survive? Worst of all … should the professor and I fail to endure our injuries, what would happen to the girl? Was it fair to her to allow her to continue on alone? And, did I have the courage to do what I knew needed to be done? I felt for the familiar weight of the revolver in my waistband … only one bullet left. I'd been saving it for myself, but, now ….

As I stared up at the quickly darkening sky, I thought of the day this horrific ordeal began ….

*

It began as all days begin – when you're in prison. A flashlight beam in your eyes, signaling a new day as the guard makes his early morning rounds. Coffee, water on the face, exercise, wait for chow release. It was late that day, I recall being mildly annoyed at the inconvenience. We got locked down shortly after breakfast, no big deal, it happens all the time. When the electricity went out – and stayed out – that was unusual.

What was particularly strange was, only a skeleton crew of guards was at work. Nobody was let out for meds or showers or anything. In the evening they came around and tossed some sack lunches through the tray slots of the cell doors. From the look on their faces and the strained demeanor of the guards, we knew something wasn't right – but no one was answering questions. Guys with batteries tried to get news on the radio, but no signal was transmitting. Cell-to-cell chatter was constant, but all we had to go on was speculation and rumor.

The next day, nobody showed up for work and during the night the water shut off. By day three we began trying to force the doors open and chip away at the walls. By day six or so, we realized no help was coming and if we were going to get out, it was up to us.

I pried off the rubber tip of a crutch I had in the cell and began working on the wall near the window. It was slow going. The Plexiglas is about five inches wide and four feet tall. It opens to a fenced-in area between buildings. I could see the guys in other buildings working as well. My hands and arms gave out before any real progress was made. My tools weren't up to the task. By rigging the TV in a sling and hanging it from the upper bunk, I was able to manage some leverage and banged away at the wall desperately. After a couple of hours the TV was in pieces and my hands were covered in blisters and cuts. The wall was unfazed.

A couple of the stronger guys had escaped their cells into the day room. They broke into the control tower and found a hand crank used to manually open cell doors. Unfortunately, I wasn't a homeboy and didn't qualify for rescue. I wasn't an enemy either – therefore, I avoided the carnage as they extracted a few chosen victims. Rotting corpses strewn about the day room were just the motivation I needed to redirect my efforts back to the wall.

The sky had been unusually overcast the entire time, and as I worked, I couldn't help but wonder what could have happened that made them abandon ten thousand prisoners. There were only a handful of reasons I could think of, but then again, I didn't have the time or energy to think clearly about much of anything. After a few more days, supplies were dangerously low, and my whole world, my entire existence, came down to one simple equation: if I could get through that wall before I starved to death or died of thirst ... I <u>might</u> survive.

*   *

CHAPTER 1: THE END OF THE WORLD

(The Professor, Cell 121)

We knew things were bad, but we didn't know how bad. When the electricity went off, we figured it wouldn't be for long. Prison is a separate reality from the outside. We're largely detached from what goes on out there. So, at first we thought that the problems, whatever they were, would not affect us, or not much, anyhow. Boy, were we wrong!

They called us late to breakfast on Monday – never a good sign. Nobody was surprised when they announced that there would be no program that day. Pissed off, yeah, but not surprised. We knew the drill. Lucky for me, yard wasn't one of the carrots in this mule's day. Likewise for my cellie.

Glen was a real son of a bitch, but at least we could live together. He was a bundle of paradoxes: a grade-school dropout, yet he had read and appreciated Shakespeare; mean as a snake one day, unbelievably kind and generous the next. When I was first put into this cell, he treated me as though he regarded me as a major imposition. But that winter (my first in prison), when he saw me shivering, he traded a cup of his best cell-made whiskey to get me a pair of thermals. Try as he might to seem a complete asshole, he was the one who came through to help others in tough times. Glen was the one who fixed your hotpot, radio, or TV if it could be fixed. He charged for his work, but he stood by his workmanship.

They cell-fed us bag lunches for dinner, which was highly irregular. The guards weren't saying much or answering questions. From the beginning we had wondered what was going on, but after a while Glen and I amused ourselves by playing dominoes and joking around – that first day. By nightfall we were beginning to worry. We went to sleep early, hoping everything would be better, or at least normal, when we woke up. No such luck.

As far as we could tell, there were only the minimum number of guards manning Second Watch (the main shift) the first day, and nobody showed up the next day. No guards, medical staff, or free staff. Things were getting too weird.

Glen had a pretty good radio, the best available – a Sony boom box. Try as we might, we couldn't get any signal, though. From scrap pieces of several defunct radios he'd been working on, and strands of wire from various cords of other appliances, he assembled a homemade super-antenna and somehow rigged the radio to pick up citizens' band transmissions. Even then, it wasn't much more than static. For one brief instant we zeroed in on a distorted communication that sounded like some truckers talking. What we heard was incredible and unimaginably grim: Stores were being looted, the highways hopelessly jammed with traffic; hospitals overwhelmed. Something catastrophic was happening. A twinge of alarm crept up my spine and coursed through my veins. Even then, I refused to consider what was creeping into the back of my mind … the worst case scenario ….

The radio soon gave out, the batteries dying quickly from the strain of Glen's contraption. Left in silence, all of Glen's characteristic bravado was gone now, and even my best efforts to find some philosophical and scientific explanation that was both rational and optimistic failed dismally. When the sink tap yielded no hot water, I had the disturbing thought that even the cold water might be cut off before long. Right away Glen and I set about filling up every empty container in the cell with fresh water. Also I made a check of our food supplies.

I had taken a full canteen draw the previous week, and I had recently received a quarterly package from my brother. The best stuff had already been eaten up, but we still had, easily, two or three weeks' worth of supplies, maybe a month's worth – if we rationed carefully. I foresaw greater problems with the water … which was prophetic, during the night it shut off.

Glen always spoke of himself as a "convict", never as an inmate. He had been in prison for over twenty years, I for less than two. He might have been clueless about grammar and abstract ideas, but he was a veteran of institutional life, and I rarely questioned his judgment on practical manners. He said that we should use the 16 ounce coffee jars for solid waste, the sink drain for urinating, the stored water in the other containers for drinking, and the reservoir of (still) clean water in the toilet bowl for washing.

Glen had far too many prejudices and ill-formed ideas and opinions. But he was a genius at figuring out mechanical problems. He understood how things worked, and – more importantly – he knew how to get most things working again when they broke down. Assessing our situation, he told me that he believed he could get the cell door open, but it would take a few days. The problem was – we didn't have a few days. Nature had dealt us both a bad hand in that: Glenn was diabetic, and a severe childhood illness had left me epileptic. Both his condition and mine were controllable with daily medication. But, in prison, medications are rationed in daily allotments, and we weren't going to be getting any more of those where we were now.

So, we had no insulin and no Dilantin, and no medical staff coming in to distribute them. Even if we managed to escape from this prison, Nature had sentenced us to a prison of her own making – for life, however long or short that happened to be.

*

Cold coffee … food from pouches … the last of the bread from sack lunches …. The belly was grateful, but the mind recoiled. By day we sweltered, by night we shivered. Emergency lighting leered at us through the window from the yard, while the cells languished without electricity, water, or ventilation. It all seemed choreographed to mock our misery.

The morning of day four, or eight, or twenty came …. Who knows? Time becomes irrelevant without hope. I couldn't wake Glen up. I called his name, shook him – nothing worked. Even through the horrible funkiness permeating our cell, I could detect a strange pungent-cloying odor on his breath. Glen had gone into acute acidosis. By noon he was dead.

I threw myself into working frantically at the cell door. I felt any other route would be futile. A few years ago this very cell had housed a prisoner known as Crazy Ike. He had managed to chip away several inches of concrete from the wall to the outside. If the rebar hadn't been there, he might have made it out of here.

I don't know how some of the other inmates got out of their cells. Glen had claimed that he knew the "secret". Years ago he had even written letters to the administration in hopes of cutting a deal that would set him free, shorten his sentence, or at least get him some cushy housing in return for such "vital" information. No one took him seriously. Obviously, the "flaw" in the door's design was not nearly as significant as Glen had thought.

It wasn't long until I gave up on the door. I stared out the window wondering what the hell was going on out there. Had they finally done it? Had the powers that be finally pushed it all to the limit? Was this, indeed, the end of the world? A lethargy of despair as well as fatigue overwhelmed me. With my waning strength, I wrapped Glen in his sheets and blanket, then lowered him to the floor. After moving my mattress and bedding to the upper bunk, I put Glenn and his bedding on the lower one. With the last of my energy I climbed up and lay down on the top bunk. I felt this strange, dissociative state that foreshadows the approach of the seizure creep over me, and I hoped that, when it came, the resulting fall and blow to the head would end this nightmare.

Hope, fear, regret – all fell away with one final thought: "La commedia e finite! It is over. God will understand."

*   *

CHAPTER 2: CHICO'S ESCAPE

(Frankie V., Cell 142)

Whatever it was that made the guards and all other prison personnel quit coming to work and leave the entire incarcerated population of California State Prison, Corcoran, to fend for themselves, must have been cataclysmic. I was worn out from working on the wall, and dreaming and waking had become a single reality. The only sustenance left was some freeze-dried coffee and dry milk that I had been eating in heaping mouthfuls for the past week, washing the gritty mix down with the few remaining sodas. My teeth were rotting, I was parched and weak, and hallucinations were my only companions.

It had become eerily quiet the past few days. The guys who had managed to get out of their cells were long gone: it was obvious no help was coming, and if you didn't have food in your cell, well … like I said, it was quiet for the most part. I'd lost track of time and all but given up on the wall. The calendar is irrelevant when you're barely clinging to life, or resolved not to. Once you make peace with it, death's not so bad; it's got to be better than what I was going through.

I drifted off into that last blissful dream and welcomed the sweet relief of nothingness. What the hell was I so stubbornly clinging to anyway? Was life so precious that grim determination outweighed the inevitable reaping? Maybe I was getting what I deserved; I hadn't exactly been a model citizen, thus the prison term. Besides, everything comes to an end sometime; it had been a good run, plenty to be thankful for. Enough wine, women, and song for several lifetimes, and the last ones spent in a cage had been a time for reflection and remorse and working on spirit and retribution if it could be had. Now, simply allow the light to fade to black and let's get it over with ... just let go.

In the dream they came for my soul on wings. Softly floating down from the sky on a gentle breeze with rustling, downy silk feathers. As they neared, I sensed the angels were, in fact, menacing and hideous. They looked like ... they were BUZZARDS! Come to claim their reward and pay me mine. Apparently, my retribution was as yet unpaid. They greedily pecked at my decaying flesh, and I was still conscious to hear the clicking of beaks on skull bone. They fought over their prized dessert of eyeballs, and all I could see was alternating shadows and light amid the flurry of carnivores. The tapping was insistent and I was annoyed and perplexed as to why I shouldn't lose awareness altogether. Peck, peck, peck, tap, tap, tap ... for God's sake! End it!

My head was uncomfortably pressed up against the window and somewhere between dream and dreary reality, I forced my eyelids open. I was only mildly shocked that consciousness was just as terrifying as the nightmares. Two large, protruding, bloodshot eyeballs peered back at me from the other side of the glass. The devil come to claim me! A moment's lapse. Confusion. Contemplation. Recognition! The eyes belonged to Chico! Chico Quintanilla, my upstairs neighbor! Wait ... Chico's the devil? No, that couldn't be.

The devil spoke, "Frankie! You alive in there, buddy?" I could barely hear him through the glass. The fog lifted from my head ….

"Chico? Is that you?"

"Hey! You <u>are</u> alive! You got any food in there?"

I scrambled to present my meager bounty, a half jar of Folgers.

"Hold on, buddy, I'll get you out of there!" Chico began hammering at the window with a four foot length of steel bar, I recognized it as the beam from the cell desk. He apparently had chipped his way out of his second floor cell, and I, apparently, was not dead after all …yet.

Chico worked determinedly on the window and the wall surrounding the glass. He appeared to have lost a lot of weight and he had dark circles under his eyes. His arms were covered with scrapes and wounds. I could do nothing but lay back and wait, watching anxiously as he made rapid progress on the wall. I thought back on our conversations ….

I met Chico about two years ago; he was a religious person now and had put all the gang stuff and violence behind him. I thanked God that he saw fit to come to my rescue. It's strange how things work out.

Chico's migration to California had been a memorable and harrowing experience. He had been just a teenager, some thirty years ago, when he found himself, literally, on the wrong side of the tracks. A group of rival gang members chased him through the rail yards of South Chicago. Just being from a different neighborhood was enough to warrant a death sentence, and he knew if he didn't get away, he was through. They'd chased him for about twenty blocks and when he hit the train yard, he was badly out of breath. Chicago's a major freight train mecca, and rows upon rows of tracks built atop gravel beds are a familiar sight in and around the city and suburbs.

As he made his way over rails and ties and gravel, he took caution not to trip and fall, one false move and he was done. In the distance, a freighter was approaching at medium speed. Chico calculated that if he didn't beat it, he'd be cut off with no place to go, and his pursuers were hot on his trail. As he neared the oncoming train his breathing became more labored and his legs were giving out from the difficult footing. It was becoming obvious he wouldn't be able to reach the track ahead of the train in time. With his escape route cut off and no retreat possible, there was only one desperate course of action—he was going to have to jump the train! As he came close to the moving boxcars, he realized that if he slipped, or his strength gave out, he could easily fall beneath the train and be crushed to death instantly. Fear and the invincibility of youth combined for one final act of desperation; with his last bit of strength, Chico threw himself at the ladder that ran up the side of the boxcar and held on for dear life. Clinging to that thin metal frame, he allowed himself a brief look back at his would-be executioners as they trailed off into the distance. He would live on, at least for this one day.

He made his way up the ladder to the top of the boxcar and collapsed, watching the sky pass overhead. He'd made it! But the train was picking up speed as it left the yard and there would be no getting off for the time being. It was early autumn and the evenings were uncomfortably chilly, the nights were downright cold. All he had with him were the scant clothes on his back, no money and no clue where the train was headed. He peered over the side and saw that there were boxcars with doors open. He traversed the catwalk carefully until he came to a car with an open door. Cautiously, he maneuvered himself down and swung into an empty freight car, relieved to be safely inside.

The chase and ensuing exertion had worn him out, and he fell into an uneasy sleep; the night was long and cold, and Chico was getting miserably hungry. When he awoke the next morning, the train was still rumbling along noisily at a brisk pace but the scenery had changed. No longer were there the familiar city streets and buildings, as far as he could see it was nothing but farmland—pastures, fields plowed over, and occasionally, wooded stretches that went on for miles. Around noon, the train pulled up amid what appeared to be an endless corn field. Chico jumped down and ran into the field, delighted to find that there were ears on the stalks awaiting a final harvest. He pulled corn as fast as he could, scarfing down mouthfuls of raw kernels hungrily. He filled his shirt with ears and began to make his way back to the train.

A voice called from the distance ... "Hey! Over here!" Several boxcars down a fellow traveler was calling. "Come and keep me company!"

Chico joined him and they both unloaded their corn harvest into the stranger's boxcar as the train geared up to move on.

"Where's your stuff?" the stranger asked.

"I don't have anything." Chico filled the man in on the events which had led to the unexpected journey. Over the course of the day, the stranger schooled young Chico on the finer points of riding the rails. He was an experienced hobo and seemed completely at home in what Chico considered difficult circumstances.

"Where's this train headed, anyway?" asked Chico.

"Washington!" the hobo advised.

"Washington, D.C.?"

"Nope. Washington State, on the west coast."

The Pacific Ocean! That was nearly fifteen-hundred miles from Chicago. Chico was scared and bewildered and didn't have any inkling of an idea what he was going to do. He'd never been away from home before, and even though he was a tough guy, he was a city kid. He had no knowledge of this kind of adventure. He was hopelessly out of his element and feeling vulnerable and desperate. On top of all that, he was getting hungry again.

The hobo had a sleeping bag and blankets, a rucksack

with canned food and utensils and all the gear a seasoned traveler might need. He obviously knew what he was doing. That night he broke out cans of ravioli and Vienna sausages, expertly prying them open with an Army knife. He ate greedily while Chico looked on, stomach growling. He didn't offer to share, and when he packed it in to sleep, again, he didn't offer a blanket to the freezing boy. It turned bitterly cold that night, the train door had to remain open as the only latching mechanism was on the outside, and if it should close, they'd be locked tight inside. By morning, Chico was cold to the bone, starving and exhausted. He hadn't slept and his mind began to play tricks on him. He believed Death was chasing him in the form of those rival gang-bangers and now he felt trapped in the boxcar, imagining it to be his coffin.

The stranger awoke rested and cheery, breathing in the fresh country air as the train sped along. As he stretched, standing in the open doorway, he exclaimed, "What a wonderful day!"

Something in Chico's mind snapped. At that moment, he truly believed that it was "him or me". Hunger, hypothermia, fear, exhaustion … all came together in one brief instant of survivalist paranoia. Chico jumped up and ran full force from across the boxcar, pushing the hobo out of the gaping doorway! Just like that, the stranger was gone. Morality and conscience didn't make an appearance. Chico dove into the sleeping bag to warm himself and dug into the food supplies. Remorse and regret didn't arrive until many years later, when Chico began to wonder about his lack of empathy or consideration for human life. At the time, however, he truly thought that if he didn't do what he did, he probably would have perished. It was survival.

When Chico relived that event as he told it to me, all those years later, I believed he honestly regretted his actions. There's no way one man can judge another without walking a mile in his moccasins. Different people, coming from different places, react based on their own ideals and interpretations of want and need, and right and wrong. I personally knew that I had failed nature's test between good and evil more times than I cared to think about. Unfortunately, when the foundation of your life is built upon quicksand, the wrong choices happen far too often. In Chico's case, growing up in gang culture where life and death are daily occurrences, I had to imagine perspectives were vastly different than those of others not from similar circumstances. He'd done what he did for whatever reasons he did them, and nothing was ever going to change that. I knew him now be a decent person, even honorable. I liked the guy, and trusted him, and that's rare on the inside.

His journey took him to Portland, Oregon, where the train finally stopped long enough for him to disembark. A stranger in a strange land. It was the late seventies and a few aging hippies littered the west coast. He met a friendly drifter who showed him how to get fresh clothes from Goodwill and find the missions for free food and at times, shelter. After a few days, Chico figured out that his best bet would probably be to head for Los Angeles, where his grandmother lived. The drifter advised him which train to ride; one to Fresno would get him to California and he could hitchhike the rest of the way.

Sure enough, the freight stopped in Fresno and Chico hit Interstate Five for L.A. He walked all day and night and finally, about sunup, a weaving Cadillac came to a swerving stop. The driver was drunk ....

"Where ya headed, Kid?"

Chico didn't want to ride with a drunk driver, but to his surprise, the guy asked him if he wanted to drive! To make a long story short, Chico ended up driving the drunk guy's Caddy, all the while contemplating another act of treachery. He thought maybe he could jack the guy for the car and drive on to L.A. Out of nowhere, fate interceded. The engine overheated, not an hour into the drive south, and they had to call for a tow from the roadside emergency box. Turns out the car was completely out of oil and the repairs would take days. They were towed to a nearby freeway town that consisted of only a garage, a diner, and a small building with a Greyhound sign in the window. The drunk had been headed for Vegas and sent Chico to the station to find out how much a ticket cost to get there. Chico was still thinking larceny and decided to tell the guy that there were no routes directly to Vegas, that he had to go through L.A. He thought, in his 'me versus them' mindset, that maybe he could get the guy alone, knock him out and take the ticket, thereby allowing himself passage to L.A.

At the time, the cost of a bus ticket to L.A. was fourteen dollars. Chico came back with the story of no direct route to Las Vegas, and the guy pulled out two twenties and told him to go purchase two tickets to Los Angeles. Although it would be many years until Chico turned his life around, he reflected during the telling of the story, how he felt divine intervention had played a hand in his surviving the journey. How, even then, perhaps he was on a path, and how he believed maybe there was a grander plan.

I had to agree with a lot of that, and as Chico steadily chipped away at the thick prison wall that had been my tomb, I was sincerely glad he'd made it. Maybe all things are interrelated after all and there's some unseen force and power with reason and purpose. Maybe what had happened, had happened for a reason and Chico was here now, saving my miserable life in some cosmic redemption for himself and me as well. Maybe not, maybe I was delusional from hunger and thirst or giddy with the possibility of freedom.

The wall was giving away now; I could hear the clunking of steel as Chico's efforts were succeeding. In a few moments I'd breathe fresh air! I had a goofy smile on my face as I looked out the window to encourage Chico onward. I expected the same look from him but what I saw there dampened my enthusiasm and sent chills down my spine. There was a look on Chico's face that was cold, expressionless …. Was I being paranoid now, or was it perceptiveness? When I looked into Chico's eyes, was I seeing my rescuer, or was there something else there?

The look on his face could only be described with one word … hunger. The hunger of a starving, desperate man. The same kind of hunger he told about when he was recalling his journey on that train all those years ago. Was I being saved by some generous, humanitarian gesture of a changed man or did the hunger in Chico's eyes reveal his true intent? It wouldn't be long before I'd find out.

*   *

CHAPTER 3: AS THE CROW FLIES

(Frankie V.)

Dark clouds hung in the dismal sky like a canopy of gray doom. A musty, disturbing aroma traced the slight breeze, and the only sounds were my own labored breathing and the pounding of adrenaline flooding my brain. I forced myself painfully through the small cragged crevice in the cell wall. I was out! Saved from certain demise by my friend Chico, who had chipped away diligently from the outside – while I impotently watched from within. With his final bit of strength, Chico kicked in the narrow Plexiglas window, and we pried it loose. The Herculean effort had taken its toll on my friend; as I scrambled out he collapsed in a fit of coughing, and blood sprayed from his nostrils. I held his sweating head in my hands … silently berating myself for questioning his motives.

"Hang on, Chico, I'll get help." I looked around desperately, wondering what to do. "I'll get you some water."

"No es necessito, amigo," Chico rasped. "Es muy

tarde."

"Come on, Ese, you know I don't speak Mexican." The tired old joke brought a slight smile to his lips.

"That's because you're a stupid Gringo."

"Yeah, well, I'm not the one using my last strength trying to bust <u>IN</u> to prison."

"Shows what you know … I only came back to get that money you owe me."

"What money's that, Chico?"

"The money you owe me for saving your sorry ass," he coughed. "Frankie, can you do something for me?"

"Sure, Pardner. Anything. What is it?"

"There's a woman I knew … a great beauty." Chico struggled to speak. "She gave me many nights of great pleasure and I've never forgotten her. I want you to find her. I want you to thank her for giving me such wonderful memories to warm me through countless cold nights. Can you do this?"

"You're going to make it, Brother, hang on," I implored.

"You <u>must</u> promise me!" Chico insisted.

"All right, all right … I promise," I relented. "But how do I find her?"

"She had the face of an angel, the body of a goddess, and the soul of a demon whore," he spoke with fond remembrance.

"Yes, Chico … but, where do I find her? Who is this woman?" I had to know.

"Your mama!" Chico said flatly.

I was stunned at my friend's ability to display a sense of humor at a time like this. I staggered to my feet and ran to the front of the cellblock. Maybe I could get help, maybe I could find water … I stopped in my tracks. What I saw there tempered my momentary elation of being freed from the death vault. The yard was littered with corpses in varying degrees of decomposition. I supposed these were the ones who had managed to extract themselves from their cells earlier. Either they had succumbed to starvation, or … or what? How in the world had so many died in the yard? Maybe there was something in the air! I ripped my shirt and wrapped a ragged piece around my nose and mouth.

Several scavenger birds stabbed persistently at the decaying bodies. Whatever ended the lives of the unlucky, apparently, wasn't affecting the birds. I felt light-headed and sick, but I didn't have the strength to vomit, and there wouldn't have been anything to throw-up anyway. I knew I didn't have the time to linger on the grotesque scene being played out before me—like some real life Dantean drama; or, some old Hitchcock film gone horribly wrong. In this movie, the beautiful blond wouldn't be plucked from peril at the last moment by the handsome hero …in this movie, Tippy Hedron would be carried off, kicking and screaming, by giant, merciless creatures.

My head was swimming from hunger and fatigue and confusion. I felt strangely self-conscious, as if the predators feeding on the dead had turned their attention to me. In my feeble state, I feared, should any − or all of them − sense my vulnerability, they would easily overwhelm me.

A big-headed crow nearby, spat out a beak full of flayed flesh and raised to full height … as if sniffing fresh meat in the air. He stared my way, unblinking, then brazenly approached. I was frozen with fear and apprehension.

"I see you finally made it out," he spoke. "What took so long?"

Momentarily taken aback by a talking bird, I scrambled to gather my wits. "I couldn't get through the wall," I answered.

"Couldn't, or didn't want to?" he challenged.

"I don't have any tools," I defended.

"Your friend got out. Then he got you out. And how'd you repay him?" the crow said accusingly.

Wide-eyed with panic, I remembered my task. "I have to get water!"

"So, what's stopping you?" asked the crow.

I looked around, confused. "Wh … where's the water?"

"Why you asking me? I'm just a crow."

"But you can talk!"

"So can you. That doesn't mean anything. You can talk, think, reason, yet … you ended up here, left to waste away. You left your family behind to fend for themselves, you deserve what you got. Superior beings, HA! It was inevitable you'd be the ones that ended up destroying yourselves and everything else."

"You know wat happened?" I asked.

"You haven't heard?"

"N … no. They just quit coming to work. Just left us here. The TV and radio's off. I don't know anything! What happened, crow?"

The bird snorted disgustedly. "Human science. Trying to unlock the secrets of the universe. They're poking around with things better left alone. Any silly bird knows the secret to life – eat, drink, mate, sleep, LIVE! And, you don't kill other than to survive. You humans… killing for greed, domination, land, jealousy … self-serving interests. Ridiculous!"

"Are you referring to me?"

"I suppose you qualify as a human, although barely," said the crow.

"What do you mean?"

"What do YOU mean what do I mean? Are you trying to forget? Leave the past behind? That's it, isn't it? You're trying to move on with your life and leave all the unpleasantness in the past … live your life in peace. Well, it doesn't work that way, Buddy. You can't leave it behind. It stays with you and never goes away. It hangs on you like the stench of death. It doesn't wash off."

"That was an accident!"

"If you say so."

"It was!"

"Was killing Chico also an accident?"

"What do you mean?"

"Chico. Was your killing him an accident?" the crow said accusingly.

"I didn't kill Chico! He saved me!" I said defensively.

"Really? Then whose blood is on your hands?"

I looked down at my hands. I felt disoriented as if seeing everything from ten feet on high. "You're crazy!"

"You're the one talking to a crow."

My mind was splintering like termite-infested wood. Reality and rational thinking fell away like loose rocks on a steep hillside. The crow taunted …

"Late one night came a rapping … tapping at my chamber door."

(His beak clicked noisily, producing a convincing tap, tap, tapping sound …).

"One more chance before I fly, to live the truth and not a lie,

Heed a needy stranger's cry, one more chance before you die."

On that enigmatic note, the crow flew up and perched on the broken-out window frame at the front of the cell block. A homemade sheet-rope hung there—used by those who'd escaped the terror within, only to meet their demise in the yard.

Before I knew where I was going, I found myself scaling the wall and scrambling through the window, tumbling back down into the dayroom. The stench was overwhelming and I couldn't believe I was subjecting myself to such a disgusting scene. There was nothing for me here. The most logical thing for me to do was to flee from this area as quickly as possible. But, as I've stated, rationality had long ago departed. Some unseen force compelled me forward. I began searching cell-to-cell, checking for any signs of life.

A graveyard of doubt clouded my head, remorseful, guilty thoughts invaded my consciousness; the kind like those that wake you up in the middle of the night, eating at your insides like maggots on garbage that's been left out in the sun.

Each cell was ghoulishly similar, I can't even describe it – I don't want to. What had caused such devastation? What had led to all of this? And why was I still alive, when, seemingly, everyone else had perished? Why the hell had I gone back into the cellblock? The only thing I wanted was away! The crow's rhymes echoed in my head …

"Two dozen blackbirds, baked in the pie,
Save another brother, don't ask why.
Four and twenty hundred, gone away to fry,
Find him and you live … and the devil flies on by."

For the briefest instant, the sun broke through the haze and a beam of light shined through the dayroom window, falling directly onto, and illuminating, one cell in particular. It was like a dramatic unveiling of a Bernini sculpture in Vatican City.

Dream? Hallucination? Providence? One or the other all in one …. I had long ago bid adieu to logic. Curiosity bested reason. I discovered and retrieved the manual cell door hand crank and began working on the mechanism. The sturdy door lurched open haltingly … like a heavy stone from an ancient tomb. I felt that whoever, or whatever lie within held my fate in its grasp. Was I unleashing Pandora's Box? Or revealing clues to my destiny? I cautiously entered the cell ….

*   *

CHAPTER 4: ABANDON HOPE

Inscription over 'The Gates of Hell'
     (Inferno, Canto III, 11. 1-9)

Unto the Woeful City pass through me.
Through me is everlasting pain brought nigh
Unto the people lost eternally.

By Justice was my Maker moved on high,
By Power Divine in Wisdom's Highest Sphere
By Primal Love created, too, am I.

The only things before me to appear
Were things eternal. Ever I abide.
All hope abandon, ye who enter here.

                    – Dante
                    (Translated by V.W. Smith)

(The Professor)

No seizure. I actually awoke feeling better. Sometimes Fate backs off. More often than not, though she's simply playing Cat-and-Mouse, hasn't really changed her intentions, just considered some way to enhance the torment by varying and protracting it, including a measure or two of false hope.

I felt better, physically. But here I was in Hell again. The first year in prison I enjoyed such vivid dreams each night, almost always pleasant ones. I would be on vacation with my son, with my students in class, or with other poets and scholars in the great cities of America and Europe. These dreams were so vivid that they were like being there. It was torment to wake and find that they were just dreams and memories. Here I was, still in prison. Since that first year my sleep had been almost dreamless. The irony did not escape me that today I would have been ecstatic to have awakened and found that, though I was still inside these walls, the world was back to normal, and the horrors of the last few days had been only a nightmare.

But no such luck. The cell was dark except for a dim, gray light struggling through the window. I was on the top bunk. Glen was below, and he was dead. I was not only doomed, I was alone.

Not quite. Through the wall vent I heard a familiar voice call: "Glen!" It was our neighbor, Big Joe Rossum. He was about the biggest man I'd ever seen, in girth more than height, but a lot of that weight was muscle and bone. Like many big men, Joe was usually patient and affable.

In contrast, his cellie, Little Pete, was one of the shortest men I'd seen inside, barely five feet tall, and, not emaciated, but with hardly an ounce of fat on him. Pete was quiet and thoughtful. On the days I did go to the yard, Pete would often walk with me. He shared my interest in history and philosophy, and we both delighted in discussing great men and ideas. I regarded both Joe and

Pete among the few fellow prisoners that I could call friends.

Relations had become strained and complicated when our neighbors had bought a quart of Glen's hooch on credit, consumed and apparently enjoyed it, but never paid. Several attempts to obtain payment had met with negative results, and Glen turned stony toward them. He expected me to do likewise. Hence, even though Joe had called to us several times during the disaster, each time Glen had refused to respond. He'd made it clear to me that if I responded to Joe in any civil way, Glen would have regarded it as an act of betrayal. Irrational, but hardly atypical in prison.

"Glen!" Joe called again. "I know I did you wrong. I'm sorry."

"Joe," I replied, at a loss to put the point subtly, "Glen's dead. The diabetes got him."

"Professor? What shape are you in?"

"Not good. I'm worn out."

"How'd you manage this long?" Joe asked. "You got food and water?"

"Some. Not much left though. How's Pete?" I asked.

Joe got very quiet. Too quiet. His next question, innocuous in itself, was alarming for the timing and the intensity with which he asked it:

"You're a priest as well as a professor, aren't you?"

"Why?"

"Could you hear my Confession and grant me Absolution? I don't want to go to Hell," Joe asked solemnly.

"Joe, I have a Divinity Degree, but I'm not a priest. I was never ordained."

"You can't grant Absolution?" he asked.

"Not canonically, not officially. Why are you worried about Hell? Starvation is a bitch, and Nature is unforgiving, but God is merciful. I do the best I can, and figure He'll understand, even when I screw up." I waited, Joe's response was protracted.

"Professor, you don't know what I've done," he stated flatly.

I thought I could hear Joe sobbing then. After that – silence. I called out to him several times, but got no answer.

I climbed down from the upper bunk and looked at Glen shrouded (literally) on the lower bunk. I almost envied him. Nevertheless, rest had made me reassess the situation. Where there's life, there's hope. Maybe I could finish Glen's task and get the door open ... if I was lucky. But, luck hadn't exactly been on my side lately. Perhaps a mustard grain of faith was needed, I offered up a silent prayer and hoped grace was still within reach. I said one for Joe and Pete as well.

Sometimes, fate, coincidence and providence arrive at a pivotal moment in one's life – most time's – unexpected. Rarely do all three collide at a crossroads with such dramatic effect. With my head still bowed, and to my extreme surprise and amazement, I heard the strained grating of metal on metal that was both familiar and terrifying. The door was opening! Of course it wouldn't be doing so by itself – someone had to be there, using the crank that staff used when cells had to be opened manually. I leapt to my feet, my heart beating furiously and felt the pounding of the increased blood flow straining my arteries. Indeed, the door was opening, ever so slowly.

I swallowed a salivaless gulp and held my faint breath. Another prayer was offered, "Lord, don't let it be one of the predators ..." referring to the horrendous acts of cruelty I'd witnessed during the first days of our abandonment. I frantically looked around me for anything that might serve as a weapon. I lunged for the TV, but I was too weak to lift it. I grabbed a book, yes, that's it! A sturdy copy of Moby Dick will surely overpower the most worthy adversary. Should a stout whack on the head fail, perhaps I might read him into a stupor! Worthless cad, I was pitying and berating myself for not being better prepared for such an encounter. I settled for the smallest, and potentially most lethal device, the trusty ink pen. Mightier than the sword, and, in this case, possibly a life saver were I dexterous enough to be able to jam it into any vital orifice, preferably, the eye. I steadied myself and prepared for the worst ….

The door creaked open wide. Now, my breathing completely halted as I stared at the figure in the doorway. It, he, was just a shadow with faint light behind. Death comes in many disguises, mine was vaguely familiar.

"Professor?"

Armed with my tiny implement and probably too weak to strike any blow forceful enough to do any harm, I chose a more tactile approach … perhaps reason and cooperation might confound and confuse my opponent. Yes, absolutely! Words to an educated man are like knives to a lowly killer … I chose mine carefully, designed to appeal to his more humane, intellectual nature….

"Huh?"

"Professor, it's me. It's Frankie. Are you alright?"

Confusion, then recognition, as I began to comprehend that my potential tormentor was actually someone I was familiar with. Someone I knew to be one of the more quiet and peaceful prisoners.

"Frankie? Is that you?"

"Yes. Yes, Professor, it's me!"

A weak sputtering of laughter and relief escaped my throat; my cell door opened by a simple prayer, and my rescuer a peaceful Samaritan. "Thank God!"

"Were you writing something?" Frankie asked.

I looked at him, dumbfounded, then realized I was still brandishing my pen. I smiled. Probably the first such expression I'd attempted in weeks, my face felt oddly stretched and I realized it was because the muscles used for the movement had become atrophied. "No, Frankie, I was …." There were no words for how I felt, I simply shook my head in relief and gratitude.

Frankie looked past me to where Glen lay. "Glen didn't make it, huh?"

"The diabetes got him," I explained. "Are there other survivors?"

"I didn't see any," Frankie answered. He seemed oddly disoriented and unsure. "We should go." Simply stated and, oh, so very true.

"Is there a way out of here? I mean, will we be able to get out?"

Frankie didn't appear unsure when responding to that question. "We'll find a way. Grab what you can carry, food if you've got any. You think you can climb?"

He glanced toward the dayroom window, several feet up from the floor. "I'll manage. Did you happen to see what shape the yard clinic is in?" I asked.

"It looked trashed. Why? What do you need?"

"I'm epileptic. I need Dilantin to prevent seizures." As I gathered a few clothing items and the scant food that remained, an anticipatory wave of fear passed through me even with the brief self-reminder of my condition. When a seizure hits, a blockage of the brain's natural electrical flow causes one to be seized by involuntary but irresistible motion. Nervous twitching, the jaws biting the tongue to keep one from swallowing it and choking. Although only lasting moments, the affects linger for days; mainly lethargy, sore muscles, and an extremely sore, swollen tongue. There is a period of unconsciousness, and, upon awakening, a brief period of disorientation. Soon, the mind and nerves return to normal operation. How I'd lasted this long without an episode, and how much longer I could manage, I didn't know. I took several long breaths.

"Professor, are you all right?" asked Frankie.

Frankie's voice brought me back to the present. It also brought me to the embarrassing realization that, while concentrating on my own most immediate problem I had forgotten about my neighbors.

At once I urged Frankie: "Big Joe — my neighbor in #120! Big Joe and Little Pete! I think they're still alive. We've got to get them out!" Frankie jumped to action and soon ratcheted their cell door open. The look on his face should have stopped me, but I failed to recognize the horror behind it. I understood quickly enough.

As I peered into that cell, the cold realization of the unspeakable horror that had been going on right next door, became abundantly clear. From the ceiling fixture, by a noosed cord he had made from a sheet, Big Joe hung lifeless. It's not easy task — especially for a big man in a small cell — to hang oneself, but Joe had managed. As for Little Pete, he no longer existed either as a living human being or even as a whole body. He had been dismembered and, to a large extent, devoured. Even in the dim light and deep shadows I could discern what had to be human femurs, humeri, and other bones on the floor of the cell. The gore was simply too horrible to describe further, and I won't insult one's sensibilities by belaboring the unspeakable in graphic detail.

Frankie turned away and whispered, "Professor, have you ever read Dante's Inferno?"

Indeed, I had. In fact, in a normal world the closest one comes to such horror as we were witnessing is reading about Count Ugolino in Inferno. Former President of the city-state of Pisa, Ugolino was arrested as a traitor for a plot against the government. He and his sons were locked in a cell – and simply left there. The sons died of thirst and the father ate their corpses. Finally, he, too, starved to death. Of all the tormented figures presented by Dante, none suffered a fate more gruesome or heartbreaking that that of Ugolino.

Unlike many, prison has made me a more compassionate, less judgmental person. As Frankie urged me to finish collecting my stuff so we could get the hell out of there, I couldn't help uttering silent prayers to the providential God, who must still watch over the world in spite of allowing Man the free will to destroy it. The first was for being spared the agony of a nonfatal seizure at this time. The second was for the brother who cared enough about me to see that I usually had a large private stock of food in prison. Otherwise, before Glen's diabetes did him in, I might well have ended up like Little Pete.

We found a hole in the fence where some others had managed to crawl through, that seemed to indicate we weren't the only survivors. It was exciting to move in open spaces again; yet, the uncertainty of not knowing the cause of the devastation which had led to our new-found freedom left an uneasiness that was palpable. Frankie and I exchanged observations and speculation as to the why's and how's ... we soon realized that neither of us had answers, and we concentrated on getting out of the immediate area as quickly as possible.

We found a rusty, beat-up old maintenance truck with the keys conveniently hidden in the ashtray. Relief filled the cab as the engine cranked over and the gas gauge revealed a half tank remaining. We were soon on the road headed towards the nearest town; what we'd find there we didn't know nor did we speak of the possibilities. Frankie was especially quiet. I posed the question that had been at the back of my mind the entire time.

"Frankie, you were out. Why did you come back? How was it that you came to my rescue?" I waited for an answer for several seconds. His response might have seemed flippant, or a vain attempt at humor ... but his demeanor was serious.

"A little bird told me," he said.

It wasn't so much what Frankie said, as much as the way he said it, that caught my attention. For the first time I took a good, long look at my rescuer. His face was gaunt and weathered with heavy creases around his eyes. His arms were marred with deep wounds and he had blood on his hands. I didn't know why Frankie was in prison, I didn't much care; what I was concerned with, was what he was going through internally. As if he sensed my inner dialogue, he broke the silence.

"How far you think it is to town, Professor?"

I thought for a moment. "I'd say five or six miles … as the crow flies."

Frankie got quiet again. He just stared straight ahead at the road, lost inside himself, wrestling with whatever demons he lived with.

After what I'd been through and what I'd seen, and thinking about what Frankie must have gone through as well … even though he'd taken it upon himself to assist me in my hour of need, I decided I'd better keep a close eye on Frankie V. A very close eye. I hoped he would turn out to be all right. On that day, at that moment … hope was all we had.

* *

CHAPTER 5: FLOWERS FOR FRANKIE

(Frankie V.)

The drive from the prison to town didn't take long. The air was thick and humid, and on the horizon, low-hanging storm clouds threatened to unleash their wrath on the landscape. Several vehicles were left abandoned along the route; dusty and forgotten, scattered like a child's discarded toys. In more than a few, rotting corpses remained as testament to the severe nature of the calamity that served as our salvation, and their bitter release from this world. The Professor and I were still acclimating ourselves to our new-found freedom, and struggling with shock and confusion over what we'd seen and experienced. Despite a lack of sleep, exhaustion and hunger – I felt exhilarated. The wind whipping through the truck window was invigorating. Hope and excitement battled fear and dread for dominance within me. A twinge of guilt invaded my thoughts.

"Professor, do you think we should have checked the other buildings?"

"If anyone was still alive they most likely would have found a way out by now," the Professor said thoughtfully.

He seemed to understand my remorseful uncertainty. "Doubts are our traitors, and guilt is the fiend that follows with whips and stings." We passed another car with a body behind the wheel. "We have our own problems ahead of us now, Frankie. It's best to leave the past where it belongs."

I knew he was right. If only words could make it so – we drove on in silence. The small town was quiet and appeared completely deserted. Lifeless street lights stood as impotent guards at unused intersections. Even with the windows rolled down we heard none of the sounds you'd normally hear driving down a main street on a weekday. No kids on bikes, no honking traffic, none of the hustle and bustle of a small town. No citizens going about their daily activities.

"Where are the people?" I asked breathlessly.

"There aren't any people," the Professor answered as we coasted past another body on the sidewalk. "Not any live ones, anyhow."

It appeared that most of the stores had been looted. We parked and began scavenging for food and water. In the freezer section of the Winn-Dixie we found several bags of melted ice. We drank our fill and poured the remainder into plastic thermoses to take with us. A few canned food items and a fifty-pound bag of dog food were the only edibles left in the entire store; we threw them in the back of the pickup and continued searching. At J.C. Penney's we exchanged our soiled prison garb for clean clothing, and packed duffel bags with extras. At Walmart we found some tools, rope, sleeping bags, matches, knives and sundry items we thought might be useful The restroom sink was still working, so we grabbed shampoo and soap and washed up.

Occasionally, we'd come across the remains of another anonymous victim. The putrid smell was always a reliable warning. At the downtown car dealership I tried to trade the old maintenance truck for a shiny new S.U.V. None of the showroom models would start. The ones I tried on the lot didn't respond either. So we syphoned gas from the immobile vehicles into the truck, filled gas cans and went in search of food and life in earnest.

The rows of residential streets could have been from anywhere in the U.S.A. Simple family homes with picket fences and swing sets in the backyards stood mute and lifeless. The slight breeze created a false sense of life as it rustled through the shade trees that lined the deserted streets. Shadows of the branches performed a funeral dance on the untended lawns of the forsaken homesteads.

We pulled up to a modest A-frame that reminded me of my own imaginings of what 'home' should be. The kind of place Dorothy Gale might be trying to get back to, Toto nipping at her heels and Auntie Em baking pies and humming a gospel hymn. "Why Dorothy, where on earth have you been, dear? And who are your friends?" Aunt Em would ask.

"Oh my, Auntie Em! You wouldn't believe what we've been through ... it's so good to be home!" My mouth watered at the thought of those pies baking.

There was no car in the driveway, meaning that maybe no one was home; which also meant, perhaps, we wouldn't have to encounter more bodies. It was ghoulish enough to be rummaging around in some stranger's home for necessities; we didn't particularly want to have to be tripping over more bodies as well.

Comically, we stood on the front porch and rang the doorbell – it didn't work. We tried knocking, there was no answer. We looked like a couple of pesky door-to-door salesmen. The Professor's calm demeanor belied where we'd come from, and I couldn't help but suppress a grin when I considered the scene. What exactly were we expecting here? Maybe June Cleaver would answer the door in a crisp, knee-length housedress, white apron and matching pearl earrings and necklace. Perhaps she'd invite us in for cookies and a randy midday roll in the hay before Ward, Wally, and the Beav got home. How ridiculous the thought! Surely June's propriety would forbid such crass debauchery. Besides, we both knew the Cleavers of this residence were long dead and rotting away. Now … Samantha! That was who we needed to answer the door! One twitch of the nose, and all our problems would be over. Or, Jeannie! "Oh, Master! Where have you been and why is everyone dying?"

"I don't know, Jeannie, but you and me and Major Healy are out of here!"

"Frankie?" The Professor was looking at me quizzically. "Perhaps we should force our way in."

I answered, distractedly. "Yes. They must be out." We broke the window and let ourselves in. It was a modest, two-bedroom with small living and dining rooms, economically furnished. The kitchen was in the back and the second bedroom was upstairs. After confirming that no one was in the house, we began collecting essentials. To our relief, the cupboards we well-stocked. We stacked canned meats, tuna and vegetables on the table – along with boxes of pasta, cereal and other dry goods. We munched on peanut butter and granola, with generous portions of strawberry preserves. It was a feast.

There was a barbeque grill on the patio that led from the kitchen onto the backyard. We built a charcoal fire to boil water and heat up some canned stew. Steaming hot instant coffee and the sudden influx of protein had us re-energized. We leisurely sat in lawn chairs, sipping coffee and watching the sun disappear over the neighbor's house. For the moment, life seemed almost normal again … or as close to it as we might ever experience, in this lifetime. A lone seagull passed overhead, bearing west.

"The birds don't seem to be affected," I observed.

"Animals possess survival skills that are lacking in humans," said the Professor.

I posed the question that had been gnawing at both of us, "Survived what though?"

"It's impossible to know, based on the available information."

I knew the Professor to be extremely intelligent, informed, and a reliable authority on a wide range of topics. He was a former college professor, writer and literary editor. Back on the yard he mostly kept to himself. I figured if anyone might have a reasonable explanation, or theory, it would be him.

"What's your best guess?"

The Professor had a unique mannerism that I would come to recognize and appreciate. When posed with a particularly thoughtful problem, he would pause before speaking and tilt his head slightly upwards – as if seeking wisdom from some higher authority, before answering. I found out later he also had a theology degree. Whatever one's beliefs or superstitions, in the dire circumstances we found ourselves in, I believe we were both open to whatever assistance might come our way, from whatever source saw fit to intervene. The Professor concluded his momentary divine consultation.

"It would appear there are only a few viable possibilities. One – a nuclear strike, or perhaps, accident … reasonably nearby, yet, not so close that we were directly affected by the wake of the blast. Two – some sort of viral infestation, or, bacterial warfare assault; which might explain the mass casualties."

"So, the deaths might be from radiation or some viral contamination?" I asked.

"Possibly. I'm not a forensic pathologist and the bodies we've seen are far too decomposed to allow insight from a layman."

"But, what about the birds? How did they survive? And why is the electricity out?"

"The birds might have wandered in from outside the impacted area. There's no one left to operate the power plants."

Why wouldn't the cars at the dealership start? And why are all the T.V.'s and radios not working – even with batteries?" Each answer seemed to spark more questions.

"A significant blast could create an E.M.P., electrical magnetic pulse, frying anything electrical. Either, our truck was fortuitously shielded in some manner, or maybe the newer, computer enhanced vehicles and mechanisms using digital technologies, are adversely affected."

I evaluated and digested the Professor's theories. It was a lot to swallow and went down like half-chewed tree bark. I had more questions. "But, Professor, why are WE still alive?"

Again, the head tilt. "It's possible, the extreme seclusion of the prison, the thick concrete walls and isolation from the outside world might have allowed us to remain relatively unscathed. Whether it was a cataclysmic blast or viral infestation – at least the initial wave didn't hit us directly. Perhaps we were just outside the mortality zone."

"But, nobody else from the prison seems to have made it. At least, we're not seeing anyone that did. Even the ones who made it out, they died on the yard. I didn't even see anybody make it past the fences. You saw 'em on the way out."

The Professor countered, "Yes, but it took us longer to escape our cells. It's possible, the delay allowed the worst of the ... contamination ... to pass."

"You mean, we survived by simple, dumb luck?" I asked.

"Could be."

I felt the Professor wasn't completely satisfied with his own theories. I probed further. "What's the fallout period from that type of blast? How long until it's safe to be out in it?"

No head tilt. "About one hundred years." We both stared at out new J.C. Penney shoes. There was a good chance they would outlive us both.

"So it's possible that we're already contaminated, Professor? That we're already dying?"

"Might be." Under the circumstances, it seemed odd that the Professor could project such an unflappable facade. It was disconcerting.

"How can you sit there and tell me this and not even comprehend what it is that you're saying? If we're in the contamination zone, which apparently we must be, judging from the bodies on the street, and the fact that nobody seems to be around … how can you just sit there and be so calm?" I was losing it.

That freaking head tilt again. "Why do you walk through the fields wearing gloves? When the grass is as soft as the breasts of doves." said the Professor.

"Huh?"

"To know pleasure, we must experience pain. To appreciate joy, we must understand sorrow," he continued.

"What are you talking about?" I asked, perplexed.

"However long, or short, our time on this Earth … however fleeting our successes, joys, freedom … one must stop to smell the roses, Frankie. Tell me, did you ever imagine you would be getting out?"

"I … I had a life sentence," I confessed.

"As did I. Life, wherever one finds oneself, is like a rose … with equal portions of beauty and fragrance and thorns. Regardless the circumstance, one must stop and smell the roses."

Despite the Professor's lofty view of the bigger picture, I was still inescapably tethered to the wants, desires and fears of my own narrow existence. Dread and trepidation filled my heart and fear-fueled doubts once again invaded my thoughts. All of my life I'd made my way through good times and bad using a combination of wit, charm and cleverness. Look where it had gotten me. Maybe, there was some truth in the Professor's words. Maybe there was some higher, unseen order to life, and all my struggling, worrying and fighting to get my way was like a minnow swimming against the current of a mighty river. In that one brief instant, I felt I'd caught a glimpse of what the Professor meant. In that one, fleeting moment of clarity, his philosophic reasoning washed over me like a spring rain. Regardless of my fears and self-preservationist thinking, I knew he was right.

"I don't know about you, Frankie, but, contamination or not – I'm completely exhausted and could use a good night's sleep in a comfortable bed. I doubt a few hours more will make much of a difference. Especially if we close up the house."

I took the upstairs bedroom and fell asleep instantly. In my dream, I was surrounded by flowers. They swayed to and fro in the gentle breeze like softly rolling waves. The sun shone brightly and a pure white dove floated down to alight on my shoulder. Several times during the night, I woke to find myself feeling as if I wasn't alone. I imagined strange, dwarfish creatures watching me through the window. They were ghoulish, gnarled and scary. I willed myself back to sleep in order to continue the pleasant dream.

I awoke in the morning, refreshed and optimistic. I dressed quickly, ready to face the day and whatever it might bring. I rushed downstairs to greet the Professor. It was a cold shock of harsh reality to find him unconscious on the living room floor. I frantically turned back toward the kitchen to grab a wet towel, thinking I might be able to revive him. As I did so, the dull thud of a rifle stock caught me directly in the forehead. Pain shot through me, then I too lay unconscious on the floor.

When I came to, I was securely tied and my eyes were covered. I was in the back of a truck, possibly the maintenance pickup, and we were driving over a gravel road. I felt the presence of another person next to me; likely, the Professor. His words from the previous day rang in my ears, and anxiety, once again, gripped my heart in its grimy fingers. I had barely begun to even consider pulling off my gloves to feel the grass – soft as the breast of doves ... and smell the fragrant beauty of the roses ... and, it was already over. Our freedom had lasted less than a day. The bitter taste of captivity filled my mouth and enveloped my entire being. It tasted like poison and washed over me like hopeless doom. I clenched my eyelids together to fight off the tears ... and thought of the flowers.

⚹   ⚹

CHAPTER 6: ACADEMIC CONSIDERATIONS

(The Professor)

Bound, gagged, blindfolded, and prostrate on the bed of some truck … head hurting like hell …. For all my efforts, I could neither escape nor even loosen my bonds. So, knowing I would need my strength later, I decided to save it. I relaxed, breathed deeply, and turned my thoughts to the Big Picture—reflecting on the paramount problem.

Frankie's questions the night before had bombarded my brain long before he had raised them. The Big One was a triad: (1) What was happening? (2) How was it happening? (3) Why was it happening? Somewhat to my surprise, what came to mind next was not some scientific treatise, but the poem "The Second Coming" by William Butler Yeats. Who could forget such lines as:

> "Turning and turning in the widening gyre,
> The falcon cannot hear the falconer.
> Things fall apart, the center cannot hold;
> Mere anarchy is loosed upon the world.

The blood-dimmed tide is loosed; and everywhere
The ceremony of innocence is drowned ...."

Even more to the point were these less famous words, with which Yeats had annotated the poem: "All our scientific fact-accumulating civilization belongs to the outward gyre and prepares not the continuation of itself, but the revelation as in a lightning flash, though in a flash that will not strike only in one place, and will for a time be constantly repeated, of the civilization that will slowly take its place."

What, or, rather, who came to mind next was Richard Adams. He and I had been colleagues at Stanford, and he was one of the few that I could also call my friend. Indeed, I considered him my closest friend. He must have felt likewise about me, since he had honored me by making me his son's godfather. With the onset of the Catastrophe, and especially since our escape, I hoped and prayed with all my heart that Richard and his family were alive and safe.

Having two Ph.D.'s – one in Physics, the other in Biology – Richard taught courses in both these sciences at Stanford and brought massive funding to both of these Departments through his research. One would have thought his position there secure, his future at the University assured. But suddenly, several years ago, he had left the school, under a cloud as it were.

He wasn't exactly fired. He received a fortune in severance pay. Even more mysterious was the absence of any mention in the media. Ordinarily the *Stanford Daily* and the *San Francisco Chronicle* would have been all over the story. Instead, as the saying goes, the silence was deafening. What surprised me no less than Richard's leaving Stanford was his selling his fine home in Palo Alto and moving to the Sierra foothills.

My patience was rewarded in mid-July, now some six years ago, when my wife and I were invited to spend a weekend with the Adams at their "compound." Cora begged off, claiming some longstanding social commitment to her Women's Group, but had not objected to my going. Even if she had objected, wild horses could not have stopped me.

Richard's cabin had a rustic look about it but was equipped with all the necessities of modern living, including its own electrical generators, water system, and fertile agricultural acreage. The living area of the sprawling main cabin was on a single story, constructed on a hillside, and had a huge basement. The side facing the expansive lake sported a splendid deck; leading down one side were stairs that descended to the beautifully landscaped garden and lawn.

As soon as I stepped out of my car I was welcomed with hugs from Richard, his wife Jane, and their small son, Lannie. He would have been about six years old at that time. He always made me wish Cora and I had children; most other kids made me glad we didn't.

The conversation before and during dinner had been filled with humor, conventional pleasantries, and the usual questions-and-answers. After dinner, at Jane's insistence, Richard and I retired to the deck, facing the lake. Now we turned to serious matters.

"You're not having some domestic or financial troubles, are you?" I asked.

He laughed wryly, then said gravely, "Jordan, I wish it was so mundane. It's far more ominous than that." His look and manner garnered my fullest attention. "We're facing the Apocalypse."

He might as well have said, 'The sky is falling'. "Richard, we're Episcopalians, you don't take that 'Left Behind' stuff seriously, do you?"

"I don't believe each and every detail literally. The writers of the Bible used imagery because the actual processes and events envisioned are beyond the scope of most people's understanding. But I'm serious as a heart

47

attack when I say that the world is about to change drastically, and that, if we survive at all, we are going to be facing <u>tribulations</u> beyond anything the world has seen for centuries."

"Does this have anything to do with you leaving Stanford and the Bay Area?"

"It has <u>everything</u> to do with it. The Physics Department is working on matters best left alone, if not forever, then until we have surer safeguards."

"Against what? There have always been risks. Oppenheimer was afraid that the first nuclear bomb detonation might set off a chain reaction engulfing the planet."

"He considered the <u>possibility</u>. This, I'm afraid, is different. They're retooling the Linear Accelerator Complex along the lines of the Swiss model at CERN, but way beyond it in complexity."

"They want to test the Big Bang Theory again?" I asked.

"Yes, but they also have all sorts of other experiments lined up. Many of them involving antimatter."

"Yeah, I even heard something about constructing a 'controlled wormhole'. Just big enough for a worm to wiggle through." I smiled. He didn't.

"Jordan, we're simply not ready for what they're proposing. There is nothing more dangerous in the Universe than antimatter."

"I didn't know it even existed in this Universe. I thought it was something purely theoretical except maybe in outer space. Don't matter and antimatter annihilate each other when they come into contact?"

"Of course they do. Can you imagine the energy released by such a reaction? If we could harness <u>that</u>, then we could generate limitless energy without the insidious pollution of nuclear reactors. Fossil fuels would become as passé as the life forms they're made from. Jordan, the scary thing is that we now have the technology to harvest antimatter, but not to assure prevention of unacceptable hazards. Yet, at the <u>new</u> SLAC they'll be performing the new experiments next year and progressing to greater goals each year after that. I don't want myself or my family anywhere in the vicinity when they do that."

"So, that's why you left Stanford?"

"Not entirely. While I was opposed to something the Physics Department was doing, the Biology Department was outraged over something that I had done."

"What on Earth are you referring to?"

Richard paused and took a long breath. "I'm referring to my son. Haven't I ever told you that I'm infertile?"

"Okay. So, he was conceived in-vitro. It's not unusual these days, Richard."

"Biologically, I'm not his father, and Jane's not his mother, either."

"So, you're telling me he was fertilized in-vitro and implanted in Jane as an embryo not from one of her own ova. Jane still carried him to term and gave birth to him. More important, legally and in all other respects except DNA, he is your son, and you are his parents, about the best and most loving parents any child could have. So, what's the issue, Richard?"

"Lannie is a clone."

<u>THAT</u>, I did not see coming.

"Of whom, Richard? And, why not of you?"

"Because, under the spell of vainglorious ambition, I did something that my conscience still has not let me live down."

"Richard, what in the world are you talking about?"

After a heavy sigh and a generous drink, Richard spoke. "As you may recall, nearly six-and-a-half years ago there was a conference in Italy where all the most eminent scientists in the fields of genetic research gathered to share information and converse about the most advanced studies and developments occurring in the various areas of their respective specialties."

"Of course. I recall you attended, representing the science department of Stanford. It was highly publicized at the time."

"Yes. Well, what wasn't highly publicized was that some of the experimentation discussed included cloning, in-vitro regeneration techniques, and the push to develop antiviral pathogens—not only to fight disease, but to prevent it."

"All valid scientific research, Richard. I don't understand what the problem is."

"The 'problem', as you put it, Jordan, isn't exactly in the science. It's more in relation to application."

"What do you mean?"

"I mean, some research presented was advancing the cause to produce a line of people who are immune to viral infection."

"Genetically altered?"

"Genetically 'enhanced'."

"A super race," I concluded.

"Yes. Blood samples were presented that actually had been successful enhanced to nearly be inviolable to disease."

"Incredible."

Richard smiled. "Not only that, there was even a presentation before a very select few of us where a sample of human pericardia tissue that was several centuries old was shown to have survived without a single sign of decomposition."

"Are you speaking of the samples from Lanciano?"

"Yes. Six times since the end of the Middle Ages and the firm establishment of the hard sciences, the material at Lanciano has been rigorously tested. The blood at best should be dust by now—it hasn't even clotted, and is identifiable as Type AB, positive."

"Fascinating! But how was that sample involved with genetic research being done by members of the conference?"

"It was postulated that this sample might conceivably be considered the most pure blood known to the human race. And, at the very least, worthy of the most thorough regards, and examination."

"Isn't that sample held under the authority of the University of Florence as some sort of Holy Relic?"

"Yes. And only by order of the Pope shall it be examined."

"Richard, I know you're getting at something … but I'm not following the relevance. How are your actions, and your conscience involved?"

"There was talk among some of us about the possibility of utilizing cells from the Lanciano sample in conjunction with super cells developed that were resistant to viral infection. It was all talk, mind you. Not only wouldn't the University of Florence allow such controversial experimentation, but we had all signed oaths of honor and agreement that no cloning was to be done using the super cells until it had been determined clinically safe and ethically acceptable."

The wheels in my mind were spinning to the point of actually making me dizzy.

"Go on, Richard."

"Well, these are highly respectable, honorable men. Men of science and above ethical reproach. And, security is extremely tight."

"You're <u>one</u> of those ethical men, Richard … aren't you?

"My 'intentions' certainly were."

"Oh, Richard! What on earth did you do?"

"I stole cell samples from the Lanciano relic."

"What? Why? What did you do with it?"

"Jordan, I cloned Lannie from a conference super cell and Lanciano sample hybrid."

My brain was exploding and I wanted to scream from the sheer shock I was experiencing from Richard's bizarre revelation. Purely on a scientific level, it was astounding

… on an ethical level, it was diabolical.

"Richard!? Are you saying that you actually got close enough not only to observe, but to physically touch, and steal samples?"

"Professor Guido Giulio and I were the only two involved in the conference who did not attend the luncheon put on by the University in all of our honor that day. Some tainted seafood he had eaten the night before had left him truly indisposed. I merely pretended to be. So, for more than two hours, we were the only ones in the lab. Professor Guilio, a representative of the University of Florence, was the designated 'overseer' of the samples, and it never occurred to anyone that during the brief luncheon that subterfuge might arise. When the professor was seized with bowel cramps and had to leave the room for a brief time, I was alone just long enough to acquire miniscule fragments of both the Lanciano and super cell samples."

"You do realize, Richard, the unspeakable treachery of your actions?"

"Something came over me, Jordan. It was as if I couldn't help myself."

"What did you do next?"

"I employed the assistance of a fellow scientist, and obstetrician, who was also at the conference – and, for a generous fee – he rendered his services and performed the in-vitro procedure."

"But you had to conduct cell hybridization and very elaborate laboratory labor prior to the implantation."

"At the conference, there were fully functioning laboratories available for general usage. I was merely one more scientist exercising his craft."

"Jane was receptive?"

"She loved being in Florence with me, the time of her monthly cycle was just right, and she was overjoyed with the prospect of our finally having our first child."

"Child? What about having this child? Did you

explain to her where it had come from?"

"No, Jordan. I let her think it was a standard in-vitro procedure. She still doesn't know otherwise."

"How could she not suspect <u>something</u>? You yourself said you're infertile."

"Infertile, not sterile."

While listening to Richard I had been watching Lannie as he played in the yard. He was such a happy, healthy child! Yet, as I looked at him, now with a hypercritical eye, I could not help but notice certain details. Everyone has some skin blemish somewhere, and some irregularity in the size or proportion of some physical feature. Moreover, almost everybody's face is in some way asymmetrical – being wider or narrower at some point on one side or the other. Yet, this was not the case with Lannie.

I noticed other things: His hair and eyes were darker than those of either of his parents. The irises of Richard's eyes were gray; Jane's were hazel. Lannie's were brown. Both Richard and Jane's hair had been blond, when I first met them. Lannie's, by contrast, was distinctly brown in summer, almost black in winter.

"You mentioned, Richard, that the Biology Department at Stanford was enraged …they knew what you'd done?"

"When I returned from Italy, I pushed for increased funding for the genetic research being done at the University. A 'rumor' spread that I'd become involved in cloning … and, there was some 'speculation' that something amiss might have occurred at Florence during the conference. Nothing that was ever substantiated, however … and most considered it idle gossip. Rather than face the scrutiny, I decided it was best to move on. And, here I am … free and independent, with a wonderful family."

*

Now, as I lay prone and bound in the back of the

moving vehicle, I once again became aware of the throbbing pain in my head. Although it was significant and acute, it paled in comparison with what I felt in my heart … for I feared I would never see my friend, or my godson again; a godson cloned from genetically altered super cells and the DNA of a man who walked this earth two-thousand years ago. A man who many believe to be the embodiment of pure spirit and the holiest of holies … Jesus Christ himself!

∗   ∗

CHAPTER 7: CAPTIVATED

(Frankie V.)

My eyes were blindfolded, my hands and feet shackled, my spirit crushed like dry dirt clods under heavy tires. After enduring the desolation of prison and the despair of abandonment, to have the elation of freedom disrupted by a return to captivity – that was nearly too much to endure.

Only a couple of times in my life had I been subjected to such gut-wrenching hopelessness and utter defeat …. So much at stake! So much lost! The temptation to just give up and accept my bitter fate flooded over me in waves of shame and sorrow.

One of those times was the day I got arrested. Looking into Marie's eyes and seeing the heartbreak, confusion and panic mirrored there made me question the reason for going on – especially when I realized that it was my own actions that had brought such inexcusable hurt to someone I cared for that deeply. It shook me to the depths of my soul, like a giant fist dropping from the sky and slapping my teeth loose. At that moment I knew I'd never see her again, and my life would never be the same.

The other experience I don't talk about. I can't afford to. The worst thing about guilt and remorse is, neither of them ever go away. They hang over you like a cloud of foreboding doom. You can try to ignore the nagging remembrances, put on a happy face, or beat it back with booze and drugs. Nothing works – it only gets worse with time. During the long nights the cold winds of regret blow through what's left of your soul and you begin to understand what Hell is. Hell is what's left after everything good and decent is gone.

There ought to be a class in school to prepare you for that kind of thing. Instead of sixth period study hall, maybe a course that points out, "Hey, Kid, before you do the deed or pull the trigger, you should understand something: IT'S NEVER GONNA BE THE SAME!" A little heads-up that actions have consequences and one day you might wake up in the back of a pickup truck, traveling over a bumpy road with the Professor knocked out next to you … at least, I think it's the Professor, and I hope he's just knocked out.

"Professor! Professor!" I call in a loud whisper. He moans slightly.

I'm wedged snugly between stacks of gear and loosely folded blankets. I roll toward the groaning, and scrape my face against the bed of the truck to get the blindfold off. Sunlight is coming intermittently through the treetops. The air is cool and dry, but the truck bed is warm and kind of moist. The blankets are damp and musty. My eyes gradually adjust to the light. Then cold chills rush through me from scalp to toenails, and bile fills my throat as I recoil in revulsion. The wet blankets are bodies wrapped in sheets! I want to scream, but don't dare. I want to run – but I can't. I yank at my bindings, but they hold fast behind my back. The familiar pain of metal against my wrists is strangely encouraging. If I can get my hands in front of me, I can get out of the cuffs!

The six years I spent in County Jail before going to State Prison gave me a Master's Degree in handcuff escape—especially when the cuffs aren't double-locked. I test the cuffs—squeezing the left wristlet with my right hand, ever so carefully … CLICK! Ah, not double-locked! In that cramped space I begin the arduous maneuver of getting my feet up to my wrists. Not an easy task, it's going to be difficult and painful, but not impossible. I have to bend my head and shoulders backward, beyond normal limits ….

"What the HELL are you doing?"

Startled to the point of shock, but too entangled now (with one foot between the cuffs) to either turn around or to cease my efforts, I continue the straining, but ask, "Who's that?"

"My name is Valerie, Valerie Fierno." The voice is deep, but feminine and is coming from one of the wrapped bodies just behind me.

"I'm trying to get my hands in front," I tell her. "If I can get them in front, I can get out of these cuffs …." I continue the exhausting effort. One final shoulder-tearing push, and my bleeding wrists slide up the front of my legs. I take a moment to catch my breath.

"Do you have a comb, or a pin?" I ask Valerie. "Anything pointy, like a paper clip or safety pin?" I can't see her, she's shrouded in a sheet, stacked on top of another wrapped body.

"There's a safety pin in my waistband, in front."

I strip the sheet from around Valerie's midsection and feel for the pin.

"Don't try nothing funny, Mister."

"Don't worry. Something about the presence of stacked corpses sort of kills the mood for me."

"Yeah, I've heard that one before. Just watch where you're touching!"

Focusing on the task at hand, I locate the pin and unclip it. I bend it straight and tweak the tip to a 90 degree angle, using the cuffs for leverage. I insert the bent tip into the lock and the cuffs pop open instantly, my hands are free! The first thing I do is to check on the Professor.

His head is bloody, but he's breathing, and even seems to be coming around. I quickly uncuff him.

"Ah, Houdini, do you mind?" Valerie says from beneath the sheet.

"Oh! Of course, I'm sorry." I help her roll over, then open her cuffs. She sheds the sheet and we both rub our sore wrists.

"Oh!" she exclaims, "You're a Munie."

"A what?"

Valerie's face is young, but her eyes are old – and odd. A bit too large, greenish, and the corneas aren't normal. They're sort of dark and the irises are oversized. Her skin appears sallow and dry. Her lips are full and badly chapped. Her teeth are slightly yellowed and a bit elongated. She shakes her mane of tangled curls, as though to hide her face.

"You're a Munie," she says less forcefully.

"What do you mean? What's a Munie?"

"Man, what rock you been livin' under, Mister? A Munie. You know, immune."

"Immune to what?" For the first time I notice the girl's unusually long fingers.

Valerie flashes me an incredulous look from beneath her long dreads, "You really don't know?"

"Know what? I don't know anything. We've been in pri ... we're not from around here."

"I don't care where you're from. Everybody knows what a Munie is. There ain't many of 'em around now, of course, because of the Curse."

"Curse? What's that? Like the Plague? Was there an outbreak?"

"Ain't no plague, Mister. It's a damnation."

"Is it contagious?" I looked around the truck bed at all the wrapped bodies. "Is that what they all died of? Are ... are they really dead?"

Valerie looks around as well. "I don't know what they died of or how it's spread. I guess they're dead." She pokes a couple of the wrapped bodies, no reaction. "If not, it won't be long."

"Where are they taking us?" I ask. "Who's driving this thing anyway? Are they Munies too? Are you?"

Valerie covers her teeth with her long fingers, then replies, "They ain't no Munies, they're Bounties – bounty hunters. We're going to the work farm. I am, anyway 'til it's too late ... 'til I turn. They're going to sell you. You'll bring a good price, too. Like I said, ain't many of your kind out here."

"Sell us? For what?"

"I'm not sure. Testing, experiments, breeding …. Who knows?"

"You said, 'til you 'turn'. Turn to what?"

"Moonkie. 'Til I go all the way Moonkie."

"Valerie, I'm not following this."

Exasperated, Valerie explains: "Look, there's three kind of folks survived the Day."

"What do you mean, the Day?"

"Some people call it the Big Blast, some of 'em call it the beginning of the end, I just call it the Day. Nobody knows for sure what happened – it was just all of a sudden. Folks started dying, the computers and cars and TV's and everything went out. Some say there was a big explosion, but I never heard nothing. We even heard that the Earth was torn open down to the core and something was spreading all over the world, it all happened in seconds! People just croaked where they stood. Others began changing."

"Changing? To what?"

"As I was saying, there's three types of folks. You got Munies, like you—immune. Them's rare. Then you got Muties—mutants, like me and the Bounties. We're slowing devolving …. Then you got Moonkies. Full-blown Moonkies."

I hear the Professor stirring and check on him. "Professor, are you alright?"

"Like I said, you got Munies, Muties and Moonkies. Them's the worst. You don't want never meet up with no Moonkies."

"What is a Moonkie?" I ask.

"The worst thing you could imagine, I guess. Not human no more. That's for sure!"

"Why are they called Moonkies?"

"Couple days after it started, some Munies come through, warning everybody to 'beware the Homunculi'! We don't know what the hell they were talking about, but we sure found out before long: Moonkies!"

"Ah, Homunculus!" the Professor exclaimed, sitting up now, apparently pain and discomfort forgotten by curiosity.

"Homunculus, Professor?"

"Yes. Scientifically it applies to hominids before and beneath Homo sapiens. The term itself means 'little man' or 'lesser humanoid', implying beings of diminished mental and moral capacity as well as less physical size. Though little known among the general public today, historically the most remarkable use of the term was its application to the semi-legendary, zombie-like being somehow bred or invoked by Paracelsus."

Valerie and I were listening intently, but neither of us had a clue as to who Paracelsus was. "Go on, Professor," I urged.

"Paracelsus is the better known name of one of the most famous (and infamous) men of the late Middle Ages. Born Theophrastus Bombastus Von Hoenheim, he became the stuff of legends, though I stress that he was a historical person. As Dr. Paracelsus, he convinced many that he was one of the few genuine alchemists, namely that he could actually transform lead into gold. Of course he had plenty of detractors who claimed he was simply a charlatan who made off with other people's gold. It was also rumored that in his laboratory he found the formula for the Elixir of Life, which could not only heal any and all injuries (short of braining or decapitation) but also literally keep a person from dying, ever, or even aging – as long as he took Paracelsus's elixir."

"His most astonishing and extraordinary feat, however, if indeed there is any truth to it, was – probably through the use of that same Elixir, applied to dead or inanimate mater – the creation and animation of a being called the <u>homunculus</u>. I'm not sure how reliable their testimony would be in a court of law, but numerous witnesses at the time attested that Paracelsus's experiments somehow produced what we would call a virtually indestructible, rather diminutive subhuman creature with little higher brain function and <u>no</u> original thought, but phenomenal physical strength. And, with unquestioning obedience, it would perform whatever task Paracelsus required of it – provided it didn't require too much or too fine an amount of cerebration. The Homunculus could collect firewood, or collect debts; clear a road of an obstacle, or rid the world of an enemy. The prospects were immense, as long as the requirements were long on brute force and short on intellectual sophistication … of course there was also a real Count Dracula, and the actual, historical Paracelsus captivated peoples' horrified imagination for centuries and ultimately served to inspire one of the most poignant and terrifying of horror stories, namely Mary Shelly's, Frankenstein."

He had either finished or just paused to catch his breath and see whether we understood or cared about what he'd just said. Appreciating – and certainly entertained by what the Professor had just told us, I nevertheless had to interject, "All that is very interesting and informative, Professor, but maybe we should focus on getting out of here."

Concurring with that practical course, the Professor asked, "Where are they taking us?"

"Nowhere I want to find out about. Can you handle a jump from a moving vehicle?"

"I suppose."

We both eyed the tailgate and estimated our chances of survival—and landing without fatal or crippling injuries.

"Perhaps we should wait until the truck slows up a bit," the Professor suggested.

His words proved prophetic. The truck began to slow, then turned off the gravel road. We passed in front of a small trailer and entered a fenced enclosure, then stopped. We might have waited too long to make good our escape; we ducked back down and listened. What sounded like a large dog greeted the Bounties, bounding after the truck. By tacit agreement we three feigned unconsciousness and simulated our original positions as our captors stepped out of the cab. Knowing that if they checked our cuffs, the jig was up, I took a quick peek to determine how formidable these guys were. Should it come down to it, a sneak attack might be the best move for us. I just hoped the Professor and Valerie were on the same page.

First, the Bounties pulled cargo from the tool compartment. Then they looked in on their other cargo, namely us – and the many in far worse shape. Discretion truly was the better part of valor for us – they were armed with shotguns. We heard them speak ….

"They're still out, Gelson. You think we whacked 'em too hard?"

"What's the difference? Munies live or dead bring the same price."

"Maybe we outta finish 'em so they won't be getting any ideas …."

"Why waste good shells? They try anything funny – Bruiser here'll let us know, won't you boy?" Bruiser, the guard dog, enthusiastically agreed – at least, from the sound of his whimpering and slobbering, that's what it sounded like.

"Did you get that bag of dog food outta their truck, Nomez?"

"Oh yeah. And everything else they had. That house was loaded with goodies."

"Where you think the Munies came from?"

"Well, that was a prison truck parked outside. They mighta come from the joint."

"Man, I haven't seen any Munies out and about since … I can't even remember."

"Yeah, either these two didn't know what they were doin', or, maybe they're not really Munies."

"It's been too long. Ain't no more human holdouts that aren't immune. Hell, ain't hardly no more humans at all. Moonkies seen to that."

"Speaking of which, let's get inside. Too much open ground out here, makes me nervous. We'll unload later. Let's get some grub, we got a long drive ahead."

Finally, the two headed off to the trailer, locking the chain link fence gate behind. Peeking out of the truck, I see Bruiser standing guard. Just as I had imagined – big, mean, and dangerous.

Valerie is the first to speak …. "Well, we just gonna sit here?"

"Professor," I ask, "Is that a bag of dog food under you?"

The Professor feels beneath him, then nods affirmatively. I pull a buck knife out of my back pocket (obtained during our shopping excursion and undiscovered by our captors) I cut a hole in the fifty-pound bag and we each grab a handful of the of the dry, mealy nuggets.

"Okay, just a few at a time." I toss a single nugget towards Bruiser. It works just as you'd expect. The dog forgets about everything except his hunger. We take turns tossing pieces. He snatches up every one, munches it down and waits for the next.

"Now what?" the Professor asks.

"I'm going to try and get close without spooking him, and you two can get away while I have him distracted."

"Then what'll you do?" Val asks.

"I'll play it by ear."

"Let me," Val suggests, "I have a way with animals."

"I don't think so."

"Listen, Mister. Outta the three of us, only one's a Mutie. I ain't especially clingin' to life here, tryin' to find out what the future brings. I mean, it's not like I'm all anxious because the Senior Prom is coming up or anything. So, let me, okay? I want to."

I look to the Professor, then back to Valerie, "All right, but once we're in the woods, work your way over to the far side of the fence and I'll get Bruiser's attention. You should be able to hit the fence and get to the woods also."

Val gives me a determined nod and grabs two handfuls of dog food. She eases out of the back of the truck, tossing one chunk after another to Bruiser and cooing, "Hey baby, baby! Hey, baby, babe. Good doggie!" She slowly creeps up on him. Meanwhile, the Professor and I slide out the back and make our way to the fence. It's only chain link, about six feet tall, we climb over the top easily. One quick look back and I head for the woods. The Professor is making good time, also, but his attention is distracted back toward the trailer. I urge him to hurry ….

"Professor, come on!"

As he joins me in the woods, surprisingly, Valerie appears, right on his heels. I'm amazed the impromptu plan is working so well, it's almost too easy.

"What happened to Bruiser?" I ask Valerie.

"I told you I have a way with animals. Let's go, Munie!"

She didn't have to ask me twice. The three of us make tracks through the woods, and don't stop for a good half-mile or so, then take a brief pause to catch our breath. It seems, for the moment, we're not being followed.

Valerie stands tall and breathes in the air. "Salt water. The ocean is near. We gotta get to the water before nightfall."

"Why is that?"

"Moonkies come out at night. But they're scared of the water. They won't go near the ocean, especially. It's not far, we gotta go!"

Valerie takes the lead. She's fast and limber as a cat. Rather than run, we hike at a brisk steady pace. Both the Professor and I, thinking ahead, had each grabbed duffel bags from the back of the truck before departing, hoping we might be lucky enough to be taking something that might be of value to us later. Even without the baggage, Valerie easily out-paced us and had enough of a lead she wasn't able to hear when the Professor tugged my sleeve and let me know he wanted to speak in private.

We halted momentarily, "What is it, Professor?"

"Valerie," he panted out, a bit out of breath.

"What about her?"

"You didn't see, back there?"

"See what?"

"You must not have been watching. When I looked back … it all happened so fast."

"What? What are you talking about?"

"Valerie … she … Frankie … she pulled that dog's throat out!"

"What? What do you mean, pulled its throat out?"

"She was right up close to him, feeding him … then, all of a sudden, she just reached out, quick as a snake, grabbed his throat and pulled it out of his body."

"We were running, Professor, surely you only 'thought' you saw that."

"Frankie, she pulled the damn dog's throat out! I mean that literally. The dog couldn't make a sound then, just flailed around, unable to breathe, it must have bled to death nearly instantly. It was … beastly."

"She saved our asses."

"But, why? And, are we sure where she's leading us?"

I opened my mouth to speak, but no answer came forth. Then, as I eyed the waning afternoon light, another thought took priority.

"Come on, Professor. We need to pick up the pace. I'd rather take my chances with what's ahead than what we left behind."

"Yes," he replied gravely. "But, if she's an indication of what Muties are, I don't ever want to find out how bad Moonkies are!"

"How bad could monsters be who are afraid of the water?" I joked, failingly.

In the distance a disturbing wail resonated though the forest. The same chill that shot up my spine must have passed through the Professor, as well. I thought I saw him shiver. Without further words spoken, were resumed our trek towards the ocean — this time with renewed purpose. Soon, the smell of salt in the air and the sound of breaking waves in the distance assured us that we were near our destination. The forest ended abruptly and a sandy rise sloped down to the beach. Valerie was already at the water's edge — hair flying in the wind and eyes ablaze. She exemplified a part of what I felt inside ... exhilaration and joy.

As the Professor and I stumbled over the sand toward the water I took in a deep breath of fresh air, filling my body and spirit with newborn vigor. It finally dawned on me — we were free. After so many years, after so much hardship — finally free. Ironically, our freedom arrived just as the world had come, or was coming, to an end. Fear of the unknown can be a terrifying demon, and this whole new world was unfamiliar. It certainly wasn't the one we had been familiar with. Everything before this day was fading away into the past ... the future was as uncertain and unnerving as the captivating Mutant girl that stood before me in the surf. With the fathomless ocean on one side, and Moonkies and Bounties on the other ... I wasn't sure where the most fatal danger lie.

*   *

CHAPTER 8: ANGEL ART THOU?

(Frankie V.)

The warm glow of the sun burned heavy on the horizon and the sea sparkled invitingly. A fresh, comforting breeze caressed our skin with salty gusts. If what Valerie said was true, that Moonkies were deathly afraid of the water, then we were safe ... for now.

By a stroke of dumb luck the knapsack I'd snatched up from the truck bed as we had fled contained enough meager supplies to enable us to set up camp on the beach. We gathered driftwood for a fire and heated up the few canned goods – peas, carrots, beans. There was enough liquid in the cans to sustain us for the night, but tomorrow we'd have to go in search of food and water. Regardless of the scant supplies and dire circumstances, as night fell, we each felt equally fortunate to be alive and free.

The Professor tended to the fire and Valerie waded into the frothy surf to bathe. She appeared completely unselfconscious as she stripped naked and washed her ragged clothes in the ocean. The waning light painted a beautiful reflecting gloss on her wet skin, and long-forgotten stirrings rumbled in my stomach. The campfire crackled and the heat built steadily. Noticing my distraction the Professor spoke …

"Angel art thou? My preservation? Or the fell demon of temptation?"

"You're speaking of Valerie, I suppose?" I asked, though I had little doubt.

"Yes," he confirmed. "I'm speaking of Valerie. Those lines are from Puskin's verse novel Eugene Onegin and from Tchaikovsky's opera based on it. Tatiana, the young heroine, asks the dashing older man, Onegin, these questions. Though, tonight the ages and genders of the respective roles are reversed, the questions remain the same, and just as valid."

We both found ourselves watching Val admiringly. "You know, Professor, I used to date models and actresses."

"And now you're wondering if you've got a shot with a Mutant girl," he concluded. We shared a simpatico smile. "A man who is a slave to his desires is like a dog chasing a bone, Frankie."

"Woof."

"She's not bad, for a Mutie," I remarked.

"Certainly spirited … not too good with pets, mind you."

I retrieved a cigar I'd found at the Cleaver's; it had survived the odyssey, none the worse for wear. I broke it in half and presented the Professor his share of the prize.

"Ah, a woman is just a woman …."

"But a cigar …."

We lit up and continued our mutual appreciation of the beauty of the scenery before us. Our senses alive again and hyper-aware of everything we'd been missing during all the years of confinement.

"She said she's turning … or, will turn into a Moonkie."

"I wonder how long until that occurs," the Professor wondered aloud, "and, how it might affect those around her?"

That, we <u>both</u> wondered.

"Interesting name, Val Fierno," the Professor mused, "Valley of Fire."

"That seems about right," I commented. "You know Professor, I don't know your real name. After everything we've been through, it just seems right that …."

"Of course. My given name is Jordan Bruno. The English variation of Giordano Bruno."

"That sounds Italian."

"Quite so. However, it was simply that my German-WASP parents liked the sound of 'Jordan Bruno' which led to the christening. They didn't have a clue who Giordano Bruno was."

I felt a story coming on.

"Bruno was the least known but most tragic figure in one of the most radical paradigm shifts – probably <u>the</u> most radical paradigm shift – in the history of science. Learning the truth is essential, but sometimes comes at a terrible price. Many believe that it was Columbus and Magellan who proved conclusively that the world is round, but making that claim for them was simplistic and inaccurate. You see, simple people may have thought the world was flat, but that was rarely the case with the thinkers and rulers. Both Strabo and Ptolemy − major geographers of the Classical Age −had no doubt that the world was <u>round</u>. They just happened to think that it was the center of the Universe. For over 1,000 years people accepted without question Ptolemy's model of the Solar System. According to that, Earth was the central body. The Moon revolved around the Earth, forming the first of seven concentric spheres, each representing one of the seven 'planets' and its orbit. Extending outward from Earth: 1) The Moon, 2) Venus, 3) Mercury, 4) The Sun, 5) Mars, 6) Jupiter, and 7) Saturn. In Christian perception these worlds were also thought to be parts of Heaven, not just the heavens. The 'planets' and the 'Empyrean' beyond them were thought to be the abode of the Almighty, the Angels, and the Saints."

"Then awhile after Columbus a brilliant scholar named Nicholas Copernicus, no longer able to accept the irregularities and inconsistencies in the calculated orbits of the worlds in Ptolemy's system, dared propound that Ptolemy had got it wrong – except for the point that the Moon revolved around the Earth. After studying the matter for years, Copernicus presented mathematical proofs showing that the Earth and five other planets – Mercury, Venus, Mars, Jupiter, and Saturn – all, in fact, revolved around the Sun."

"This ran afoul of the cosmology in the Bible and Church tradition. Copernicus' theories were so radical for their time, that he published them only when he was literally on his deathbed. He was the first of what some historians call 'the Galileo Triad'. Copernicus died on the same day that he got his book from the printer. Ironically, he could have lived for years without persecution for his theories – if he had lived. The thing that saved him from condemnation and arrest, besides his own death, was that nobody understood his theories. They were presented in such dry, scientific terms, with so much advanced mathematics, that the meaning eluded almost everyone. If he had presented his data and conclusions in plainer language, it's quite likely he would have been tried and convicted of heresy and burned at the stake!"

"Like Galileo?"

"No. That's a common misconception. Galileo was not burned at the stake. Giordano Bruno was, however. Bruno was one of the outstanding poets, philosophers, and scientific thinkers of the Renaissance. He was one of the few of his day who understood Copernicus' theories – and one of the even fewer who were brave enough, or foolish enough, to affirm them publicly."

"Why?" Why would he risk it?"

"It's complicated. Ordained a priest while he was a young man, Bruno rose quite high in both the Catholic hierarchy and in the Dominican Order. Yet, he could not abide the stodginess of the Dominicans, and impatient with the Church in general at that time, he resigned from the Dominicans, then left the Catholic Church altogether. He returned to both Italy and the Catholic Church years later, but the Dominicans had long memories. They found it intolerable when Bruno defended both the cosmology of Copernicus and the humanism of Erasmus. He was arrested on charges of heresy, tried before the Inquisition, and condemned to death. He was burned alive at the stake in Rome on March 8, 1600. The Inquisition probably thought that this 'example' would silence anyone else from coming forth in support of Copernicus."

"But, along came Galileo. Although he didn't actually invent the telescope, he applied it so well, that he convinced others that Copernicus was right – or, a lot closer to right than Ptolemy ever was. Yet, old beliefs die hard. At the time there was a new Pope, a fairly liberal man, and not unsympathetic to Galileo. But he did not dare risk alienating conservative elements in the Church, especially the Dominicans. (The Inquisition consisted largely of Dominicans.) So, he effected a compromise, which enabled them to force Galileo to recant."

"On one hand, he categorically forbade the Inquisition to harm so much as one hair on Galileo's head; on the other hand, no one told Galileo of this constraint. Moreover, the Inquisitors were allowed to show Galileo the full array of the many instruments they had on hand to use for torture; and they explained in painstaking detail to him exactly what each and every one of these devices were designed to do …. In less than one hour a white-faced Galileo signed a detailed Confession of Error and a full recantation. He was not physically tortured, however. He was not burned at the stake nor left to languish in prison.

But he did spend the rest of his life under house arrest."

"Good story, Professor. I guess we've come a long way in the past five-hundred years."

That made us both pause and consider.

"Maybe not."

Another pause ....

"You think this is all man-made devastation, Professor?"

He poked at the fire. "Could be, Frankie. Could be. I've been considering that question. I have a friend, also a colleague, he lives, or lived … in a compound in the sierra foothills. I don't know exactly where we are, but I estimate it can't be all that far. If we could get to the main highway, we'd be able to determine exactly how far Richard's compound might be."

"Richard?"

"Yes. Richard Adams. An esteemed professor and scientist. If anyone might know what precisely has occurred, it would be Richard. If, he's still alive. Do you have a pencil or pen?"

I searched through the knapsack and discovered a small pencil. "What happened to that duffel bag you were carrying, Professor?"

"I … must have lost it during the run through the forest. Perhaps we might locate it in the morning. Have you thought that far ahead yet, the morning?"

"I know we're going to have to find food and water. After that, I'm not sure."

The Professor began scribbling on a scrap of paper. "I believe I can make a rudimentary map leading to Richard's compound. We'll need transportation."

Valerie approached. The canned food was already hot, we divided it up and ate hungrily. I couldn't help but be fascinated by Valerie – so lithe and graceful in her movements. In some inexplicable way her increasingly feral features and actions made her more, not less attractive. She sat on her haunches, completely at ease in her nakedness. She sensed both the Professor and my uneasiness.

"My clothes are wet."

I reached for the knapsack and searched, no clothing items. I shed my shirt and offered it to her. "Thank you."

The congenial silence, broken only by the lapping of the waves and the crackling of the campfire, was delightful – for a time. Then it became awkward; the uncertainty of so many things – where we were, where we'd go, what might happen ….

Finally, fatigue set in and we realized that no matter what, we were going to have to sleep sometime. The Professor spoke …

"I'm just going to the tree line for a few moments, I'll be right back."

"I don't know if that's a good idea, Professor."

"I'm just going to use the facilities, Frankie. I'll be within earshot, if I need any assistance."

Valerie and I, left alone in the firelight, not as uncomfortable as I had anticipated. It was nice being next to a woman again, even if she was a Mutant. In that light, with the campfire reflecting in her eyes, she seemed more human than not. I don't know whether Muties have any telepathic ability or other hyperawareness, but I had the strongest feeling that she knew what I was thinking ….

"I'll take the first watch," I offered. "You two get some sleep."

"You want me to go with you?" Valerie asked.

"You should get some sleep. We'll have to find food and water tomorrow. You'll need your strength."

"I won't bite, you know."

I didn't know what to say – so, I said nothing.

"Is it 'cause I'm a Mutie? Am I disgusting to you?"

"What? No! Of course not. It's … I'm, I put all those kind of thoughts and feeling and desires away a long time ago. So far away, I don't think I know how to find them again."

She shook her tasseled curls over her face and stared into the fire. The flames flared up and crackled angrily.

"You're not disgusting, Val. You're … very beautiful."

"You should walk down the beach, stay near the water and circle back. Moonkies aren't too smart, when they come, we'll hear them."

"You mean, if they come, don't you?"

She didn't answer.

I waited until I heard the Professor coming back and headed down the beach a short distance. I set up watch on a mound of rocks halfway between the trees and the water. I had a good view of the campsite and the rocks were uncomfortable enough so I knew I wouldn't fall asleep. The sharp edges against my backside matched the gnawing guilt I felt inside for so callously rejecting Valerie.

The stars illuminated the night in frosted elegance, as if taunting humankind for our recklessness. How could we have been so careless and fucked off a world so divine? Nature had given us all we'd ever need to survive and flourish, what more had we wanted? An hour into the watch, Val was standing at the fire and motioning me back. I jumped down and ran back to the campsite.

"What is it?" I asked concernedly.

"The Professor! He's had a seizure, or something!"

His breathing was shallow and I felt completely helpless. I knew that without anticonvulsant mediation, the chance of more seizures was problematic. The risk of serious injuries and complications was just too great to ignore. I had to do something ….

"His seizures might recur, might even come close together or he might also just wake up and be perfectly fine. If he comes to, don't alarm him; just tell him I didn't see how we could make it to his friend's compound without a vehicle, or even get very far away from here if the Bounties come after us. They might well leave us alone tonight. But they'll probably be after us tomorrow.

We'd be sitting ducks for them if we stay here."

"So, what are you saying?"

"I'm going back to the Bounties' place for the truck."

"What? That's insane! What about the Moonkies?"

For a moment, I couldn't form words and stared into the darkness. "It's about a two-hour hike back, pretty much a straight shot. I can't just let him die out here, Val. We've got to get him some help. If I can get the truck, we might have a shot. I gotta take the chance. If I'm not back by morning …."

Val looked at me, waiting for the rest of it. The 'what if's' and the 'what if not's' … I couldn't bring myself to say them. I hated to leave the Professor. I hated to leave her. Most of all, I hated the circumstances we were in. But, I knew this had to be done.

I moved fast and made good time. At least I was a moving target, should Moonkies be around. I pushed out all the lingering doubts and focused on the task. If the Professor could just hang on for another day, maybe he'd be fine.

By some miracle I made it back to the Bounties' trailer without incident. At the edge of the clearing I paused, concealed by darkness. My heart was pounding in my ears, and I felt dizzy and sick. No lights were on and nobody stirred. If I could get the truck out of the fenced area by rolling it in neutral and get it down the road a bit, then I could hotwire the thing and get away undetected. Luckily, the gate had been left unlocked; likely, after discovering that we'd escaped, Nomez and Gelson figured why lock it. As I crept through the gate, I stumbled over something mushy. In the moonlight I recognized it to be a mass of bones and leftover innards of some animal … disgusting. I wiped my shoes on the grass and made my way to the tool compartment of the truck. In seconds I discovered just what I needed. A length of wire and a screwdriver … everything needed for the hotwiring.

The terrain was flat enough to allow me to push the

truck a couple of hundred yards down the road. After fumbling around in the dark for a while, I managed to connect the wires accurately enough, sparked the alternator to the coil with the screwdriver, and the old truck fired right up. I drove toward the ocean as far as the road would go, then made my way through the woods to the beach. Parking on the sandy slope, I unloaded the sheet-wrapped bodies, leaving them for nature or whatever else was out there to deal with them. Morbid, but I had my own problems.

I figured I was about a mile or so north of the campsite and simply followed the beach until I found it. I was back by morning. Valerie ran towards the truck as I pulled up. Her eyes were watering ….

"Are you all right? How's the Professor?"

She struggled to speak, shaking her head. "He's in bad shape, he had another attack. I don't know if he's going to make it."

When I got to the Professor, his skin looked ashen, and he was barely breathing. We quickly loaded him into the back of the truck and secured him in sheets still scattered there. I found some rope in the tool compartment and tied him down so he wouldn't be rolling around. I latched the tailgate securely, and we drove away from that spot that would forever seem both blessed and cursed in our memories. We found a passable secondary road and headed toward the main highway. If we could figure out exactly where we were, and decipher the Professor's map, maybe we could get him to Richard's compound for help. It was the only place I knew of that seemed to hold any semblance of hope.

"Was it hard? Getting the truck?" Valeria asked.

"Naw, not really any problem at all."

"You didn't run into any Moonkies?"

"No."

For some reason, Valerie seemed apprehensive. "You cut yourself."

"What?" I looked down at my right arm, then at the left. I had been so pre-occupied with the mission, that I hadn't noticed the fresh blood. It was the second time in as many days that significant amounts of blood had appeared on my arms and hands without my having any memory of how or why. My shirt was also smeared with blood.

"What about the Bounties?" asked Val.

"What about 'em?"

"They didn't hear you driving away? They didn't try and stop you?"

"No. I slid the truck out in neutral and hotwired it out of earshot."

"You hotwired it?" Val asked, sounding dubious.

"That's what I said."

I was feeling defensive and irritable. Probably the lack of sleep was getting to me, as was my concern for the Professor.

"If you've got the key, why'd you have to hotwire it?" Val asked bluntly.

"What?"

Val looked from me to the ignition. I followed her gaze. A rabbit's foot key chain hung from the key in the truck's ignition slot.

I felt light-headed and dizzy again. Confusion swarmed around me like bees in a hive. Nothing made sense.

Val leaned over and examined the bloodstains and cuts on my arms. When she sat back up, I recognized the look on her face. It was only momentary, fleeting – like a ghost passing through an open window. She tried to conceal her true feelings.

"What is it, Val?"

Her eyes were big and mournful. Her lips opened to speak, but no words came out.

"Val, damn it, what is it?"

Finally she spoke: "That's not your blood. Not all of

it, anyway."

"What the hell are you talking about?"

"That's not all human blood on your shirt."

"What do you mean? How can you know that?"

"I'm a Mutie, I know what human blood is ... and what isn't."

"IF it's not my blood, then whose is it?"

She didn't have an answer for that. Neither did I. My head and thoughts were swirling. Why couldn't the Professor be conscious when I needed his logic and reason the most? I felt hot, too hot – like my brain was on fire. What had happened back there? I suddenly felt unsure of everything. Where were we going, and how did I really expect everything to work out? What dangers lay ahead of us and how might I deal with them? Even while attempting to do what I felt was right, my hands were, once again, covered in blood. But, whose?

I felt Valerie's stare; it was penetrating and unsettling. I dared a glance her way and was instantly hypnotized by her overpowering presence. It was as if the entire cab was filled with her energy – it enveloped and filled me and my blood seemed to boil within my veins. Her enormous eyes shot sparks that electrified my very soul ... awakening some long suppressed primordial longing. Who was this fascinating creature and what powers did she possess? For that matter, who was I? What was I becoming? What kind of beast was hidden inside me? And, who was the more human being here? The Professor's recitations came back to me:

> "Angel art thou? My preservation?
> Or the fell demon of temptation?"

*   *

CHAPTER 9: BEASTLY BARGAIN

'Captive Beasts'

We are wild beasts held captive,
And howl as we might,
But can't open our cages,
For the doors are locked tight.

When our hearts can remember tradition
And our barking consoles, bark we do!
We don't know; long ago we've forgotten
How foully it stinks in this zoo.

Hearts numbed by routine now, we cuckoo
Our monotonous song of ennui.
All the zoo's so impersonal, habitual,
We no more even long to be free.

We are wild beasts held captive,
And we howl as we might,
But can't open our cages
For the doors are locked tight!

- Sologub

(The Professor)

What price glory? What price honor? What price survival? Is all negotiable? Maybe not. Last night had been dramatic and eventful, especially for me. I'm not by nature a brave, or secretive man, but I must admit ... when I excused myself from Frankie and Valerie to 'use the facilities', I had ulterior motives. Frankie had done well, very well in grabbing the knapsack from the truck as we had fled. I too, had the same idea, and had gathered up a duffel bag of the Bounties' pilfered loot. Unfortunately, I had laid my bag down during a brief rest stop and in my haste, forgotten it. I felt absolutely foolish and even worse when Frankie had the good manners and grace not to even mention it. We were scrambling for our lives out here and I certainly wanted to do my part.

Frankie had saved me, Valerie had saved us all, and now, I felt obliged to take it upon myself to find that lost bag. Perhaps it contained enough supplies to stave off starvation for another day or so. I knew the others would vote down such a risky expedition, especially at night. Also, I didn't feel it right to have them put themselves in such extreme peril, should they by chance agree to such an undertaking. I had some idea of where I'd left the bag and felt reasonably certain I could locate it. Moonkies be damned! It was, without a doubt, a foolhardy mission – and I was just the man for the job.

Up the sandy slope, through the scrub, then oaks, then redwoods and pines – I entered the dark woods. I halted momentarily, listening for movement or other evidence that I might not be alone. Hearing nothing, I continued on ... finding the path we'd followed earlier that day. I found the trek so difficult in the darkness that I scarcely had time to be frightened. Whoever or whatever was out there that might do me harm surely wouldn't have much of an opponent; so, what was the sense in worrying over it?

Soon enough I came to a spot that seemed familiar, a grassy clearing of sorts. This appeared to be the place where Frankie and I had paused this afternoon. I felt around on the ground behind the log on which I had sat. An instant of good luck and momentary elation. I felt the familiar canvas pouch and snatched it up; I'm sure I was smiling with delight. Holding my treasured prize to my bosom, I set out in the reverse direction stumbling awkwardly through the brush and foliage. Thoughts of a hero's welcome and grand reunion were quickly interrupted when my foot became caught in an outgrown root and I fell face-first to the floor of the forest. My duffel bag cushioned the fall, however, I immediately became concerned for the condition of my cargo – whatever it might be. I ventured a feel around inside the bag, to see what damage was done.

Nothing seemed to be broken, at least, nothing I could discern. I pulled a few of the items out for closer examination. Within the bag was another bag of some synthetic material, cinched with a tied drawstring. There wasn't adequate light for a thorough examination just then; but no odor emanated from within, its contents seemed solid enough and inert, and their shapes intriguingly familiar. The drawstring had enough give that I was able to stick my right hand in and feel around. Saints above. I pulled out a silver-capped flask of what could only could be liquor! I quickly unscrewed the cap and sniffed … it was a strong, mellow whisky, most probably name brand. I contented myself with a brief swallow, then screwed the cap back on. Next I pulled out a plastic cylinder, exactly the size of a Havana Perfecto. Oh my Lord, this was a treasure trove. A twelve-ounce canister of Buglar tobacco followed, then tins of what I imagined must be some edible delicacy … perhaps even caviar! No weary traveler ever had the thrill of discovery as I was experiencing, I was sure of it! I packed the treasure back into the bag without searching further, so anxious to share the good news with my friends. That's when I heard the strangest, saddest, most unnerving sound I've ever heard in my life. I froze where I kneeled.

I'll call it an ululation, perhaps not nearly so vigorous. It had a thin, agonizing quality to it, like a very sick man crying out in pain and trying to sing at the same time – except whatever I heard was definitely not human. I didn't want to think it, but any analytical man would have drawn the same conclusion. Moonkies. It had to be Moonkies. And judging from how Valerie had described them they were quite likely skilled night hunters … and most definitely, traveled in packs. The direction of the wailing led me to believe they stood somewhere between me and the ocean – my route back was closed-off. To divert from the path would mean attempting to navigate thick forest and brush, in the dark, with no tools. To retreat further back into the woods seemed futile. I might try and hide; surely the Moonkies' animalistic natures would allow them to sniff out my scent. I took a few steps forward on the path again, leaving my bagged bounty behind. Then I heard the footsteps.

Panic is like a flash flood and one's actions during are unexplainable. For some incomprehensible reason, I bounded back to my duffel and quickly hid it behind a thick stand of trees. Then in an instinctive hunter-prey maneuver I proceeded to run around in circles in the little clearing, obviously having completely lost my mind. I likely would have run headlong into some tree or probably induced a heart attack except I was suddenly seized from behind by a strong arm around my neck. Whatever had hold of me tightened the grip and the blood and air were cut off from my brain and lungs. I was out in seconds.

I came to rather quickly, struggling against grogginess and dizziness. During that time I heard the ululations of several of those terrible, mysterious denizens of the woods. It seemed they were only a few yards away! Then I heard hissing and snarling, mixed with what sounded like horribly slurred human speech. Next came a series of zapping sounds, each followed by a yelp. Then silence. I was staring into the darkness, not able to make out any figures here, when someone grabbed me roughly by my collar. A huge, hairy hand was reaching down into my shirt pocket. I fully expected to be eaten or bitten to death any second.

Instead I was released. Whoever had been searching me so roughly set me down almost tenderly. Finally the darkness briefly illuminated, the moon shone through the clouds and forest ….

What I saw there was both terrifying and mesmerizing.

Never before had I seen anything so incongruous; so hideous on one hand, so banal on the other. About me on the ground lay three of the most loathsome, repulsive creatures imaginable. On two of them the only clothing was filthy rags around their midsections. The third one was quite naked. They could not rightly be called human, but they were definitely humanoid. Each appeared to be a creature quite distinct from the others. The first resembled a gnome, the second a goblin; the third one − the naked one − looked like a perfect specimen of a Neanderthal. These three were all unconscious. What caught and held my attention was the fourth figure. He was fully dressed and even wearing boots. He wasn't wearing just ordinary clothes either. He was wearing the uniform of a State of California Correctional Officer.

Having found the book of safety matches in my pocket, he had lit the small stub of cigar I still had (used to have) secured in my breast pocket. He deeply inhaled the smoke − sucking it down in great gulps as though he never wanted to let it out again. There was almost a blissful look on that indescribably hideous face!

Then, the most horrifying realization dawned upon me: This creature and I were no strangers. I remembered him all too well – at least who and what he <u>had</u> been.

"Shavers," I exclaimed, "Officer Shavers!"

"Bruno," he rasped. "You son of a bitch. I didn't know you smoked, what are you doin' with a cigar?"

Absurd question, ludicrous situation, laughable response. "It's complicated."

"I stopped them from killing you." He motioned his large head toward the creatures lying about. "They woulda' et ya right here and NOW if I hadn't tasered 'em."

"Why'd you stop them?" Not that I was arguing or complaining.

"I dunno. Sentimental, I guess."

"But, you didn't know it was me … did you?"

"No. But I knew you was human. Like me … well, like I used to be. And, I smelled this cigar on you." Grinning hideously he took another drag.

"You saved my life for a cigar?"

"For a cigar, I let you live a little longer. What I do for you now – and what I do or don't let them do to you depends on what you have to offer me."

"Your buddies here don't have any say in the matter?"

"Shoot," he exclaimed in disgust. "Dicklick, Nutsack, and Jetlag there ain't no buddies o' mine. If'n I didn't have this taser, they'd probably just as soon eat me as look at me. But, in the meantime I got the advantage. They went a little crazy with the full moon and all, but usually they'd do anything to avoid getting zapped."

Another penny dropped, as the British say. And since I'm using that metaphor, I'll specify that it was one of those big, heavy, old-fashioned English pennies. What I mean is I suddenly realized who the other three monsters had once been.

"Shavers," I asked, "Are you telling me that these three Moonkies here are what's left of Officers Dickel, Nutzach, and Jederlach? I thought it was only the inmates who referred to them with derogatory nicknames."

"You thought a lot of things," he said scornfully. "Anyway, yeah, those bastards turned into them things, and it serves 'em right. They always thought they's better than me and looked down on me – just because I took a little nip now and then."

"Now and then?" I mumbled.

"What's that?"

"Nothing."

"So, back to business. What are you gonna give me for saving your miserable hide?"

"Nothing," I replied, "Unless you can guarantee the safety of my companions as well."

"Those two back at the beach, huh?"

Just as I thought, he'd been trailing us. "That's right."

"Bruno, I can't keep all the mule heads in line, these three here are a fulltime job. And the offer's only good for tonight and holds only if you give me something really good. And you'd better be quick. They're gonna come to soon."

"Shavers, in your whole life you never loved anything except booze and tobacco."

"Come up with either of those, and we've got a deal."

"What does your word mean to you?" I had to ask.

"I ain't all the way gone yet," he said. "Motherfucker, you'd better accept my word as a man. Otherwise, you and both your friends are gonna be a three-way breakfast for my three amigos once they come to."

"Calm down, Shavers. No need for hostility, we're all civilized men here." I suppose I was being ironic. We both scratched our respective heads. "Alright, Shavers, what's your preference—a good pint of bourbon or a full can of Bugler?"

"Bugler? You got a can of tobacco? And bourbon? Are you shittin' me?"

His mouth was literally watering. "I'm on the level."

"Okay. Both. Give me the Bugler and the bourbon, and I'll be your best friend – until sundown tomorrow."

"Swear to God?"

"Word of honor."

Just like that the deal was made. I located the bag, handed over the tobacco and whiskey and was afforded safe passage back to camp. I swear, there were tears in his eyes when he opened that flask and smelled the liquor. Simian tears of delight and wonderment.

We heard the cries of homunculi in the distance. Not in the immediate area, but not that far away either. "Don't worry about that," Shavers said gruffly. "I'll take care of them bastards. You and your friends best be clear of here tomorrow, though – the further, the better."

By the time I got back to camp I wasn't feeling my best.

"You don't look so good," Valerie exclaimed. "Five more minutes and I was coming to look for you."

"Sorry I took so long," I said sincerely, then told two lies. "I took a wrong turn on the way back, it took me a few minutes to find the right path. But don't worry – I'm fine. Where's Frankie?"

"He's keeping watch. Did you hear the Moonkies calling?"

"Yes." As I sat down I was suddenly seeing strange geometric shapes in my peripheral vision, the campfire had taken on rainbow colors, and … Oh, no! My eyes were involuntarily straining to the right, my head trying to keep pace with them to relieve the pressure. Now the contortions were constricting my windpipe, and my jaws were cruelly forcing my teeth to bite my tongue to keep it from sliding down my throat. I knew all too well what would come next. It could not be fought, only ridden out … the convulsions … the descent into blackness ….

*

When I awake, the night has passed and I am still alive … I think. Once again, I find myself in the back of a truck traveling to who knows where. I can tell by the way I'm comfortably wrapped and secured, with a rolled blanket under my head as a pillow, that I'm being – or have been, cared for. Possibly by Frankie and Valerie.

As the truck rumbles onward the treetops that are shading my eyes from the sun give way to open sky. We come to a stop, momentarily, then a sharp right hand turn and the bumpy ride transitions to a smooth, steady glide. Overhead, a falcon sails on the breeze confident and strong … keeping pace with my iron chariot – chained to the ground and never to be as free and mighty as one of God's most elegant and noble creatures. My eyes follow my winged companion as long as I'm able … my body, weighted to the earth and failing – my mind … drifting, flying, and free.

*   *

CHAPTER 10: THE LUCKY ONES

(Frankie V.)

"Frankie! FRANKIE!!"

I guess I had drifted off. The dry wind blowing through the truck window and the steady drone of the tires on pavement had induced a hypnotic daze. I couldn't remember the last time I'd slept.

"I'm awake!"

"You sure? I can drive you know. You could get some shuteye."

"That might be a good idea. You sure you can drive?" The look Valerie gave me let me know it was an inappropriate question. "Can you follow this map?" I pulled the Professor's hand-drawn directions to Richard's compound from my shirt pocket and handed it over. Valerie gave it a quick once over.

"Yeah, I know these roads. It's not all that far from here."

We'd been lucky, for the most part, the roads had been passable. It appeared as if someone, or some group of like-minded individuals, had come through and cleared the highway – in a manner. In large part, most of the discarded cars and other vehicles had been pushed to the side. Big rigs and buses and the larger trucks remained right where they stalled – clogging lanes in spots. We'd been able to pass on the shoulder or center divider in those cases. I'd grown accustomed to seeing cars occupied by cadavers. It's odd how the once gruesome and grotesque can become the norm and mundane through repetition.

Several miles up I pulled over behind a Greyhound bus where several other cars had been pushed to the side. I siphoned gas with a hose and can the Bounties had in their truck and managed to extract enough to give us about half a tank. I checked the luggage compartments of the bus, and discovered several suitcases of clothing and personal items. I grabbed a few items I thought we could use and pushed the lingering thoughts about stealing from the dead from my mind. I also refused to think about how that bus was probably filled with bodies ….

I tossed some clean clothes to Valerie. "I think these will fit you, Val." She seemed a bit perplexed, but wasted no time in stripping down and trying them on. Simple jeans and a knit sweater made her look almost … never mind.

I checked on the Professor. He hadn't moved, and wasn't responding to my voice or even gentle nudging. I checked his pulse and breathing, it was barely discernable. Finding a half bottle of water in the corner of the truck bed hidden under supply sacks, I tried to pour a little into his mouth. No response, it just ran down his chin. I have no medical training but it was evident that he was in pretty dire straits and we needed to get to Richard's, or someplace safe, or else he surely wouldn't make it. I checked his ropes and made him as comfortable and secure as I could, then grabbed a couple of the supply bags from the back. Valerie was already dressed and behind the wheel.

As we headed out, I watched her movements and how she handled the truck; she knew how to drive. "How far to the turnoff?" I asked.

"About twenty miles up, then we head east across the valley, then north along the foothills. Depending on the roads, we should be there before nightfall."

I found a little coffee in one of the bags and mixed it with some of the water and handed it to Valerie.

"Thanks." She took a long swig and passed it back. "How's the Professor?"

"He doesn't look too good. The sooner we get to Richard's, the better."

"He's going to be all right," she said with conviction.

"How can you be so sure?"

"Because Muties are clairvoyant. I can sense it."

"Really?" I asked, intrigued.

Valerie turned to face me directly. "No, you idiot. You really are gullible, aren't you?"

I didn't know what to say. I didn't know how to tell her that all those years locked up in a tiny cell had deteriorated my communication skills and likely damaged my perception regarding interpersonal relations. I tended to just go on what people told me, for the most part. Lies or truth, I just made up my own mind instinctively as to what to believe. Small talk, humor and kidding around were unfamiliar to me.

"I'm sorry, that wasn't right," Val apologized, "I was just trying to be optimistic."

"That's cool."

As Valerie drove, I snuck a quick look at her now and again. The glaring sunlight made her squint, giving her face the appearance of smiling. It occurred to me that I'd never seen her genuinely smile. With good reason I suppose.

It felt good to sit back and let her drive – let somebody else take the lead for a while. Survival can be exhausting. Was it really only two days ago since the

Professor and I had relaxed in lawn chairs, that he had commented on the need to enjoy the moment – that life is fleeting. I'd finally met someone who had a perspective on life beyond selfish greed and ego dominance, someone who could impart knowledge and wisdom, and now ….

I felt that familiar out-of-control swirling of confusion and doubt threaten to overtake my thoughts. A panic generated maelstrom that often erupted into self-destructive or delusional behavior. A point where intellect and understanding end and violence takes over. Days, weeks, and months of lucidity thrown to the dogs of discontent – manifesting in acts of ignorance. A fear-driven need to exert control of momentary situations and not recognizing that such behavior actually increases the odds of losing all control. The uncertainty of life throwing these situations at me like grenades of confusion and torment. Then, came the inevitable guilt and remorse and pangs of desire for another chance at redemption.

I shook it off. We were making good time, it was still possible to get to Richard's, still possible to save the Professor. Still possible to … I was getting too far ahead of myself, deep breath ….

"What did you do before, Val?"

"Before what?"

"Before …." I hadn't thought the question out, I was just making conversation, or trying to. "Before the Lions won the Super Bowl."

Val nodded her head affirmatively. "Good. Humor … very good."

I felt like a dog who had just learned his first trick.

"I was a cashier at Walmart."

"Did you like that type of work?"

"It was a job. I was waiting to hear from the Art Institute in San Francisco. I'd applied there a few months back."

"An artist then. That fits you."

"How so?"

"I dunno. You know how some people just seem right for their chosen vocation? Like a dancer looks like a dancer … a soldier looks like a soldier …."

"What about you, Frankie, what did you do?"

I had to think about that …. "I did a lot of things."

Valerie was courteous enough to leave it at that. Some people have a knack for knowing when to speak, and more importantly, knowing when not to. Those are the ones you're comfortable being around … the ones where no conversation is necessary.

As we turned onto the eastbound exit, the sunlight assaulted our eyes with renewed fervor. It revealed deep lines on Valerie's face. Her lips were badly chapped, as were her hands. I dug in one of the bags from the back and found a bottle of lotion among the many items. I poured a generous amount into my palms and rubbed it over my hands, then asked Valerie, "Do you mind?"

She was compliant as I took her right hand and began massaging—carefully at first, then deeper. I poured another portion and slid over beside her, pulling her hair back and applying dabs onto her cheek and around her eyes. She stared straight ahead, intent on driving, but allowed me to attend to her without resistance. She seemed soothed by the attention, like a partially trained wild animal yielding to the trainer's gentle touch.

Her skin absorbed the lotion like a sponge and I applied several layers. Valerie adjusted the mirror and examined the results. Her skin appeared discernably softer and seemed more natural. Her eyes were still large and fierce-looking, and her fingers seemed longer than any I'd ever seen on a woman, but her skin did seem softer.

As I spread lotion onto her chin and neck and slid my hand under her collar to massage her shoulders, I felt a troubling surge of something unfamiliar, yet not unpleasant pass through me. A lump formed in my throat and it became difficult to swallow. Valerie sensed my uneasiness and flashed me a look that shot sparks through me all the way to my lower gut. I felt as if I'd been hit with a stun gun. Electricity coursed through her to me in throbbing jolts; for a moment, I thought I might pass out. Animal attraction hung in the air like mating season on the Serengeti. I pulled back and retreated to my side of the cab, shivering from the adrenaline rush

Testosterone was flooding through me in waves. Valerie reached over and grasped my wrist. It felt like a bear trap ….

"You're not getting away this time, Munie."

She pulled me to her in a single hug, crushing against me tightly. Her nostrils flared as she inhaled deeply, as if testing my scent.

"Val … I …."

"Shhh …." She pressed an elongated finger to my lips and pushed me back on the seat until my head rested firmly against the door. Her hand slid to my chest and she felt my pounding heart.

One of us was a convicted, dangerous felon serving a life term for unforgivable violence. The other was a former Walmart cashier and just short of one hundred pounds; yet, there was little doubt as to who the dominant predator here was. I recalled what the Professor had told me about how Valerie had dismembered Bruiser the guard dog. I trembled like a schoolgirl trapped in a backseat at the Junior Prom. I knew what was going to happen next. It was wild and intense and inevitable. I knew I wouldn't be able to stop it. I also knew I didn't want to ….

What I wanted, or didn't want, turned out to have little effect on what was to be. Just as Valerie licked her lips, one hand on the steering wheel, the other on her prey … the sudden appearance of a fast-moving vehicle headed in the opposite direction on the other side of the freeway broke the spell.

It appeared to be a mid-sixties Chevy with at least two occupants. There was little doubt that they had spotted us. Val saw them also and jerked her head around to look.

"Bounties!"

The Chevy was skidding into a screeching U-turn. Valerie floored the accelerator. The old truck haltingly gained speed but we instinctively knew we wouldn't be able to outrun our pursuers. There was an exit ramp just ahead and Val raced for it as fast as we could go. I looked back and saw that the Chevy was rumbling over the center median and burning rubber as it hit the pavement. They were about a good quarter mile behind, but it wouldn't take long to catch up. We hit the top of the exit ramp and took a right hand turn that nearly flipped the truck. Val straightened us out and we headed down the road desperately looking for a way out ….

"There! In the trees!" I had spotted a wooded area just off the right side of the road, there was a space between two of the trees that seemed just large enough for the truck to pass through. Val swerved off the road and bounded for the spot, we bumped over the grass and into the woods. She slammed on the brakes and I jumped out, tearing off a small branch as I ran to the road. I quickly erased the tire marks from the side of the roadway and ran back to the trees, kicking the grass and hand-raking it to try and cover our tracks. I grabbed brush and tossed it on the truck, helping to further blend it into the heavy foliage. I could hear the heavy drone of the Chevy engine and in seconds it also hit the top of the exit ramp, hot on our heels. We crouched in the brush.

By sheer dumb luck, the muscle car sped right past. We looked at one another in astonishment and panted heavily. Val collapsed in the truck cab and I went to look in on the Professor. He was still securely tied down, but, upon closer examination I discovered that he wasn't breathing. I attempted CPR, in a vain attempt at revival. I even pounded on his chest, listened for a heartbeat, blew air into his lungs again, felt for a pulse … nothing. He was gone. My friend had gone.

After everything that had happened, the highs and lows of escape and survival, it didn't seem appropriate that the Professor's life should end this way. There was absolutely nothing I could do. I was helpless. Finally, I covered his face and crawled out of the truck bed. I couldn't bring myself to speak and Valerie knew instinctively what had occurred. She held out her arms and I fell into them. Human sorrow comforted by Mutant empathy. I buried my grief and loneliness in her warm embrace.

We hid out in the truck until past sundown. I managed a few minutes sleep while Valerie kept watch. The moon rose bright enough to allow us to drive without headlights. We reached what had to be Richard's compound before midnight and parked outside the gates. What should have been a joyous occasion was palled by my friend's death.

"Well, I guess we're safe now. I mean, if anybody is alive in there."

Valerie didn't respond or even react.

"Val," I said, "I think we'll be alright, now."

From the look on her face, I could tell she didn't share my sentiments.

"Frankie … I can't go with you."

"What? What do you mean?"

"I can't go in there with you."

"What are you talking about?"

"Munies don't mix with Muties. I'm sorry, I should have told you that. They'll never accept me."

"What are you saying? These are friends of the Professor, educated people. Of course they'll accept you."

"It doesn't work like that, Frankie. Not everyone's like you and the Professor."

"That's ridiculous."

"Is it? You say they're educated. That means they'll know what I'll become, what I'm already becoming. It's better like this, Frankie. You're safe now."

"I'm not going in without you!"

"Then you're an idiot. What do you think is going to happen here? What would happen if we stayed together? There's no happy ending here, Frankie. In a month, or a week, or tomorrow … I'll turn. And where's that leave you? I'll turn and you'd be …."

"Be what?" I already knew the answer. "Maybe they have a cure. Maybe there's a cure."

"There IS no cure. I'm cursed. That's just how it is. That's how it'll always be. It's not fair, but that's how it is. Don't you see, Frankie? Don't you see how lucky you are? You're a Munie. You still have a future. You still have … hope."

She opened the car door and put a foot out ….

"Valerie!"

Her too-large eyes shone in the moonlight.

"I was lucky too, Frank. You know that? I was able to do something good in my life before it was too late. Meeting you and the Professor … helping you to get away. Most like me never get a chance like that. You made me feel beautiful today, Frankie. I felt like a woman again … not an animal. Thank you for that. I feel fortunate for meeting you and the Professor."

"Val … Valerie … please …."

"Goodbye, Frankie."

In an instant, she was gone. I stared into the darkness and listened as Valerie's footsteps disappeared into the night. I'd never felt so alone. I'd escaped prison, somehow survived whatever it was that had killed everyone else, gotten away from the Bounties … yet, it felt as though I'd lost everything in the world I cared for. I'd gained and lost a best friend. I'd discovered something I thought I'd lost forever, with the help of a beautiful Mutant girl – my heart. And now, it was broken.

I'd long forgotten, and I suppose given up on the healing power of love. Quite unexpectedly, Valerie had unlocked the chains with which I'd bound tender emotion.

She had reminded me that only by caring for others more than for myself, might I overcome the self-created demons that restlessly haunted me.

Luck is subjective and defined by circumstance. Good fortune can change at any given moment and can be as fleeting and uncertain as one's grasp on reality.

I sat alone in the truck, my dead friend in the back and my best girl running away through the woods. What Valerie had said was true … I'd been lucky to have made it this far, damned lucky. The night hung over me like a shroud. I couldn't help but feel, at the moment, that I'd lost far more than I stood to gain.

*   *

CHAPTER 11: RESURRECTION

(The Professor)

The really frustrating thing about being dead is – you have no control over where you are or where you're going. Make no mistake about it: It's <u>not</u> a terrifying experience. The first thing you feel is an incredible sense of relief. Whatever was tormenting you – that terrible backache, headache, or toothache – any kind of ache (except heartache) is suddenly gone. You feel ... normal again. Only, you don't get hungry or thirsty anymore. You do still feel emotions. Boy, do you ever! If you don't feel a tidal wave of wonder – or panic – when you first realize you're outside of your body, then you're not just dead, you're hopeless.

Something extraordinary had occurred. One moment I was on the beach, suffering a seizure. The next, I was back in the Bounties' truck. At first I thought I was standing. Yet, something was unnatural. The truck was moving along at quite a good speed, sometimes on poorly paved secondary roads, even on gravel tracks. Somehow I was not the least affected by all the jolting and jouncing.

Then I got the shock of my life (or should I say afterlife?) when I looked down and realized something. By the dim light I, at first, did not recognize the figure lying on the floor and wrapped in a blanket. Indeed the question that went through my mind was, "Since he dumped all those other bodies that were in the truck, why the hell did Frankie leave this one?" Then with the aid of a fleeting sunbeam as we went around a curve, I saw the prone figure's face, and a shocking realization dawned at last: That body on the floor was mine! There could be only one reason why I wasn't in it.

My next concern was Frankie and Valerie. Where and how were they? I could neither see nor hear them at the moment, but by some new sixth sense I seemed to be detecting emanations from them, indicating their presence nearby. Ergo they were in the cab. Moreover, I now saw that the blanket had been carefully, not too snugly, wrapped around the feet and body, and a makeshift pillow placed under the head. This was the work of someone who felt not indifference nor malice, but respect and concern for me. There was little more that I could ascertain just then, so I "faded" into the ether.

In death – at least the stage I experienced – I found that I was neither conscious nor asleep all the time, but – much as in life – periods of intense awareness of everything around me alternated with either a dreamlike state of crystal-clear reminiscence or absolute oblivion.

When I reemerged from the latter state, day had passed into night. The truck had stopped on a broad paved area in front of massive gates in a tall redwood fence. Detecting the emanations from his aura, I knew Frankie was not far away. No sign of Valerie, though. I wondered ….

Then, through the opening in the rear of the truck, I saw Frankie. He looked exhausted, dejected … haunted! But he still had some remnant of that same strength and resolve that had enabled and driven him to persevere, even in the face of seemingly insurmountable obstacles. To the right side of the gates I noticed the barrel of what appeared to be a shotgun protruding. I heard someone say …

"That's far enough there, partner!"

One of the gates swung open. Out came three robust-looking men, all dressed in boots, jeans, jackets and hats. The tall one in the middle I immediately recognized as Richard. He and Frankie spoke, then shook hands. I could not hear from the distance and from inside the truck. After conferring for several moments, they approached and Frankie opened the tailgate. Richard climbed in, and at once he knelt beside my body. In his left hand he held a leather satchel. He called my name several times. Then he pulled back the blanket, checked my wrist for a pulse, listened to my chest for breathing and/or heartbeat, and finally held his hand close to my face to try and detect any indication of breathing. Negative on all counts.

"He's gone," he said solemnly.

"We ran into some Bounties, that caused the head injuries. But he had a couple of pretty bad seizures last night; I think that's what really did him in. It took me this long to get him here …." Frankie shook his head. I could detect that he partially blamed himself.

"I'm sure you did all you could, Son." Richard was conciliatory.

A woman with dark hair and blue eyes came through the gate and approached. I heard Richard say to her gravely, "It's Jordan. His remains, anyhow." He embraced the woman. "Carol, would you get quarters ready for company? This is Frankie, a friend of Jordan's … he'll be staying with us for a time."

"What happened, Richard? How did he …."

"I'll explain later. And Carol, please don't tell Lannie. This will be terribly hard on him, especially after losing his mother. I'll tell him later, in private."

Even as Richard was speaking, another figure, this one barely five feet tall, came running through the open gate and dashed toward the truck. This, however, was a boy. It was Lannie.

Richard saw him right away. Looking terribly pained himself, but doing his best to maintain his composure, Richard jumped down from the truck. He wrapped both arms around his son, not to restrain him so much as to comfort and console him.

"Uncle Jordan!" Lannie cried out.

"Yes, Lannie." Richard explained in that not insincere but unnaturally calm tone of voice that parents use, "Uncle Jordan tried to reach us, but he didn't quite make it. He had a bad seizure last night and … Lannie, I'm sorry."

With his last words the composed tone was gone from his voice, and Richard sounded noticeably distressed. In contrast, Lannie's clear, ringing pre-adolescent treble sounded no less concerned, but strangely more hopeful. Far from bursting into tears, the boy calmly requested:

"Dad, let me see him."

"Son, he's <u>dead</u>. Wait until he's fixed up to look more like you remember him – more the way you'd want to remember him Believe me, you don't want to see him as he is just now."

Lannie wasn't accepting this. With unwavering resolve, he declared, "Dad, please. I need to see Uncle Jordan now. I have to see him. Let me."

Faced with such persistent determination, Richard relented. Frankie and the others stepped aside as Lannie climbed up and into the back of the truck.

As I looked down from where I floated, I was struck by what I saw when I got my first look at my godson in several years. While physically he did not look at all like either Richard or Jane, he communicated with similar intelligence and refinement, and he endeared himself to many with his rare combination of enthusiasm and gentleness. His eyes were filled with concern and compassion as he looked at me intently. I wanted so badly to console him, to tell him not to be sad because of me, to reassure him that I was no longer in pain, and that I had faith somehow I would pass from here to some place better … But as I was, I could do – nothing.

Lannie did something, however. He reached out, put my hands together, and, while grasping both my hands with his left hand, he laid his right hand on my forehead. Then he said gently but with profound seriousness:

"Uncle Jordan, wake up. You're home now, Uncle Jordan. Wake up!"

The enthusiasm and optimism of life is very much a part of what distinguishes the very young from the seemingly mature. As we get older we become less sure that everything will ultimately work out for the best, and more and more skeptical of the concepts of invincibility and forever …. Few escape this world without losing much, or most of the wonderment of our early years. Cynicism seems to grow as trust in the impossible recedes. Sometimes, however, if we're lucky, the unwavering faith of another can help us overcome our own doubts ….

In a flash, I was back in my body, wide awake, and feeling just fine.

"Lannie." The memory of being outside of my body began fading immediately – it was if hours had been seconds. "I thought I saw you there. But I couldn't move, couldn't speak …." I tried to explain – more for my own sake than his. He didn't seem the least bit puzzled or confused.

"That happens, I understand," he said simply but profoundly. "You're well now, Uncle Jordan. That's all that matters."

I was speechless, dazed, and delighted to be alive.

"What's the matter, Uncle Jordan?" Lannie asked as he helped me to my feet, noticing the expression of deep concentration on my face.

"There's nothing, wrong, just something most

unusual. I got hit hard on the head yesterday, and had at least one severe seizure last night. But neither my head, tongue nor body is the least bit sore. It's a miracle."

Lannie just smiled.

Words can hardly describe Richard's astonishment as he saw us step out of the truck. Frankie looked understandably bewildered. He rushed up and grasped my shoulders. Richard hugged me as warmly as in the old days when we'd been friends in graduate school.

The two unfamiliar men, Richard introduced to me as Andy and Hawk, stepped forward as well. My initial impression, born out in the next few days, was that both were – or had been – bikers. Both free spirits, one not evil. At a loss as to what to make of what had just happened, they made a joke:

"Hey man, good to meet you. We heard you were dead. You look pretty good for a corpse."

I responded good-naturedly, "Gentlemen, although I believe I WAS, it appears that rumors of my demise have been greatly exaggerated."

*   *

CHAPTER 12: CHILD OF THE FOREST

(Frankie V.)

To say I was amazed and astonished when the Professor stepped from the back of that truck with the boy, Lannie, would be a gross understatement. It seemed other-worldly. But much of what I'd experienced recently had been that way. I guess I took it for granted that the Professor's revival was just another bit of bizzaro that the world was throwing my way. Still, I had checked him for vital signs, several times over. Even in my exhausted, diminished state I knew, or thought I knew, that the Professor was ... or had been, dead.

Richard and his people took us in graciously. The compound was more than I expected. Even in the dim light I could see that besides the main house there were several smaller cottage-like structures and out-buildings on the property backed by a large lake. Kerosene lamps and candlelight were augmented by carefully rationed generator powered appliances. There was running water, and after a quick snack we were finally able to take a real shower. It felt really good to be clean again. They even had an ample stock of fresh clothing. I chose jeans and a cotton shirt, thick socks and work boots. We decided that we'd catch up on the details of our adventures in the morning – sleep was badly needed above anything else. I was shown to a bedroom in the north wing. Although modest by normal standards, to me it was grander than any accommodations I might ever have dreamed of.

Before the door was even closed I was already under the covers and ready to pass into oblivion. Under the circumstances, you might think I'd be out like a light. That, however, was not the case. I tossed and turned and for some reason, could not fall asleep. Every thought that might prevent me from resting body and mind seemed to be assailing me from every angle, foremost … Valerie. Finally, I quit trying to sleep and just let the thoughts flood over me, through me. I let my mind take me wherever it might. From previous experience I knew this might not be the best thing to do but fuck it, I was tired of fighting …. I surrendered and just let it happen …. I had an idea of what was to come, some idea. I didn't know, though, it would be that vivid!

Fantasy, dream, hallucination, vision – call it what you want. All those years in that prison cell, my imaginings had become as real to me as a 'normal' person's reality. People on the outside don't really understand that in circumstances where you're cut off from people and things that you've spent your whole lifetime becoming attached to – your mind learns to adapt in order to not suffer the paralyzing effects of isolation. The mind is hundreds and thousands of times stronger than the body, and capable of things that mankind isn't nearly ready to understand or accept at this stage of our development. I've read and studied many of the metaphysical, spiritual and philosophical teachings that are out there. It is so true that there are so many things in Heaven and on Earth that mankind has yet to understand. Therefore, if I allow my imaginings to become my reality, at times, so be it ….

In my dream I was miles away from the warm hugs and handshakes of new and renewed comradery shared by those enjoying refuge within Richard's compound. I searched for my lost Mutant girl. As moonlight filtered through the treetops, my mind's eye focused on a clearing where a shivering forest creature stood motionless and alone – watching, listening, sensing the other inhabitants of the darkness. A hunter in the night, doing what comes naturally – instinctively … stalking.

The rustle of a dried leaf betrayed the hiding place of a wayward rabbit who had ill-advisedly wandered too far from home base, too late into the night. He immediately knew that he had pushed his luck beyond reasonable limits. Predator and prey froze in anticipation … did she hear? If he didn't move again would she lose patience or interest and move on? With her first silent step in his direction, the cowering rabbit sprang from the hiding spot and dashed frantically through the underbrush, disappearing into the trees. She was fast on his trail though and within seconds he felt the heat of her breath as she bore down. The bunny frenziedly maneuvered left-to-right, right-to-left, around the trunk of a large oak and into a patch of thistles; too dense and sharp to allow the much larger foe entrance. He lurched to a stop, breathing heavily, heart pounding furiously – but satisfied the formidable fortress would provide ample sanctuary.

I imagined he hadn't seen many creatures like the one giving chase now, not up close anyhow. At first, he probably wasn't all that concerned.

How could a two-legged creature be a threat to a four-legged one? How could she possibly keep her balance? In a race, it shouldn't even be close. She was much faster than he had given her credit for. Still, she didn't have very much fur, she shouldn't be a threat as long as he stayed in the underbrush. His heart calmed down a bit and he settled in for the long wait. Might as well get some rest.

This will surely be one to tell them back at the burrow – how he had outrun and outwitted the tall two-legged beast with no fur. Yes, a very good tale to tell ….

Unfortunately for the gloating rabbit, long claws darted into the thistle bush and wrapped firmly around the little fellow's throat. Thorns tore at his coat as he was yanked up through the bushes. He kicked and fought furiously in vain; razor-like teeth tore into his midsection and his entrails spilled out as the she-beast devoured the warm, bloody mess before he even lost consciousness. I'm sure he wondered then what creature this was with such cunning, speed, and ruthlessness. It was the bunny's last thought.

Valerie hungrily devoured every bit of the meat and organs and licked the blood. She found a clear pool of rainwater and drank deeply, wiping blood from her face and hands. The water mirrored the full moon sky and she admired the beauty of the clouds' reflection as moonbeams danced on the ripples of the pool as if painted on the surface. Her own reflected features were dark and shadowy – her hair hung limp and wet over her face. Deliberately, she pulled strands back and peered intently at the face there. Her too-large eyes shined brightly. Her thoughts were my thoughts, her pain - my pain. The girl in the pool stared back and Val remembered for a fleeting moment who she was, and who she used to be. She used to play and sing and dream and love. But that was before. How long had it been since she had dreamed?

She knew how long it had been since she loved. She smelled her shoulder, my scent still lingered there. She collapsed in a fit of convulsing sobs. A sorrow born of humiliation and loss and bitter torment spread through her in waves of anguish. She cried for the little girl lost, and the hope and love that would never be again. The crushing force of despair overwhelmed her being and refused to withdraw. If this was how life was going to be … how and why would she go on?

She stripped off her sweater and jeans, letting go of the last remaining vestiges of civilization. There was no need for modesty or vanity now. The children of the forest know not of love and hate and heartbreak and loss or nakedness. There is only survival. Naked, blood-streaked and alone – Valerie mourned what was lost and dreaded what was to come.

I tossed and turned, falling in and out of an uncomfortable sleep. I woke up several times crying those soundless sobs that accompany dreams where the pain and sorrow are too acute to bear. Each time I forced myself back toward somnolence; knowing that a return to unconsciousness meant certain misery. It was the only way, however, to be with her – my Mutant girl – now irretrievably lost to the night, and forever a child of the forest.

*   *

CHAPTER 13: SANCTUARY

(The Professor)

At first I hardly recognized the place. Richard had modified the house and grounds considerably from the comfortable, rustic cabin I visited only a few years ago. He'd added a wing onto each end of the main house, and several cabins and a large barn were new to me. The north wing had four bedrooms with two adjoining baths. The south wing housed a communal dining room with a large table capable of seating a dozen or more. An over-sized fireplace took up a whole wall in the adjacent den/library which opened onto a glass-enclosed hot house of sorts. There an abundant variety of fruits and vegetables grew.

Always the considerate host, Richard recognized our extreme exhaustion and insisted we eat, shower and sleep before relaying details of our recent adventures. Although Carol kindly offered to cook for us, Frankie and I opted for a sizable portion of crusted bread and generous slices of tomatoes and cheese—washed down with cold, fresh milk. Possibly the most satisfying meal I've ever experienced.

During a refreshing shower, I contemplated whether Lannie had, indeed, brought me back from the dead – for compared to all that Frankie and I had seen and experienced, not just recently but for many years until now – this place seemed like Heaven! To once again sleep in a normal bed with a comfortable mattress, clean linens and down comforter, was oddly disconcerting. Compared to the one-inch synthetic pad atop a metal sheet that I'd been sleeping on for the past two years, I felt as though I was floating on a cloud of cotton. Bumped and bruised from riding in a truck bed, my body quickly acclimated and I fell into a blissful sleep that lasted into mid-afternoon the next day.

I awoke groggy but rested and spent the better part of an hour shaving and grooming myself in the bathroom – making good use of the various ointments and lotions stocked in the medicine cabinet to tend to the myriad cuts and scrapes that extended from head to toe. When I finally came out, fresh clothes had been laid at the foot of my bed, and hot, dark coffee steamed from a large cup on the dresser. The door to Frankie's room was still shut when I passed by. No doubt, it had to be blueberry muffins, cooking in the antique wood-burning, cast-iron stove. I hadn't seen one like it since my old Grandmother's.

"Good morning."

"Good afternoon. How are you feeling?"

"All things considered, never better."

"The clothes fit alright, then? There's plenty more in your closet and in the other bedrooms. We managed to stock up pretty well."

"These are more than adequate, thank you."

"Sit down, I've got muffins coming out of the oven." Carol poured me a large glass of orange juice and filled up my coffee cup, laying out cream and sugar.

"Thank you."

"I'm going to make you bacon and eggs and toast,

would you prefer ham?"

"Don't go to any trouble."

"No trouble at all." She slid over some hot toast, butter and jam.

"Thank you."

"You know, if you keep thanking me for every single thing, I'm gonna start thinking your brain's gone soft and that's all you can say ... and I know that's not true."

I instantly liked Carol. She was charming and vivacious with a hint of mischief in her blue eyes. She made me feel right at home.

"Has Frankie been out yet?"

"No, not yet. I looked in on him earlier ... figured you guys need your rest. From the looks of you, you all had a pretty rough go of it."

"It's been trying ... but, things could always be worse."

"That's my old Jordan! The world's come to an end, yet, forever the optimist."

Richard appeared suddenly, entering from the patio.

"Richard!" We shook hands heartily.

"Just finishing up some chores. Jordan, I'm so glad you made it here. None the worse for wear, eh?"

"Yes, well, I ...." Overcome with emotion, to be among friends – it all hit me at once.

My old friend put a comforting arm around my shoulder. "It's all right now, Jordy. It's gonna be alright."

"Is it, Richard? Is it really?"

Carol presented a tray loaded with food and drinks. "Why don't you two take this out to the deck and get some fresh air. I'm sure you have catching up to do."

Richard and I settled in, and as I ate, I gave him a condensed version of the events that had led me to his sanctuary ... including the encounters with Valerie, the Bounties, and Shavers.

"You are fortunate to have survived, Jordan. Once a Mutie enters the advanced stages of genetic transmutation they become unpredictable. They're very much like an animal gone rabid."

"Is there any treatment? Any cure?" I asked.

"To be honest, Jordan, I don't know. From what I've seen, and experienced, I don't hold out much hope for their kind."

"What causes the mutation? What in the world happened, Richard? What happened?"

"Do you recall the conversation we had on this very deck the first time you visited here, Jordan?"

"As though it was yesterday."

"Well, with the greatest sadness and humility let me say I was wrong only in how much I underestimated the scope of such a potential disaster. I knew that an 'accident' involving antimatter could wreak havoc, but I had hoped that the complications could be contained. I was wrong."

"How so?"

"It was an unbelievably freakish concatenation of bad decisions, bad planning, and simply bad luck. In the last six years the retooled SLAC particle accelerator produced almost a kilogram of antimatter. That's an absurdly large amount to have on hand anywhere … but ambitious and 'progressive' men had grandiose plans."

Richard paused for a breath, needless to say he had my full attention.

"Public opinion has long been against nuclear power plants. Even the minor problems with the one at San Diego were enough to initiate research and covert development of a cleaner alternate fuel."

"Why 'covert'?"

"Because if the public knew what the government and scientific community were up to they surely would have created enough outcry to prevent it. The solution of our country's greatest minds was what was to be the first U.S. power plant fueled by antimatter."

"I didn't hear anything of this, Richard."

"Of course. The whole operation was completely 'Top Secret', shrouded in mystery and guarded vehemently. The day before the plant was scheduled to begin its first trial operation, one-half kilogram of antimatter − 1.1 pounds of the stuff − was transferred to a special safety container designed so the contents were suspended exactly in the center of a vacuum. It was to be taken from SLAC to San Diego, under the most rigorous, extreme security. It was at the precise moment of the most delicate period of the transfer when the earthquake struck."

"Earthquake? I recall a very minor tremor, Richard, several days before the power at the prison went out. But it was nothing more than a 3.0 or so, nothing more than we get at least a half-dozen or more times a year. I suppose in the back of my mind I considered it had some correlation to the catastrophic events …."

"Yes, it was only about a 3.5 or so. But it wasn't the magnitude so much as the location that was the problem. The epicenter was just south of San Francisco, directly under SLAC …. Whether the vacuum container was faulty or the suddenness or violence of the quake was simply too great for the device design to maintain absolute stasis, once the material was destabilized, it couldn't be brought under control no matter what measures were employed. The fail-safe mechanisms in place called for the antimatter to be buried in an underground bunker with a 50-foot concrete walls. No one had a way of knowing that wouldn't be sufficient. Regardless, most of the facility was evacuated."

"What about the surrounding areas? The communities and cities?"

"It was determined that the panic would have wreaked more havoc and confusion than was acceptable. And the hope was that the bunker would hold."

"But it didn't."

"No. Within thirty-six hours the antimatter's kinetic

motion caused it to implode in the vacuum container, and in an instant all of Stanford, Menlo Park and much of Palo Alto, Atherton, and Portola Valley disappeared in a brilliant energy ball of matter-antimatter reaction."

"We still didn't notice any grand explosion or massive event, Richard."

"That's a part of the enigmatic nature of antimatter – with energy released on that scale, the effect is unlike anything we've ever experienced, heard of, or imagined. It's destructive force is so devastatingly powerful that the impact isn't even detectable on an auditory level. The force is so substantial, that material simply disintegrates in its path. Not only that, but it appears that the very molecular structure of whatever it hits is altered."

"Richard, are you suggesting that the destruction is at a molecular level?"

"Yes. Things in its path and even wake are torn apart molecularly."

"Incredible."

"As bad as the initial impact was, it got worse. All communications in the western states were immediately knocked out. Within minutes, world-wide transmissions were disrupted as well. President Cyrus moved to institute Marshall Law, and reach out to foreign governments, but there was no way to contact them. Before any order could be restored, North Korea snapped. They launched preemptive missile strikes from submarines, against Russia, China, and the U.S. Four of their arsenal of six missiles found targets. Shanghai, Moscow, Hong Kong, and Colorado Springs."

"Colorado?"

"The U.S. Military bio-tech weapons facility is in Colorado Springs. That bomb killed millions and left Colorado and much of the plains states west of the Mississippi a contaminated wasteland. The electro-magnetic-pulse knocked out most of the electricity and fried most of the computer chips in the Western

Hemisphere. Then, it got even worse."

"The bio-tech facility!"

"That's right. The military had just developed a nightmarish pathogen engineered as the ultimate weapon in the event that any nation ever used bio-weapons against us. It was never intended to be used, just make everyone aware that it was there, to insure perpetrators knew we had the capability."

"What exactly is 'it'?"

"A virus," Richard said bleakly, "A genetic virus."

"Genetic warfare, Richard? Are you talking about genetic transmutation? A virus that turns people to homunculi! A Paracelsus virus?"

"That's an appropriate name for it, Jordan. The Paracelsus virus."

I was shaking with rage at the thought that the terrible "curse" that had smitten Valerie and so many others was in fact man-made.

"I learned about the virus only after it was a fait accompli. Seth Edelstein of Berkeley was the scientist who engineered it. I read his research. Even the die-hard activist who gave it to me wouldn't post it on the Internet for fear of the panic it might cause. And, by the way, it doesn't turn everyone into Muties or Moonkies."

"No, apparently it kills most of the infected!"

"It may seem cold comfort, but approximately 1.0% of us, apparently including everyone on this compound at present, are blessed with a natural immunity to the pathogen."

"Actually, that anyone has some immunity to it is extremely hopeful news. Still, it utterly outrages me to think that anyone turned this loose on our own people."

"Jordan, in all fairness, it wasn't turned loose on purpose. It got into the environment through an unforeseeable combination of disasters. No one – not even a madman – would deliberately release this thing under any but the most extreme and final scenario I mentioned."

"I've already seen what it can do. Can you explain more about how the virus and the antimatter are interacting, or if they are?"

"I certainly don't have all the answers, and, I don't have the facilities to do the research needed to come up with the answers …. However, based on what I do know and all the available data, my hypothesis is that the extreme molecular debilitation of those affected by the antimatter in combination with the Paracelsus virus, as you call it, could possibly be the cause of the hyper-genetic alternation of those turned mutant."

"How far has it reached? How long will it continue?"

"There's no way of knowing that. But from what I've heard," Richard's look was intense and blank at the same time, "This swept around the entire Earth in waves of chain-reacting devastation … it went through and around the entire planet!"

"Are you implying that the whole world is gone?"

"As we knew it. Of course, there are survivors and patches of civilization out there … like here."

"Are people elsewhere similarly affected? I mean, are there Muties and Moonkies everywhere?"

"I believe there are. Communications are poor. The best we've managed is through couriers and the occasional CB radio transmissions. It appears that most, or all, of anything using digital or computer chip technology is wiped out. Anything using modern composites didn't survive. Particularly susceptible is anything synthetic or comprised of silicone. That's why the only vehicles still working are the older models with simple engineering."

"It astounds me, Richard, that some of us are immune …. How in the world?"

"Location, happenstance, fortuitous genetics, luck …."

The word 'luck' made us both stop and consider. Indeed, fate, fortune, luck … all had played a hand in the symphony of tragedy and survival.

"Richard, what sense do you get of … what I mean to say is, do you believe that this is the end? Is there any possibility, any hope for us? For man? Will the planet even endure?"

"I don't know, Jordan. Never in the course of recorded history has the human race faced such dire circumstances. Human beings have become the most violent beings in the world and the source of our own destruction. What a mess we've made of it. Scientific advancement has endangered our very existence. As long as man is driven by selfish ignorance, greed and vengeance, we'll insure our own extinction. Despite scientific and technological advances the world is further from being peaceful and safe than ever before. Continuation of life is anything but certain."

"It seems as if in attempting to gain control over the forces of nature, man has lost control of his own nature," I reflected. We shared a moment of silence, as if mourning for a mutual sorrow.

"Richard, is it possible that Muties and Moonkies will out-survive humans?"

"Not if I have anything to say about it."

"What do you mean?"

"Jordan, it's one of the most agonizing assessments a scientist and humanitarian can make. Especially if there's some chance of developing a cure, then every consideration should be given to helping and saving even the infected. However, once a Mutie has gone past a certain point, once they've gone feral, for all practical purposes they're Moonkies. When an infected becomes homunculi, they're no longer human. You can't reason with them, you can't bargain with them. They have lost the capacity to speak or to understand written or spoken language. The most humane solution for our kind is to eliminate their kind."

"Genocide?"

"They're genetically altered mutants, Jordan. They

prey on humans. If we don't exterminate them, they surely will slaughter us ... to extinction."

"But …."

"Do you know what a Moonkie would do to you, me, Carol, or Lannie if it got a hold of us? To be honest, Jordan, any Muties or Moonkies that wander onto the property, we shoot."

"That's murder! I've told you of my acquaintance with Valerie, a mutant girl. She saved my life! And the life of my friend as well."

"Jordan, it doesn't matter what happens BEFORE they turn ... and they turn in an instant. Once they go Moonkie, everything changes. You're no longer an acquaintance, or friend ... you're food."

"But Richard, if we determine to kill on sight, what form of 'humans' have we become? Where's the humanity in that?"

There was a pall of some vague sadness that had befallen my friend. I'd sensed it from the moment we'd arrived. It was only now that I began to understand the source ….

"Jordan. I know you've noticed that Jane isn't here."

I had. But for some reason, I felt obliged to not mention the fact, to allow Richard to tell me in his time. "Yes, Richard, I've noticed."

"In the beginning of the 'events' we thought as you do … that humanity compelled us to reach out to the unfortunates. To feed, or even house those who had been infected. The few that happened upon the compound we allowed in."

Richard stopped for a moment, his eyes clouded with tears and the pain on his face was excruciating to see. "What happened, Richard?"

"The first Mutie I saw turn Moonkie was a child, Jordan, just a child. Jane was her caregiver and provider … she would do anything for that little girl. They were in the garden, just down from the house, playing, tossing a ball or something. At first, I thought the screams were merely playful laughter … but, before I realized it, it became all too clear. By the time I got to her … to them … Jane was …."

"Oh, Richard …."

"She was torn in half, Jordy. That little girl had torn her in half and was eating her insides."

I was, quite naturally, in shock. The chills I felt from hearing Richard's story ran through me and ignited a queasy, ill-feeling that's difficult to describe.

"That, Jordan, is why Muties and Moonkies are shot on sight."

After Richard's final word, I stared blankly at him in mournful condolence. He stared back barely able to contain himself.

We both turned when we realized we hadn't been alone. Frankie stood in the doorway, his face suddenly pale and grim.

*   *

CHAPTER 14: KEEP THE FAITH

(The Professor)

"Frankie!" I don't know how much my friend had heard, but apparently it was enough to have an impact on him. He disappeared from the patio doorway, obviously distressed.

"Frankie developed quite a bond with Valerie, Richard. You understand."

"I'm sorry, Jordan. I didn't mean to be callous, but sooner or later you must know the truth about mutation and face up to it."

"Yes, of course. Richard, I'm terribly sorry about Jane .... Words can't adequately express my condolences. I can only imagine the traumatic effect this has had on you and Lannie."

"Well, actually, Lannie doesn't know. I mean, when his mother died ... was killed ... we told him she had been involved in an accident."

"I see."

"A drowning."

"Oh."

"You don't think that was the right thing to do?"

"Oh no! I'm not questioning your judgment, certainly not under the tragic circumstances. It's just … eventually he'll find out. And, well … he IS aware of the dangers of Muties and Moonkies, is that correct?"

"Yes. I've made it clear, and he's witnessed other events."

"In the world we find ourselves in, I suppose the whole paradigm of what a normal childhood is has been turned upside down."

"I doubt it'll ever be as we knew it, Jordan."

"Tom Sawyer meets Frankenstein's monster on the Island of Dr. Moreau."

"… during the Apocalypse."

"I'd better check on Frankie, Richard."

"Of course. Jordan, I've got perimeter duty in about an hour. I'd like it if you would join me. It would give me a chance to show you around."

"That would be splendid. I'll check on Frankie and be with you shortly." I got up to return the food tray to Carol. "Richard, again, I'm just so sorry …."

"I'm all right, Jordan." Richard's brave lie cut me to my heart.

As I entered the kitchen from the outside deck, Carol met me and took the tray. "I've got that, Jordan. I hope everything was all right."

"Wonderful, Carol. You're an amazing chef."

"Yes, well, eggs and bacon are my specialty." She read the concern on my face. "He went back to his room, Jordan, do you want to take him some food?"

"That would be a good idea, I'll just take whatever you have already prepared."

Carol loaded a tray with fruit and hot toast, coffee and juice. "Here you go. Tell him to come on out anytime he's ready."

"Thank you, Carol. You're quite gracious."

Frankie's door was closed tight. I knocked gently. "Frankie, I've got some food for you. There's toast and coffee, piping hot, and …" The door opened.

"Come in, Professor." He took the tray and sat it on the dresser. "Thank you, this looks good." He bit into the toast and drank the coffee appreciatively. "I don't mean to be antisocial or anything. I guess I'm just not used to being around people. Sorry I just left like that. Sometimes I don't know what to say."

"Of course, I, if anyone, fully understand. Even the brief two years I served dulled my social skills. I can only imagine what you're going through." A break in the conversation had become normal for us, neither Frankie nor I was uncomfortable with the silence. "I'm sorry if you overheard Richard out there. I'm sure he wasn't referring to anyone like Valerie."

"I'm sure he was."

"Frankie, they've been out here with mutants much longer than we have. They know better than we what goes on. I know Richard, I've known him for a very long time, and he's not a ruthless man by any means."

"He would have killed her on sight, he still would … given the chance."

"We don't know that, Frankie."

The look on Frankie's face told me that he didn't share the sentiment.

"Frankie, the important thing to remember is, we've found a safe harbor. We're free and alive. We have to have hope, and faith …."

"FAITH? What the hell are you talking about, Professor? Faith in what? Faith in God? What God is that?" Frankie moved to the window, looking out onto the property. "What do you think? They've got their own little Garden of Eden here? Gonna start up the world again one perfect human baby at a time? Maybe kill ten Muties for every baby born in celebration. What kind of world would that be, Professor? Is that how we're going to get it kicked off? Teach the children well how to kill and live in hell?"

"Frankie, you're upset."

"Execution on sight for anybody that doesn't meet up with human standards, Professor? It's only just begun and already the 'most civilized' of mankind are planning genocide. It was 'man' who caused all this, isn't it? I'm sure Richard has filled you in on the grisly details."

"It was an accident …"

"A man-made accident …."

"Yes Frankie. That's right, man-made. But that doesn't mean all men are responsible. You can't condemn the whole human race for the mistakes of a few."

"Then how can you condemn all Muties for the act of one?"

My friend's logic was valid, while I also understood Richard's rationale. Although I couldn't completely buy in to the killing of mutants without provocation. "Frankie, I'm not arguing with you here. Richard has his own reasoning for his position. Certainly there's room for a middle-ground, you have to have faith that …."

"There you go again! Faith in stone temples and pillars of salt and walking on water is what got us to this point."

I let Frankie vent, he needed to get it out.

"What kind of God would allow this to happen, Professor? Surely you see that it's all a myth. Another man-made lie, a fairytale. Only in this one, Hansel and Gretel don't even make it to the gingerbread house. They're shot in the forest, mistaken for Muties."

"I'm on your side, Frankie."

He crossed to the dresser and looked in the mirror, leaning in closely. "I never noticed I have grey hair." A deep breath. "I got old in prison and never knew…. I'm sorry, Professor, I didn't mean to attack you. I don't even know what I'm mad about or who to fight. There are so many things I'm not sure of. Inside, you just live day-to-day and don't think about what's to be. Now, it's complicated."

"Well, Frankie, when things are complicated I've always been able to follow one rule that never seems to fail."

"What's that, Professor?"

"Follow your heart, my friend, you can't go wrong if you just follow your heart."

*

I joined Richard and we began the trek around the perimeter. He carried a loaded shotgun and presented me with a heavy .45 revolver – which I carried awkwardly, never having actually fired a weapon. I wasn't sure if I'd be able to be of much assistance if trouble erupted but the walk was uneventful and pleasant. As we rounded the other side of the lake, a woman and two children about Lannie's age were walking from one of the cabins toward the main house. From the distance I could detect that the woman was not unattractive, her hair was long, black and shiny and she walked with grace and agility … like a dancer.

"Who's that, Richard?"

"Donna Quinones and her two children, Roberto and Angela. They'll be having dinner with us. Donna's been with us for quite some time, her kids are Lannie's age and they get along like siblings … well, like sibling that actually like one another."

"No husband?"

"Actually, he died at the onset of the virus."

"That's terrible, a wife and children left behind."

"Yes, but he wasn't the only one. You see all those cabins? They were all filled to capacity. We were beginning to grow as a community, everyone pitching in to do the farming and sharing responsibilities. Now there's just Carol, Lannie, the Quinones, Hawk and Andy and their women, and Joe Rivera."

"I haven't met Joe."

"He lives on the south end, near the border with the rock quarry. We'll pass by his place when we get over there. Good man. He's down in Bakersfield today, meeting with Lieutenant Governor, now acting Governor Maximo Mierdamonte."

"There's a government in place?"

"Of sorts. Not that there's much left to govern … still, it's essential to reach out to other survivors We need to get organized and see exactly what kind of numbers we're looking at here."

"You mean, Munies?"

"And mutants. We've gotten a few messages from the Bakersfield area, via courier. And, you get the occasional Bounties coming around, but many of them are Muties themselves, beginning stages. They're only interested in rounding up other Muties or Moonkies."

"What for?"

"They turn them in for a bounty. There's a work farm outside of Bakersfield and I hear they have them working in the fields harvesting the crops and tending to livestock."

"What about Munies?"

"What do you mean?"

"What do Bounties do with Munies?"

"I've heard stories, but nothing substantiated, that occasionally Bounties will go after Munies. For testing."

"Testing?

"Lab testing … to find a cure."

"Where's the lab?"

"On the farm, at least that's what I've heard. I'm planning to go down there myself, well … I've considered it. But I just couldn't bring myself to leave Lannie and Carol. Especially since …."

"Since what?"

"Well. As I've said, we lost a lot of people from the virus. A lot of men. The reality is, Jordan, no one outside of the compound knows exactly how many men we lost."

"Why is that significant?"

"It's my opinion that we've not been raided, by Moonkies, or ... otherwise, because those outside of the compound believe we have many more forces than is the reality."

"You believe there's a potential threat of that happening?"

"It's possible."

"So you believe all that's keeping them out is an illusion of formidable resistance?"

"I'm afraid so, Jordan."

"How long do you believe you can keep up the charade?"

"Well, with you and Frankie here, that's a couple of extra bodies. And I told Joe to see about rounding up some other Munies while he's down in Bakersfield. He'll be back late today, early tomorrow. It's not really the Moonkies that pose the biggest threat of an organized raid; as you may have concluded, they're not very sharp – intellectually. It's the Muties I'm worried about."

"Has there been any indication of hostility?"

"Not really. Nothing I can specifically point out. It's just that ... well they're still part human, and it's the human part, ironically, that makes them dangerous."

"How so?"

"They still have a mind that functions, they can read the writing on the wall and know they'll eventually turn to Moonkie. They're liable to utilize their brute strength to overpower a weaker human for whatever they deem necessary to survive, or even out of frustration, or spite, or jealousy."

"Human frailty."

"Precisely."

We walked on and the trees began to thicken, turning to forest. A worn path wove through the foliage. "It's fortunate we're situated out here, off the beaten path. Everyone flocked to the cities in the beginning – looting for supplies. So when the mutating began ... it was a slaughter house. Most of the Moonkies remained in the cities. Moonkies out in these parts are locals."

We began the ascent of a steep hill. At the apex the trees suddenly opened onto a huge pit, about the size of two football fields. It was filled with clear rainwater.

"Here's the old rock quarry, Jordan."

"It's beautiful! The water's nearly as clear as a swimming pool."

"Yes, well, I wouldn't advise swimming in it."

"Why so?"

"When the virus hit, as I was saying before, there were a lot of casualties. There were also many men left alive, mutating, but alive. We formed burial details. I couldn't supervise everyone, of course. Somebody got the bright idea that the rock quarry would be a convenient burial site."

"Oh my God."

"They weighted the bodies down with rocks and threw them in there, Jordan. At the bottom of that rock pit, I can't say how many bodies there are."

Suddenly, the beauty of the tranquil setting wasn't quite as enticing. I began to notice that on the edges of the water, among the overgrown grass and reeds, were a few bloated bodies. A stark reminder of the gruesome plight we were facing, as individuals and as a society …. That's if there were enough others out there to form one.

We passed a small cabin located on the top of a knoll near the quarry, Joe Rivera's place. Richard peeked in to make sure everything was in order and we headed into the final stretch of our perimeter tour. It took us near the main gate. Before we reached it, however, the sound of an approaching vehicle caught our attention. It pulled up to the gate and Richard and I halted where we were, hidden in a thick stand of trees several yards south. We watched and listened as two men, Muties, actually, exited the vehicle and began examining the front gate of the compound. They weren't grotesquely mutated, obviously not in the advanced stages, but we could tell they were Muties. Their foreheads were slightly distended and eyebrows thickened. Their mouths seemed slightly enlarged, as if the teeth within were somehow, overgrown. They seemed to lean forward as they walked, as if their arms and shoulders were heavy.

As we watched, Andy and Hawk appeared from the compound, carrying rifles.

"Who's that there?" Andy hollered.

The Muties stayed back from the gate but responded, "This here's Bounty Ortiz and Bounty Perez. We're lookin' for a couple of escapee's from the State Prison."

"Why you lookin' around here?" Andy asked. He hadn't opened the gate and it didn't appear as though he was going to.

"They mighta' passed around this way. You see anybody out of the ordinary?"

"Just you."

The Bounties looked at one another. "They murdered a couple of Bounties up in the woods toward the ocean sector. Might be traveling with a Mutie girl. We spotted 'em up the freeway yesterday ... but they got away. You sure ain't nobody come around recently?"

"Mind if we look around your property?" The Bounties took a tentative step forward.

"That'll be far enough." Andy raised his rifle. "Richard don't allow no Muties on his property, you know that. And if these here escapees are traveling with a Mutie girl, then you know they sure as hell ain't gonna be welcome here. So why don't you just get in your little race car there and go look someplace else."

"You got somethin' to be hiding up in there?" the Mutie persisted.

"Everybody knows that Richard runs a clean camp, Bounty Ortiz. What makes you so certain it was escapees that murdered them Bounties, anyway?" Hawk spoke up.

"Their log book. Says they picked up a couple of

Munies in the town of Corcoran; they'd been lootin' a residence there—the escapees was drivin' a State Prison vehicle. The Munies must have got a jump on 'em, killed 'em both. Bounties Nomez and Gelson were slaughtered and shot, their guard dog too. Gelson musta' been fillin' out his log just when it happened ... it cuts off there."

"Can I see the log book?" Andy asked.

"It's State property now."

"What state's that? There's no official government," countered Hawk.

"Provincial authority. We're duty bound and sworn to uphold the law in the name of Acting Governor Mierdamonte. Any escapees or murderers or looters or other law-breakers, we're authorized to apprehend."

"I guess you mean 'provisionally authorized', and I bet you don't even know what that means," Andy said.

"It means, if you're standing in the way of me upholding the law, I'm authorized to use any force necessary to carry out my duty."

"I've got my own orders, too. And there ain't no Muties allowed on the compound." Andy stood firm, gun still raised. "If we see any escapees traveling with a Mutie girl, we'll let you know."

The tension in the air was palpable. Both duos were armed, but no one appeared to want to be the first to resort to gunfire; especially since there was little to gain from violence – and much to lose.

"They're driving a tan pickup with a utility compartment, stole it from them Bounties they killed."

No acknowledgement or response, it seemed Andy and Hawk were tiring of the dialogue. It was clear the Bounties weren't getting in, not without force.

"We'll be back," the lead Bounty vowed.

"We'll be here," Andy responded.

After the Bounties had left, Richard and I joined Andy and Hawk near the entrance.

"You hear any of that?" Andy asked Richard.

"Yes, we caught it all." The three turned toward me. "You know anything about what they were talking about, Jordan?" Richard asked.

"Well, you already know my version of events (as I had relayed them earlier), but other than the guard dog, we left their encampment without confrontation."

"How'd you get the truck?" Andy asked.

I had to consider that, as I had been comatose when Frankie had gone back to retrieve the truck – in order to save my life, no less. "I'm afraid I was blacked out during that episode … all I know is, I woke up here."

"Frankie musta' gone back and did in the Bounties to get the truck," Andy said.

"Now, let's not jump to conclusions," Richard interjected. "We don't know that to be the case. We don't know anything until we talk to Frankie." Richard asked me, "Jordan, is Frankie capable of that kind of violence? Do you know what he was in for?"

"I'm quite certain that Frankie was acting in my benefit. He certainly wouldn't resort to such violent behavior unless it was absolutely necessary. And, as Richard pointed out, we don't know for certain whether he was involved."

"What's this about a Mutie girl?" Hawk asked.

"Valerie. She helped us get away. I don't know what happened to her. We're going to have to speak with Frankie. Richard, if you don't mind, let me talk to him first. It's been a … difficult time, you must know. We've been through much in order to get here. I certainly don't want to be the cause of any conflict between your community and the authorities."

"Jordan, those Bounties aren't of any authority that I recognize. And besides, our friendship trumps Bounty jurisdiction. We'll just have to talk to Frankie and see what the real story is …."

The sound of a rumpling truck motor and tires skidding on dirt, coming from the compound, made us all turn.

"Speak of the Devil," Andy said.

The very truck that had been the topic of conversation, the Bounties' old pickup, with Frankie behind the wheel, was careening down the driveway, lights flashing and horn honking.

"I think … we'll have to speak with him later." I said, hypnotized by the sight of the truck coming straight for us.

"Why's that, Jordan?" Richard asked.

"I think you better open the gate," I advised.

"Why? Where's he going?" Andy asked.

"I don't know, but you better open the gate." The truck got closer and its speed increased.

"What do we do, Richard?" Andy asked.

"OPEN THE FRICKING GATE!!!"

There was just enough time for all of us to dive out of the way as Andy unlatched the front gate and gave it a good push. Dust flying and pandemonium in full effect, the truck barely missed us and clipped the gate as Frankie sped out of the compound and down the road. We all stood aghast, surprised and perplexed.

"What the Hell was THAT all about?" Andy asked.

I opened my mouth to respond, no words came out at first. "I don't know, I have no idea." As Frankie disappeared into the dusty distance, I suddenly became acutely concerned for him, and Valerie … and all of us. God help us all.

* *

CHAPTER 15: FLIGHT OF THE FAITHLESS

(Frankie V.)

The old pickup bounded over bumps in the dirt road, barely managing to avoid careening off either side. Dense woods lined the twisting path for several miles, giving way to open spaces near the main highway turnoff. I leaned on the brakes and lurched to a noisy stop at the intersection. The sun was a big orange ball in the sky, threatening to drop off over the horizon soon. It would be gone in a few minutes, and once again, the cloak of night would descend – enabling the hunters to hunt and the hiders to hide. I was neither and both. I didn't have a clue where I was headed when I fled the compound; I just knew I didn't belong there.

At least the Professor was safe now; brought back to life by some miracle, or the healing power of his godson. I was sure he was gone. How in the world .... Well, what's important is that he's all right now. He'll be safe and secure with Richard, Carol and Lannie. That kid most certainly was "something" out of the ordinary. He seemed immune to the whirl of personal turmoil that everyone else was so often swept up in. How could a child manage so serenely as the world crashed all around? I guess kids just naturally adapt, it's the adults that have a hard time adjusting.

The accommodations were agreeable enough, more than comfortable. Food, a shower and a bed in a safe place were more than anyone might ask for, considering the circumstances. Yet, in spite of extreme exhaustion, I just couldn't get to sleep. The thought of poor Valerie out there having to fend for herself …. I shouldn't have let her go, but what choice did I have? She hadn't left me any. She'd made the call, and all I could do was sit there with a stupid look on my face as she disappeared into the dark.

I tossed and turned but couldn't get comfortable. As I finally began to drift off – I was awakened by a familiar sound. A big-headed crow was perched in the window sill across the bedroom, it was pecking noisily on the window frame.

"Son-of-a …."

"Sleeping well, are we?"

"You, again! What the hell do you want?"

"Just checking in on you."

"I don't need checking on."

"Getting along fine on your own, are you?"

"I'm managing."

"How's your girlfriend doing?"

"You scurvy fuck …."

"Now, now … no need for name-calling. I'm not the one who let her go."

"I didn't 'let' her go. She made up her own mind. How was I supposed to stop her?"

"Not your fault then, again?"

"What's that supposed to mean?"

"What's what supposed to mean?"

"You said 'again' … why'd you say that?"

"Sensitive, are we?"

"You said, 'again', Crow. I know what you're talking about. You're talking about Chrissy, goddamn you. You're talking about Chrissy, aren't you?"

"Am I?"

"You don't ever bring her name up to me, you hear me? You don't deserve to say her name!"

"I didn't say a thing."

"You know I couldn't stop her …. I couldn't stop her…."

"Valerie?"

"NO, Chrissy. You know I couldn't stop her!"

"Did you even try?"

Thirty years passed by in a flash, right before my eyes. As I stared into space, the memory of that day … that horrible, gruesome day came back to haunt me, again.

"What do you see, Frankie?" asked the Crow.

When I finally spoke, it was a hoarse whisper …

"The house was engulfed in flames. We were in the front yard. I remember it was cold outside, the first snow had just fallen, and the girls had built a snowman. It was melting from the heat of the fire. Chrissy was holding Ally, she must have been about three years old at the time. The look on her face…. I'll never forget the look on her face."

"What look?"

"Panic. And the worst expression of fear and sheer terror that anyone could imagine. She looked right at me, screaming … screaming and crying."

"Screaming what?"

"The baby. Where's the BABY?"

"What baby?"

"Chrissy's baby. My niece, Jennie Jewel."

"Where was she?"

"Inside. She was still inside."

Even the heartless Crow had no comment or response to that.

"Next thing I knew, Ally was in my arms and Chrissy was running back inside … right into the flames. It all happened so fast … I didn't even get a word out, I just stood there … holding Ally. She was crying uncontrollably, calling out for her mother and the baby. But …."

"But, what?"

"She never came back out. Chrissy never made it out. They found her in the baby's room, cradling Jennie Jewel in what was left of …."

"That's a terrible story, Frankie. I'm sorry."

"It should have been me. Chrissy was the smart one, the pretty one, the good one."

"Carrying around that sorrow, Frankie, even if it's hidden inside … it'll drag you down you know. How old were you?"

"Sixteen. I was sixteen. Chrissy was twenty-one and the star of the family. My hero, my guiding light."

"Sounds as if more than you realize burned up in the fire that day, Frankie. You lost a part of yourself there as well."

"Yeah, the good part."

"Grief is like a sickness, Frankie. At some point, you have to allow it to heal … you have to move on."

"You don't understand. That's not even the worst part. The worst of it is … how the fire started."

"What do you mean?"

I couldn't answer. Silence hung in the air like the pause between tolls of a heavy church bell. Words were caught in my throat ….

"I … can't. I can't say it."

"You shut it up inside and it'll eat your guts out, Frankie. Like it's been doing. You gotta let it out."

"I can't. I'm not that brave."

"Maybe that's where the violence in you comes from."

Emotionally spent, I stared at the Crow, confused. "What?"

"The evil that flows out of you when you're set off. The hatred you wreak on your victims – it's a projection of the guilt and self-loathing you feel toward yourself. You have to forgive yourself, Frankie. In every tragedy, from every sorrow, there's a lesson to be learned."

"Unless the lesson is that life sucks, I missed it."

"The dead live on in our hearts."

"In this case, my heart died with the dead."

"Is that when you went bad?"

"There were, 'instances' that gave me a clue as to what was inside of me. But, I always thought that in the end, I'd even it out. That day I just went cold inside and shut the world out. I began to close everybody and everything out. It was the only way I could get by."

"You never talked to anyone about this?"

"Just you."

"That's not healthy. There's only one thing a man can control in life, Frankie, and yet, it's the most difficult to master. If one can gain control though, he has found the key to unlock the universe."

"Do tell …."

"It's his own mind. If a man can control his own thoughts, the world is his oyster, and he may lead a good life. A normal life."

"Well, that ship has sailed, don't you think?"

"How so?"

"I got a best friend risen from the dead, my most recent romantic interest is a Mutant, and apparently it's the end of the world. Oh yeah, and I'm talking to a crow. Nothing normal about that."

"You're not even going to try, then?"

"What's the point?"

"It beats the alternative."

"I've thought about that … more than once."

"What's stopping you? The gun's still under the front

seat of the truck."

"What gun?"

"The one you found back at the trailer. The one you used on those Bounties: Gelson and Nomez."

"One minute you're my psychiatrist, the next you're Dr. Kevorkian. Who, or what, are you exactly?"

"I'm just trying to help. What, or who, do YOU think I am?"

"I haven't quite decided yet."

"What? Whether I'm your conscience, guardian angel, or the Devil?"

"No. Whether you're Heckle or Jeckle."

"At least you haven't lost your sense of humor."

"Comedy and tragedy go together, kind of like drinking and driving. Now, if you don't mind, I'm going to get some sleep I think."

"Pleasant dreams, my friend."

I managed to fall asleep for a while, a good while. When I woke up it was afternoon. It was disorienting to awaken in new and unfamiliar surroundings. When I wandered out to the kitchen and saw the Professor and Richard conversing on the deck, I meant to simply pour another cup of coffee and join them. Their conversation, however, stopped me in my tracks. Apparently, in the world I'd awakened in, civilized men had a 'shoot-to-kill' policy toward Mutants. At least in the world I'd left behind they gave you the illusion of justice with their three-strike legal system and beyond-life terms following a one-sided charade called a fair trial

I didn't handle that cold splash of reality in my face very well. I retreated back to my room – back behind closed doors, confined and secure in a small space. When the Professor tried to console, or counsel me, his words concerning 'faith' hit a sour note. I'd known something of 'faith' before. My mother was a religious person. Well, in a sense. We actually never went to church, but she must have been a very devout follower because she surely spent enough hours praying to her God. I remember, from a very early age – I must have been about three years old ….

"Frankie, honey, you go out and play in the cornfields now, Mama's gotta pray."

"But, Mama, I don't want to go out there. There's snakes and bugs and all kinds of crawly things. And, the others."

"What others, Darlin'?"

"The Crows." They were big, black, shiny creatures. Almost as big as me. A first, they were cautious and kept their distance. But as the summer wore on, me being out there every day, they got brave. They'd come right up on me. I didn't have any friends to play with, the nearest neighbors were miles away …. I tried to make the Crows my friends. But, they were scary and mean.

"You don't come in until I call you, Honey."

"But, Mama!"

"Go on, now. Mama gotta pray."

It was getting late summer. Those corn stalks were heavy with ears and the Crows came in droves. I hid out in the far end of the field, maybe they wouldn't notice me. Maybe they wouldn't taunt me today. It was hot out there. I was sweating and scared and knew it wouldn't be long before one of those Crows figured out where I was hiding and told the others …. Then, they'd all come to get me.

I couldn't take the tension anymore, I ran home. I was almost as scared of my mother, I didn't want to interrupt her praying. So, I crept around to the back and peeked in the window to see if she was done. The preacher had come by and was praying with my mother. She was really going at it, too. He was standing over her, she had her head bowed and her dress pulled up to her waist. Her front buttons were all undone and he must have been feeding her communion because he kept telling her, "Swallow it." Except we weren't Catholic, that I'm aware of.

I think it was Mama's praying that finally made Daddy

leave for good. He just left one day and never came back. I was sent off to live with my aunt and her family. She was religious too. When I got bigger she always made me pray with her. Long, hard hours of intense prayer. I had to swallow communion too. At least I didn't have to go out to the cornfields anymore. But, the Crows still came. When things got bad, they always came around ….

"Planning a trip, are you, Frankie?"

"Go away, Crow. I ain't got time for you now."

"Where you headed?"

"I'm going after her."

"It might be too late. You might not like what you find."

"Would it be any worse than sitting around here, wondering?"

"It might be. You're safe here. You'd be crazy to leave this place."

"Yeah, well, I'm not the one talking to a human."

*

I watched the last sliver of the sun disappear over the horizon, then looked left to the south, then right to the north. How long had I been at Richard's? How far could she have gotten on foot in that time? And, how on Earth would I find her? It'd be a one-in-a-million shot.

I looked at my reflection in the truck mirror. "So you're saying there's a chance?" At least now I was talking to myself; that was an improvement. I turned the rusty old truck onto the freeway heading south. What I was heading into I didn't know. What I was leaving behind, I hoped stayed there … by God I hoped it stayed there.

*   *

CHAPTER 16: POETIC IRONY

(The Professor)

Frankie's unexpected departure and the Bounties' blatant threats had added an extra helping of uncertainty to an already unceasingly ambiguous atmosphere. I had no answers to everyone's question of why Frankie had flown the coop in such a manner. And Richard, likewise, couldn't assure me that the Bounties' intentions would or would not be carried out. I didn't want to be a burden, even though most of the community members did their best to assure me that was not the case. Still, there was a pall of apprehension and uneasiness around the dinner table that night.

After dinner, Andy took the first perimeter sweep, each watch lasting about two hours. Each of the men would take turns, allowing for several hours sleep in between. Carol and Donna cleared the table; Roberto, Angela, and Lannie helped with the dishes and clean-up, and Richard asked me to join him in the library. He laid out a detailed map of the compound grounds and the surrounding area. He pointed out the key defensive spots, and we discussed options.

"As you can see, Jordan, the rear of almost the entire compound is fortified by the presence of the lake. And the south perimeter is protected by the rock quarry. Moonkies won't be trying to gain entrance through either of those ways and they're not apt to be inclined to simply attempt to storm the front gate. The north property is so heavily overgrown with thistles and thorn brush that it's unlikely anyone would be attempting to get through there. Even Muties or Bounties would find it difficult to maneuver through the natural defenses that are around three sides of the compound. The fencing with razor-wire along the west entrance side, could be thwarted with simple wire-cutters, but we'd see anybody coming that way easily. We have a series of escape routes through the woods, indicated here by the blue markings. There are also caves in the rock face of the outer quarry hills that would take days to search. I haven't even been in all of them myself."

"Do you think they'll be coming back? I mean, looking for me?"

"I'd say the chances are about 50-50. Just surviving, even for Bounties, is the main objective. There's a good chance those two were more interested in getting a handout than actually looking for escaped Munies."

"I don't know, Richard, they seemed pretty intent on finding whoever killed their brother Bounties. I wouldn't underestimate the justice element."

"Well, Joe Rivera ought to be back from Bakersfield tomorrow. Maybe he'll have some word on what the atmosphere is like down there. Bounties still take orders from somebody, and they're not likely to make any significant moves without authorization. There's something else I wanted to show you, Jordan."

Richard moved to the side wall and opened a large sliding door that had been hidden by a curtain. Inside was a cozy work area, about the size of a spacious walk-in closet. He lit a kerosene lantern and placed it on the work table that extended the length of the space. There were several glass lab beakers, a propane gas set-up, several books and pages of equations written in pen and pencil. From a metal cooler under the work bench, Richard produced a test tube and held it up to the light. It contained what appeared to be a red-colored liquid, too thin in consistency to be blood, too thick to be water.

"What is it, Richard?"

"Jordan, I don't have the facilities here to do the proper research. I don't have adequate data relating to the exact composition of the original virus. What I do have are samples of infected victims, and my own knowledge of biophysics. I'm trying to develop an antidote to the Paracelsus virus, but it's arrows against cannons. Take a look."

He retrieved a droplet of the liquid from the tube and placed it on a glass sample slide and carefully mounted it onto the microscope that stood near the lantern. He held the light close from one side and pulled down a battery operated flashlight from the overhead shelf, shining its beam from the other. I adjusted the focus and peered into the lens.

"What am I looking at here, Richard?"

"That's a sample of AB-positive blood, fortified with every antibiotic and viral-fighting component or compound I could lay my hands on. Now, watch."

Richard added an extremely small droplet of another fluid to the slide. Almost instantly the original sample began deteriorating, cells from the added sample 'ate' or 'consumed' the cells of the host sample.

"That was the Paracelsus virus. At least, contaminated blood from a Moonkie, applied to common AB-positive blood."

He then produced another sample and applied it to a slide. "The O-negative." He let me look into the microscope as he added the tiniest droplet of contaminated blood to it. "What do you see?"

"Well, it appears that the contaminated cells are cohabitating with the O-negative. They don't seem to be infecting the sample."

"Give it a few seconds."

As I watched and waited, the cells on the slide appeared to be transforming before my eyes. "It looks like the virus is mixing with the O-negative, but not destroying the cells. It's as if they're both existing in the same space."

"Precisely. The virus doesn't destroy the O-negative, but it does lie dormant."

"Do you mean, Richard, that at least with this sample, the virus does invade the host body but doesn't 'destroy' the cells? In other words, persons with O-negative may have the virus, but not show symptoms?"

"I can't categorically say that. My tests are limited to the few samples I've tested. But, in this case, at least, that is true."

He pulled out yet another sample. "Now, watch this!"

He repeated the previous procedure adding the virus to the sample. I watched through the lens and waited. I adjusted the light to make sure I was seeing properly. It was amazing.

"Richard, this sample isn't being affected at all. The contaminated blood isn't able to either invade or attach to the host."

"Yes, it's the only sample I've tested that is truly immune to the virus."

"Where or from whom did you get it?"

"This is Lannie's blood."

I couldn't have been more intrigued or fascinated by any bit of information than I was at that very moment. It was astounding and opened up a whole realm of questions and possibilities.

"Richard, if you could break down both Lannie's blood and the infection to its core elements, map the genetic code, you'd have the antidote."

"Precisely."

"Are we saying that Lannie is the only person on Earth that's truly immune to the Paracelsus virus?" I asked incredulously.

"I'm not willing to assert that claim, Jordan. It may very well be that is merely true of the few samples I've tested. It would be highly unlikely for that to be the case on a worldwide basis. I'm sure there must be others."

"Are you?"

He didn't answer. We were both allowing our brains to consider the possibilities and compute the multiple algorithms that might be involved. Our meditations were disturbed by the slightest discernable movement near the doorway to the work space.

"Who's there?" Richard called out.

From behind the half-closed curtain, Hawk appeared like a phantom. "It's me, Richard. I was just wondering if Andy and I were still going into town tomorrow to pick up supplies."

Hawk looked interestedly at the scattered samples as he spoke. Something about him seemed uneasy.

"Yes. Just search for essentials: food, fuel, tools. But make it a quick trip. I might need you guys close to home later in the day … just in case."

"Alright then." He nodded his head but made no effort to leave.

"Thank you, Hawk. You're up next for rounds when Andy gets back, then me." Richard checked his watch, "You'd better go ahead."

"Yeah, I'd better go."

After Hawk left, an uneasiness hung in the air that was palpable. "That was odd," I remarked.

"Yes. Nobody usually comes in the library unless invited. It's sort of my private space … that's why I set up this little archaic lab here."

"Did you get the impression he was … eavesdropping?"

"I'm not sure. Did you notice him come in?"

"No. He was just 'there' … all of a sudden. Tell me, Richard, how well do you know Hawk? Is he a trusted friend or employee?"

"He's an acquaintance of Andy's. He rode up soon after The Day and we naturally took him in. I wouldn't call him a friend though. And as far as trust goes, I don't know. I get bad vibes from him sometimes. I can't exactly say why …."

"Richard, do you think he heard? I mean, about Lannie?"

Concern was written all over my friend's face. "I'm not sure."

"That's not the kind of thing you really want to get around. I mean, it's amazing, monumental news … but, for Lannie's sake …."

"Yes. It was not meant to be a matter of general knowledge."

"Perhaps you should speak to Hawk about keeping it confidential."

"Yes. To be frank, Jordan, I've never detected a strong sense of personal integrity from Hawk, certainly not the same feeling I get from Andy, however, at the moment we desperately need as many able hands as possible to guard and maintain a citadel of safety and civilized life in the midst of a moribund and ever more barbarized world. Even though I couldn't say I trust Hawk with any certainty, the times dictate tolerance."

"I understand." Richard began clearing the work table and putting everything away. "Richard, you have generators. I was wondering why you're not utilizing electric lighting, at least in the more critical areas?"

"We only run the generators about four hours a day, for refrigeration and to freeze ice or do whatever otherwise couldn't be done without electricity. The main issue with the generators is gasoline. Although we have a pretty significant stock, I feel it's better to conserve and get used to doing without wherever we can."

"So you keep your samples refrigerated then?"

"Absolutely. With chemical ice – blue ice."

"What are your plans in regard to an antidote?"

"I've developed a tentative game plan: First, I must complete my experiments using samples from all available sources. I have to exhaust all the potential remedies that are currently available to me – test blood samples of every person on this compound against the virus, and every combination of conceivable antigens. Second, I believe I'll need to travel to the Bakersfield area, to see if their lab facilities are more conducive to the type of research that's needed to find an antidote – and to see what they've come up with. Third, and I may have these items out of order – as this step might better be executed first – I need to retrieve Seth Edelstein's research data from when he was developing the virus."

"How is that even possible? Weren't Stanford and Berkeley completely destroyed from the antimatter explosion? Even the military medical laboratories in Colorado, where the actual virus was likely manufactured is a total wasteland."

"My thinking is that Seth very likely kept his original notes and formulas very close to him. I believe there's a distinct possibility that the information we're looking for might be at his home."

"His home." Now that Richard mentioned it in fact, it was a logical conclusion. I know that anything of significant value I'd ever produced was usually kept close at hand. "Where does, or did, he live? He's not still living, is he?"

"I seriously doubt it. However, Seth lived in Daly City, southwest of San Francisco. It's possible that Daly City escaped the devastation, at least the worst of it. It's far enough from the main event to potentially have escaped total destruction."

"Do you know his exact address?"

"As a matter of fact Seth and I corresponded on a number of occasions and I do have his return address." Richard crossed from the mini-lab to the desk of the library and pulled out a stack of envelopes, selecting one and handing it to me.

I read the return address … "Seth Edelstein, 1666 Heaven's Angel Way, Daly City, CA." I looked at Richard and him at me, both with a hint of irony in our expressions.

"Prophetic, or ironic, Richard?"

"I'd venture to say, Jordan, a generous portion of either and both."

*

After a few hours of much needed sleep, it was my turn to make the rounds – patrol the compound perimeter. In the dark it was quite spooky, to say the least. I took the same route that Richard and I tread earlier, down the fence line of the front to the north side, rounding the briar patches and thorny thickets to the eastern corner which led directly to the far side of the lake. As I made my way along the ridge the sounds of the night began to become apparent to my ears and other senses. The stars shined bright and the moon was over half full. It was actually a brilliant and beautiful night and my nervousness gave way to enjoyment of my surroundings and contemplations on my discussions with Richard.

It appeared that, at some point, a road trip would be essential. Perhaps more than one. I thought it highly likely that Richard and I would eventually have to travel to Bakersfield in order to meet other survivors and interact with the powers that be. It was also imperative that Richard be allowed access to a well-equipped lab. The other potential excursion, to Seth Edelstein's home in Daly City, I wasn't as enthused about. Then, there were the logistics of taking a trip – leaving the others to fend for

themselves and insuring our own safety. There was a lot
to consider.

I thought of my friend, Frankie, and wished I had
done more to make him want to stay. He would have
been invaluable on such missions, they were his specialty –
dangerous and foolhardy.

As I neared the rise that led to the lower hills of the
rock quarry, I rested for a moment. It was a good little
climb up to the ridge of the quarry and at night, potentially
dangerous. I stepped carefully and nearly lost my balance
several times before summiting. Up on top of the rocky
perch, overlooking the tranquil water below, I felt, literally,
on top of the world. It only fleetingly passed through my
mind – the thought of all the Moonkie bodies floating or
submerged in the waters there. I quickly decided not to
think about that.

I could see Joe Rivera's cabin from my roost. I
imagined it must take an especially brave soul to choose to
live out here – all alone and independent. I supposed one
could get used to the solitary lifestyle, not having to answer
or deal with anyone else; just you and your inner drummer
to march to. I raised an appreciative eye to the heavens,
inspired at that moment to compose an ode to the self-
reliant soul … it should be strong and reflect the
determined nature of anyone who has struck out on such
an arduous course. Heavy with courageous thematic intent
and marbled with a spirited weaving of adventure and …
OH! AHHHH!!!!

In my reverie I had inadvertently stepped forward one
too many steps and quite inexcusably walked over the edge
of the rock quarry ledge. I was now hanging on the cliff
that fell straight down to various rocky edges before
meeting the deadly waters of the quarry lake. I had
somehow managed to grasp a tree root, and was praying it
was strong enough to continue holding my weight. It
dawned on me that it probably wouldn't matter, however,
as I wasn't strong enough to hang on to the root much

longer myself. As I kicked and desperately attempted to gain any footing, I rammed my right leg into a protruding rock that happened to be extremely sharp and positioned just so that my shinbone caught it at the worst possible angle. The pain was excruciating and for a moment I thought it would be better to simply let go and let whatever happen, happen. Luckily, my inner guidance somehow overrode that directive and I continued to cling to my precarious lifeline.

There's one thing that's good about being in a life and death circumstance that there just seems to be no way out of … things can't possibly get worse. Well, usually that's the case. In mine, however, it just seemed natural that it would not, could not, be the case. As I writhed in pain and clung to my last little shred of hope, above me, quite oddly, appeared two little heads. Looking down on me from the perch I'd just fallen from were two strangers. In the dark I couldn't quite make out their features – I was a bit distracted. However, by sheer concentration of will, I forced myself to focus and slowly the moonlight allowed me to see who my observers were … or, who they appeared to be. Based on my brief experience during my new found freedom, I determined that the two heads staring down at me were Muties, in advanced stages of mutation. Or, quite possibly, MOONKIES!

The heavy revolver I'd been carrying had long ago fallen out of my waistband and dropped down the face of the cliff into the water below. I was less than defenseless, I was helpless. Without a weapon, I wasn't merely vulnerable … I was dinner. The irony didn't escape me – even in the current circumstances. Man had gained dominance in the world through higher brain function and the development of tools and sophisticated weaponry. He'd also destroyed the world with the penultimate of those weapons – once again to find himself at the mercy of nature's less intelligent, but physically superior beasts.

As the monsters of the night adroitly crawled over the ledge above and made their way toward me … I realized the irony was poetic.

*   *

CHAPTER 17: THE DEAD BURY
THEIR DEAD

(Frankie V.)

The freeway heading south from Richard's compound was littered with cars and trucks pushed or dragged to the side of the road to allow the few remaining travelers to pass. Not that there was any traffic. The first several hours were uneventful – not a soul in sight. At least, none inhabiting a living body. There were plenty of corpses, though. The remains of the unlucky lay entombed in Chevys and Fords and Toyotas all along the way. Rusting final resting places. I'd quit being affected by the sight of them. When you think about it, does it really matter what happens to your body after you're done with it? Dust to dust. The line from a long-ago Sunday sermon came to mind: "Let the dead bury their dead." I didn't know what that meant when I'd heard it as a kid, and I didn't have the mental energy to analyze it now. Just one of those itinerant thoughts that passes through one's mind when you feel like you're one of the last remaining few survivors of the apocalypse. Which reminded me … I wasn't the only one out here.

I'd been on pins and needles watching out for oncoming vehicles. I didn't want to run into any more Bounties. I had it worked out that if I did see anything, I'd just pull to the side of the road and lie down in the seat. The shabby truck would easily pass as just another stranded vehicle, with just another dead driver. I'd fit right in. I'd already stopped several times to siphon gas from discarded junkers. I'd managed to find enough to get me this far. What I really needed was to find some food and water, and soon. In my infinite foolishness, I'd left the compound with barely a day's rations. I'd have to take the next turnoff and raid some unfortunate's residence for anything edible. But then what?

Where was I going, and what did I expect to find? Clarity? Closure? Peace of mind? Sanity? Doubtful. Those things had eluded me my entire life; did I really think the path I was on would bring me to a more satisfying place? Sometimes, you just keep moving forward just to be moving, fooling yourself into believing that you're getting somewhere. Some people go through a whole life that way. I knew that from experience. Did I truly believe I'd find Valerie? And how long would I be able to dodge Bounties and Muties and Moonkies?

I checked the revolver on the seat next to me. Four bullets. Four bullets to fend off whatever is out there that I need protection from. Well, three. I thought I'd save one, just in case. Night was falling and I was a sitting duck out on the wide-open road. There's a turnoff just ahead, leading to some no-name town. They're all pretty much the same now. Everybody's dead or hiding, or worse. All I'm concerned with is getting off the road and finding some food and avoiding contact with anyone or anything.

Halfway up the exit ramp the inevitable happens – the engine sputters and steam billows from under the hood. Great! Just what I need. Car trouble and a smoke signal declaring my location. Hey, blood-thirsty monsters and greedy bloodsuckers, come and get me.

A quick examination reveals a busted radiator hose, not fatal. I can probably find a suitable replacement on one of the abandoned vehicles back on the road. I could even walk into town, it's only about half a mile east. I opt for the trek back down to the freeway; the evil I'd already trod. About a quarter mile back I'd seen an SUV that likely had what I needed. Escape transportation is worth the risk of being out in the open, I hope. I grab a screwdriver, pliers, and a mini-crowbar from the utility bin and trudge back down the highway. I watch out in all directions for any movement. Daylight's wasting and I break into an easy jog.

When I get to the SUV I realize I'm going to have to reach into the cab and pull the hood release under the dash. That means close contact with Mr. Gruesome Corpse, who's stuck snugly behind the steering wheel. He's a smelly one, and the wife's not any better. The door's unlocked and I hold my breath and avoid eye contact. I don't think he will mind, and he's not objecting, so I pop the hood and get to work. Sure enough the SUV's hoses are in good shape, and I take both the radiator hoses and a couple of fan belts. The battery is relatively new and I consider taking that as well, but decide that traveling light is probably my best option. Still, while I'm here, I unlatch the rear door and rifle through Mr. and Mrs. G's belongings. Waste not, want not. I'm in luck. Under the carpeting of the rear compartment is a sunken storage space, just like the one in my old Ford Bronco. Apparently, the scavengers before me had missed it.

Inside I find a flashlight – still working, a pair of leather gloves, and much to my delight, a small cooler (normally used for a six-pack). What I discover there surely would have brought tears to the eyes of any hardened post-apocalypse survivor. Inside the cooler are five, well-preserved Snickers bars, six cheese and crackers mini-packs, and two Hostess cupcakes! My head gets light for an instant; riches can best be defined by need. I suddenly feel wealthy beyond belief. I grab the loot, look around like a guilty shoplifter, slam the back door and head back up the highway.

During the short walk, I dine on one of the cheese cracker packets and the most delicious slightly melted Snickers I've ever tasted. I couldn't help but flash back on memories of dining at the 'Top of Five', a fancy rotating restaurant in the Bonaventure Hotel in downtown Los Angeles. Nothing I was ever served at the exclusive eatery outshined the banquet I was enjoying at present. I was eternally grateful to the couple in the SUV; and momentarily wondered when it was my time to go, if there would be anyone around to share the final moments with. While at least those two had each other, I couldn't think of a soul who would mourn my passing.

I wasn't ready to tap out just yet, however, and I devoured another Snickers bar, savoring the gooey mess. When I got back to the truck, I tossed the lot on the dashboard and got to work on the hose. After I crawled underneath and removed the busted hose, I got an unexpected surprise when the backwash of water still left in the radiator poured out all over my face, neck and hands. Antifreeze and putrid radiator water do not taste good, even when washing down chocolate. I came out spitting and gasping and cursing myself for being so stupid. I frantically wiped my eyes and washed them out with the last of the water I had. I'd have to be more careful, there weren't any clinics or pharmacies or hospitals to go to for medical attention. Even a simple injury could be fatal, if left unattended.

I tested my vision and wiped my face with my shirt. Luckily, the worst of the mess hadn't directly flooded my eyes. No permanent damage. Not so luckily – the brief distraction had taken my attention away from my primary responsibility and just like that … I had company.

A large, slack-jawed man-beast stood before me.

Shock and paralyzing fear flooded through me. His slumped shoulders heaved with each labored breath. He had large, dark eyes with a protruding forehead and thick brow. His teeth were slightly elongated and a mat of hair stuck out of his shirtsleeves. He was wearing a mechanic's coverall with a name patch that read, "Hodges". I believed myself to be in the presence of a Moonkie … or, at least, a Mutie in the advanced stage of mutation. There was little doubt that this creature could literally tear me limb-from-limb, but I felt no malice or sinister intent on his part. He just stood there. The look on his face might be described as sad or docile. My fear subsided and turned to curiosity.

If the creature attacked I wasn't completely sure even a bullet would stop him. I didn't reach for the gun. It became apparent that Hodges was interested in only one thing. He was staring longingly at the Snickers bars on the dashboard and drooling. I reached through the truck window and grabbed the bag, pulling out a candy bar. I extended my arm and his huge eyes followed my every move. When I tossed the candy to him, he caught it deftly and gobbled it down in one gulp, not bothering to remove the wrapper. I pulled out another and unwrapped it, tossing that one to the beast as well. It was like feeding time at the zoo and although no cage separated us, I didn't feel threatened by Hodges.

He made quick work of polishing off the chocolate, taking care to lick every trace from his long fingers. Then, without prompting or formalities he picked up the replacement radiator hose from the ground and proceeded to install it efficiently and expertly. As he climbed out from under the truck, I realized that the virus, or whatever it was that caused mutation, had significantly damaged Hodges' communication skills, but had little impact on his mechanical abilities. He made no attempt at speaking and avoided eye contact. He wiped his hands on his coveralls, as if out of habit, and closed the hood.

"Where do you stay?" I asked.

No answer.

"Would you like to come with me?"

Again no response, but he grabbed up the tools and other items scattered on the ground and hopped in the passenger seat.

"All right. It's settled then, you'll come along." I cranked the old truck to life and we headed to town. A couple of eligible bachelors on the prowl – not exactly Starsky and Hutch – but with the world in its present state, what can you expect?

"We gotta find water, Hodges. For the radiator, especially; but, we need drinking water, too. You know this area?"

The main drag revealed another ghost town. Everything had been looted and it looked as though somebody had come through and cleared out all the bodies from the streets – because there weren't any. At the edge of town Hodges abruptly grabbed the steering wheel and guided the truck into a deserted gas station. I slammed on the brakes and yelled at him …

"What the hell, Hodges?"

He just sat there with a blank expression on his face, staring out the window. It didn't take too long to figure out that he knew this place. He got out, I followed. He went directly to the garage doors and yanked the nearest one open. He disappeared inside and I stayed back surveying the surroundings. I didn't want to be surprised again. I could hear him rummaging around in there and he soon reappeared carrying a five-gallon water container. It was full of clear water and he sat it down in front of me and returned to the garage. I filled the radiator and tasted the water, clean enough for drinking.

Hodges came back out carrying a large, red gasoline can with a hand pump and coil of rubber hose attached; he also had a big pipe wrench. He went around to the side of the building and rolled away a rusty fifty-five gallon drum, revealing a hatch cover to what had to be an underground gas tank. Sure enough, he cranked the lid with the wrench and the cover popped off. The smell of gasoline filled the air and he began pumping gas into the can expertly. It took four trips to the truck to fill the tank, then we filled up every container we could find with gas and loaded them into the back of the truck. Hodges brought out a well-stocked tool box, gloves, rags, quarts of oil and transmission fluid. He checked the tire pressure and added oil to the engine, then dived under the hood-checking everything over.

I took a look around the gas station office. It was extremely dirty and dusty; apparently no one had been there in a while. There was a metal desk in the middle of the tiny room with sundry car parts scattered about, old calendars with smiling bikini girls, a file cabinet and an old-fashioned cigarette machine with a mirrored front against the wall. I found a cigar box in the back of one of the desk drawers that had a bunch of quarters in it. I took a handful and deposited them into the cigarette machine – pulling the lever on a pack of Camel non-filters. I could've pried the machine open and looted the whole thing, but somehow, that just didn't seem right. As I stood there unwrapping the pack of smokes, I took notice of my reflection in the mirror. I didn't recognize the face I saw there.

The accident with the radiator hose had left smeared grime all over my face, neck and arms. My hair was sticking up and covered in goo. Dirt was caked around my eyes, and my hands were black with filth. I realized then that Hodges had likely mistaken me for a Mutie. That's probably why he approached without fear. He seemed sedate and comfortable around me, so rather than clean up, I decided to continue to let him think that way. I found matches in the desk and lit my first smoke since the beach cigar. It made me light-headed and I sat on the desk, taking a breather. It had been a wild time the past weeks. Now I found myself casually smoking a cigarette in an abandoned gas station while a Mutant man-beast expertly tuned our getaway vehicle. Somehow, none of it seemed all that strange anymore.

I noticed some photographs on the wall. There was one of a smiling Hodges with an older man. Hodges with an elderly lady. Hodges with a happy-looking dog. All the pieces fell into place and I understood that this was Hodges' family business. His mom and dad and him and the dog …. He probably grew up in this little freeway town, working at his dad's gas station since he was a kid. Just living life slow, one day at a time. Just a regular family. Probably went to church a couple of times a week and had a big Sunday dinner with fried chicken and potatoes and gravy. Then everything fell apart with the catastrophe.

Now, Hodges was all alone and a Mutie.

When I came out, Hodges was done with the truck and wiping off the windshield.

"Hodges, you live around here?"

He didn't ever look me directly in the eye, and never really responded to any question or said anything. But he got in the truck and as I drove, he reached over and turned the steering wheel this way and that, directing us to a tree-lined street and to a little white house with a picket fence. He just stared at the place and I understood this was his home, or, it used to be.

Hodges got out, and, before opening up the gate in the fence, he checked the mailbox. No new mail. Apparently he wasn't cognizant of the interruption of mail service. I followed him inside. He didn't seem to be all that aware of my presence. He just went about his regular routine, I guess. He checked the house (for intruders, I believe). He tested the windows and the back door to make sure they were locked. Then he settled into a comfortable looking easy chair in the living room, right in front of the TV. Of course, it wasn't working, but he just sat there, staring. He pulled a shotgun from behind the sofa and laid it on his lap. But, none of that was the weirdest thing in the room.

The smell alerted me before I noticed the rotted remains of what I believe must have been his mother and father sitting together on a small couch on the far wall of the room. TV trays were placed in front of them. Hodges sat guard over the family without qualm or complaint. The fact that this gentle giant had allowed me into his irregular inner sanctum was both disturbing and heart-warming.

Before nightfall I pulled the truck into the garage and locked the door. There was canned food in the kitchen and we ate green beans and ravioli that I heated up over a charcoal fire on the grill in the backyard.

Hodges slept on the sofa in the living room. I took the back bedroom at the other end of the house – Hodges' room. It didn't smell too bad over there. I blocked the door and cracked the window. It was an ordinary room, the kind of place a regular kid grows up in. Baseball mitt, records and CD's, a poster of some blond pop star, old magazines and dirty clothes strewn about. Relics of a once ordinary life, now anything but ordinary. My heart ached for Hodges and his family, and me and the memories of a once happy child. All that was gone now. Yesterday a memory, tomorrow just a dream.

I looked out the window from Hodges' bed that night, counting stars until I fell asleep. I didn't know what tomorrow would bring, or the next day – if I made it that far. I figured tomorrow would just have to take care of itself and I'd face it just as Hodges had, one day at a time.

The next morning we gathered up all the useable gear and food and packed it into the truck. I handed Hodges his old baseball mitt as he sat in the passenger seat. He took it and held on to it tightly. I stashed the shotgun behind the front seat and thought for a moment about maybe we should've buried Hodges' folks. I didn't think Hodges had a thought on it one way or the other, but I asked him.

"Hodges, you want to bury your folks?" He didn't respond.

"All right then, Buddy. We'll let the dead bury their dead, right?" No answer.

As we backed out of the driveway and I threw the old truck into gear to head out, Hodges tossed the baseball mitt over the fence into the front yard of his old house. We drove away in silence. Whatever we were to face in the immediate future, at least we wouldn't have to face it alone.

*   *

CHAPTER 18: THE BEAST WITHIN

(The Professor)

"Professor! Professor Bruno!"

I could hear my name being called. I could even feel my face being lightly slapped. I was aware that I was no longer clinging tenuously to the tree root lifeline on the quarry cliff. The last thing I remember, I had let go … preferring to drop and risk physical harm (or even death) than to suffer the unthinkable at the hands of the gruesome beast that inched nearer. The creature's eyes seemed to glow in the dark. I smelled his rancid breath and caught a glimpse of his razor-like teeth; then, I let go – not only of the root, but of my resolve to face the terror that confronted me. I believe I was literally, or quite nearly, scared to death.

Now, as I lay on some form of cot in a small room that appears to be lit by a single candle, I feel a pulsating pain throbbing through my leg all the way to my hip. I recall ramming it into a sharp rock that protruded from the quarry wall. The pain is a reminder that I'm still among the living. In the far corner of the room, a man is conferring in hushed tones with two other smaller individuals. He seems to be issuing orders, then approaches and leans over me – wiping my head with a damp cloth ….

"Professor Bruno …."

"Yes. I'm … yes."

"How do you feel, Professor?"

"My leg … it hurts like hell!"

"You split it open pretty badly, I'm afraid. I've cleaned it but I don't know if it's broken. Don't worry, I'm going to get you some help. Just rest up and gather your strength. I'll get someone from the main house."

"Who are you?" I ask.

"I'm Joe Rivera."

"Joe!"

"I just returned from Bakersfield and saw you standing at the top of the quarry. I guess you got too close to the edge."

"<u>You</u> saved me?"

"Yes."

"But, what about the Moonkies?"

"Moonkies? Ain't no Moonkies around here. Moonkies don't go anywhere near water."

"Muties, then?"

"Nope. No Muties, either."

"Joe, your cabin's all the way at the far side of the quarry from where I fell. I'm telling you, there were Moonkies, or at least Muties in advanced stage mutation over there at the top of the cliff. I saw them."

"You must be mistaken."

"Maybe the others saw them."

"What others?"

"The ones you were talking to just now." I looked around the cabin. Other than Joe and me, it was empty.

"Ain't nobody else here, Professor. Maybe in all the excitement, you got … confused."

Or, maybe I had fallen down the rabbit hole. Because

things were getting curiouser and curiouser.

"How'd you get me out of the water?" I noticed for the first time, that I wasn't wet. Which I surely should have been … unless I somehow got caught up on the rocks of the cliff.

"You didn't fall into the quarry. I grabbed you off that root you were hanging on to."

I didn't wish to appear ungrateful or dispute Joe's account of events – but logical reasoning dictated that something here was, I believe the appropriate term to be – whacked. For Joe to have seen me at the top of the quarry and have gotten all the way to the other side, in the dark, covering that much distance through thick foliage … humanly impossible. I took careful notice of Joe Rivera. He was a stout man in his late forties, early fifties. Dark eyes and hair and pretty much regular features. Joe was, to my best estimation … a Munie. Human.

"I'm a good climber."

I knew, that <u>nobody</u> was <u>that</u> good.

"Joe, in no way do I mean to appear unappreciative, or doubt your word … but, how is it that you know my name?"

Joe noticeably stiffened, but he did not respond.

"I told him, Señor Professor."

From the shadow of the doorway appeared a young man of similar size and proportion to Joe.

"Mijo, no!" Joe exclaimed.

As the younger man stepped into the candlelight, I could see his features were distinctly, irregular. Long hair hung over prominent cheekbones and his eyes were overly large … similar to Valerie Fierno's. He had a large mouth with elongated teeth. His shoulders were slightly hunched forward and his arms and fingers were unusually long. From behind him, another boy appeared, a carbon copy, except a few inches shorter. The realization was clear … Muties.

"I am Topo Rivera, Señor. This is my brother, Nieto.

We know who you are. Forgive my father, he was just protecting us."

"Your father?" I looked from Joe to the boys and let the shock dissipate. "You saved my life. Thank you."

"It is our honor, Señor. Lannie has told us of you. We have watched you and the others on your patrols around the compound. We know you hold none of the prejudices that the other Munies have for our kind, you are welcome in our home."

"You know Lannie?"

"Of course. He is our close friend. We grew up here together."

"After the catastrophe and the ensuing plague," Joe spoke, "when the mutations began, and especially after Jane Adams' death, it was better to hide the boys from the others. I just told them that they ran off. I understand Richard's grief. I lost my wife, also. But, not all Muties are the enemy, Professor."

"Yes, of course."

Topo interjected, "A shadow life of wicked sin … beware the beast that lies within."

"Where's that from, Topo?" I asked.

"'The Beast Within', Eduardo Carrochio. It's a poetic commentary on civilization, and how advanced culture is man's way of training himself to repress his natural tendencies. That's why the most popular books and movies are of killing and lust and murderous violence. That's why there's still war, or was war; a 'civil' manner of acting out the most basic of instincts."

"Continuing that line of thought, then the virus and even the catastrophe isn't so much of an accidental occurrence or deteriorating mutation as it's a way of taking us back to what we really are … stripping us down to our true selves."

"Perhaps. Maybe it's cause and effect of what went wrong. Man became so civilized it was impossible to maintain the illusion of civility. We'd strayed so far from our own natural condition, that it was inevitable we'd destroy ourselves – and our world. Sympathetic self-loathing en masse; subconscious murder-suicide to cleanse the world-mind conscience and the universe through self-annihilation."

"Where did you study, Topo?"

"Fresno State."

"A philosophy major, I assume?"

"Zoology."

A fresh wave of pain washed over me, it must have been apparent on my face.

"Let me tend to your leg, Professor."

"There's no time," Joe stated. "They'll be missing him soon, and come looking. You must take your brother and go to the woods, Mijo."

"How long do you expect you can keep hiding them, Joe?" I asked. There was so much more to that question that could be implied. Like, what would become of all that remained of this family once the boys mutated to Moonkies. It was evident that Joe had considered that question himself; it likely kept him awake into the darkest hours when the rest of the world – human and otherwise – faded into distant slumber.

"As long as we can, Professor. As long as we can."

Joe and the boys managed to load me into Joe's jeep and before I could utter a 'thank you' or 'goodbye', Topo and Nieto had disappeared into the darkness. We rumbled from the quarry heights down to the main house where Richard and Carol met us and helped me into the house. After the initial surprise of seeing me incapacitated had subsided, I explained how I had fallen during my rounds and how Joe had luckily found and rescued me. Needless to say, Joe's secrets were best kept confidential. Using the first aid provisions available, Richard tended to my leg and made me as comfortable as possible.

"Well, Old Horse. You nearly did yourself in that time, didn't you?"

"I tried."

"You're out of commission for the time being, Jordan. I don't detect a break, but there might be damage that only an X-ray could discern. We'll get you to Bakersfield, they'll surely have more elaborate facilities there." He turned to Joe.

"Is that right, Joe? Is there a hospital intact and operational?"

"I believe there is, Señor Richard."

"I'd know if my leg was broken, Richard. Honestly, I'd rather give it a day or two and see if I don't feel any better. It's feeling better even as we speak."

"Yes, well, the painkillers might have something to do with that."

"Still and all, Richard, let me make the call on this one. I don't want to be the cause of any rash moves, especially at a time like this."

"I was planning a trip down there anyway, Jordan, as soon as Joe can fill us in on his excursion. Were you able to meet with Mierdamonte, Joe? I saw your headlights when you got back and I was just on my way up to your place. As you might imagine, we're all anxious to hear what's going on down there."

"Of course, Señor. I just wanted to stop in at the cabin for a moment, make sure everything was in order. As it turns out it was fortunate that I did."

"Amen to that," Richard and I almost spoke in unison.

"Now Joe, fill us in. Carol, will you bring Joe some food, please."

"Of course. It'll only take a few minutes."

I was reclined on the sofa in the library, my wounded leg elevated. Joe settled in the easy chair near the desk, Richard poured us each a tall bourbon and Joe began an account of his trip to Bakersfield ….

"Well, as you know, Richard, Governor Lohan didn't survive the catastrophe and Lieutenant Governor Mierdamonte has taken control of whatever form of government you call it that's in place. They've got, I'd estimate, about two, maybe three-hundred police-type enforcers surrounding the provisional government buildings. Spread throughout the city there are other personnel that are loyal to Mierdamonte and keeping order. Their forces have confiscated most of the supplies that were available in that area. Most of the mutants, both Muties and Moonkies, are keeping out of sight. You only come across them when they're out looking for food. Some of the Muties are still partially civilized, I'd guess you'd say, not all the way gone. These are the ones that Mierdamonte has recruited as Bounties and lackeys. They're armed, most are taking orders from Mierdamonte."

"How much area do they control?"

"All of Kern County, for sure. Once you get up near here, it's pretty desolate. You see the occasional Bounties out looking for whatever they can loot, or rounding up stray Muties, or even Munies. There's a bounty on whoever they can bring in. The word's out that we've got a civilized compound here, they're not trying to mess with anybody who are still law-abiding citizens, just rounding up the troublemakers, I guess."

"Do they have lab facilities? Are they working on a cure?"

"For the virus? Yeah, they've got a lab set-up right in the main building. Mierdamonte was asking about you, Richard; if you've got any idea on how to find a cure. He remembers you from before, I guess."

"Yes. We've met, briefly."

"He gave me this." Joe pulled a folded letter from his pocket and handed it over to Richard. It was a letter of safe-transit signed by Mierdamonte, giving the bearer and his passengers safe transport to and from Bakersfield. It specifically designated Richard and members of the compound as having immunity from prosecution for gathering supplies as needed in order to provide for the benefit of the community. Otherwise, looters were arrested and, depending on their 'condition', either taken to the work camp, or executed on sight.

"Did you have any trouble on the road? With Bounties, I mean."

"No. I guess they just see me as one of them, at least none of them stopped me. Just looked me over pretty good."

"What about south of Bakersfield, what's going on in L.A?"

"Oh my God, forget it. They told me it's a nightmare, a war zone. Between the Moonkies, Muties and gangs, which have recruited a lot of the mutants, the place is a living hell. You and I'd see it that way, anyhow. Thugs and freaks overrunning the place. According to refugees, the city's a nonstop fight for life zone."

"Mierdamonte hasn't sent in his militia to restore order?"

"No, and it's not likely that he will any time soon. There's no more LAPD, but all its ordinance seems to have fallen into the wrong hands, including dum-dum bullets and armor piercing shells. Mierdamonte's militia may seem – even be – formidable enough to the Bakersfield population, but he could have ten times the troops he has now, and it would still be suicidal to send them against the armed resistance they'd meet there, something tantamount to guerilla warfare. No, for the time being they have a working arrangement with L.A., an unwritten truce. Mierdamonte leaves them alone – and they stay out of anything north of L.A. County."

"Do they know about our numbers?" Richard asked, quite concernedly.

"I was able to avoid answering that directly. They believe we've still got about the same number of men as before, give or take. They don't know how bad the plague thinned us out. I just let them keep thinking that."

"Were you able to discern if any of the neighboring

areas still have any Munie population?"

"Well, the Gonzales' farm had their rep there and we were able to talk. They still have about seven Munies and ten or eleven Muties that aren't too far gone. Their neighbors, the Gutierrez clan has around twenty folks that are hanging on. I told 'em we'd be sending over somebody to meet with them, talk about joining forces. We can use all the people we can get."

I could tell by Richard's reaction that he was considering what Joe had said very carefully. "I know Mike Gutierrez pretty well, I think I'll go over there first thing in the morning and talk to him. Then we've got to let Jordan heal up a bit so we can make our way to Bakersfield. I've got to get into that lab."

"Richard," Joe Rivera said solemnly, "I don't know if we've got that much time."

"What do you mean, Joe?"

"Well, what I mean is … I guess I should have told you this sooner. The thing is, Mierdamonte …" Joe paused.

"Is what?" Come out with it, Joe."

"Well, of course this is my opinion, but I met with the guy and I've seen him with my own eyes. And you know me, Richard, you know I'm not one to give to exaggeration. The thing is, Mierdamonte is turning Mutie. Nobody down there is saying anything, of course but, darn it, Richard, I know Muties. You <u>know</u> I know."

Richard was looking at Joe incredulously, but nodded his head.

"And darn it all, Mierdamonte has all the signs. He's turning, Richard. And once he begins turning … well … think about it. The mutants outnumber Munies about ten-to–one. Mierdamonte's got all the political power, all the guns and troops and followers. Once he goes Mutie, then advances to Moonkie, it's gonna turn into a different sort of situation."

Richard and I were thinking … thinking of all the

terrible, worst case scenarios. Joe continued ... "You know no Moonkies are smart enough to produce their own food, and sooner or later, as you know, all Muties become Moonkies. After all the ready-made food is gone, after all the fruit is off the trees and crops out of the fields ... ain't but one thing left to eat."

"What are you getting at, Joe? What's left to eat?" I asked, a bit too innocently.

"Why, us, Professor. Us. We'll be the only thing left to eat. We're Moonkie food. Or at least, we will be, once the other stuff runs out and we run out of ammunition or are overrun by the sheer numbers of 'em."

The simplicity by which Joe had cut to the heart of the matter hung in the room like a fog of tragic realization. I felt heavy, my limbs hung like lead and my heart weighed down the center of my chest, pressing me into the sofa. The fact that all Muties became Moonkies, up to that point, was a fact that had eluded me, the natural conclusion being, of course, that humankind was doomed. No wonder I had avoided that entire line of thought.

The three of us sat silent for a time, deep in thought about the scenario we faced; of what all of humankind faced. The weight in my chest felt heavier than ever. As I lay on the comfortable sofa with a glass of bourbon in my hand and my leg evincing my own human frailty – I faced the grim reality of the magnitude of what was. I realized the heaviness I felt in my chest was the weight of the dying embers of the fire that once burned fierce for my belief in mankind. The belief that had been handed down from one generation to the next that man would always rise up in the face of adversity and conquer whatever foe that presented itself ... never conceding that there could ever be an unconquerable enemy.

I sensed that the ego-driven beast of invincibility no longer roared in defiance and pride – but now cowered and wept with grief, when faced with the possibility of defeat. The beast within, whimpered and trembled with sorrow and fear.

*   *

CHAPTER 19: SOMEONE WHO CARES

(Frankie V.)

Where was I going and what did I expect to find or do, once I got there? In the harsh light of day, with the oppressive heat bearing down uncomfortably, the enormity of my insignificance overwhelmed me. In all the tragedy of the grim new world, the problems and concerns of one man were far over-shadowed by the combined heartbreaking misfortune of all the souls who'd perished, and all those currently suffering their own personal hell. And, what if by some outlandish happenstance of luck, I should somehow successfully accomplish my fool's mission and find Valerie ... would it be too late?

I'd risked personal safety and abandoned the security of safe harbor to rescue her from ... from what? The inevitable? Would she look on me as the sap I surely am – a hopeless romantic hanging onto some celluloid fantasy of a moon rising over a balcony as the heroine pines for her love-smitten Romeo? Might the fleeting look in a lover's eyes as she acknowledges the harrowing sacrifice be a just reward and payment for efforts expended? Or, was what beckoned me even more elusive? Something as ephemeral and unattainable as redemption, absolution, forgiveness? And would she even care? Would anyone?

I looked over at my traveling companion. Hodges hadn't moved or altered his distant gaze since the trip started. He stared straight ahead, intent on his own vision of the world and what was to be. I almost envied him. No protracted meanderings of thought or conscience, guilt or remorse. Just existence.

The twisting road proved difficult and tiresome to navigate. To be on the safe side, we had cut over to the Pacific Coast Highway and headed south. I believed there would be less chance of encountering Bounties on the coastal road, and we'd be near the water come nightfall. I never forgot Valerie's advice that Moonkies are afraid of the water. Hodges apparently still had enough Mutie left in him that he wasn't noticeably affected by the expanse of sparkling ocean that bordered our entire right flank. By noontime my arms and shoulders were worn out from the constant right and left turns. I needed a break. We found a small off-road that veered down the steep incline from the highway.

The roadway ended abruptly, suddenly turning to rocky cliff that fell straight down about forty feet to the ocean below. The scenery was indescribably beautiful. The water crashed violently into the rocks and the wind rushed off the sea in vibrant gusts. The air was salty and took the edge off the heat of the brilliant sunshine. If I could choose but one place to live … or die, I'd surely found it.

Good fortune had unexpectedly befallen Hodges and me. A few moments after we'd left the main road, the ominous sound of tires on blacktop caught our attention. Halfway down the hillside, we were completely hidden from view of any passing vehicles back on the road, but we instinctively crouched down to avoid detection just the same. The steady drone of tires seemed too loud to be just one car or truck; we crept up the embankment and sneaked a peek.

A small caravan consisting of a van, two SUV's and two larger military-type transport trucks was slowly weaving its way along the road, heading south. Hodges stayed back while I dared a closer look. They passed by within just a few feet, but I was sufficiently hidden by a stand of tall grass to allow me a satisfactory view. The drivers and occupants of the cabs seemed intent on the road apparently, a gorgeous ocean view held little interest for them. Most appeared to be Bounty types; dressed in khaki garb, none in advanced Mutie stage.

The last two vehicles, the military transports, particularly caught my attention. They were about half the size of regular semi tractor-trailers, with canvas covered trailer beds. The lower portion of the truck beds were open-fence slats, or railings. As they passed I could briefly see into the back to discern what the cargo was. It was a chilling sight. Sunlight passing through the fencing revealed the terrified faces of dozens of what appeared to be Muties and Moonkies. Armed guards rode on the tailgates. Ropes and chains hung from the roof, securing the prisoners. Fear and dread filled their eyes, and memories of my own life as a prisoner flooded through me. I was filled with empathy for the poor wretches, and hatred for those who would impose such cruelty upon the unfortunates.

After the last truck disappeared around the bend, I descended back down the hillside. Hodges was sitting on his haunches, idly scratching the dirt with a stick. He'd seen the trucks, and he seemed to be more withdrawn and distant than usual. I sensed that he may have been reminded of something, something too painful to acknowledge. I felt a mournfulness seeping into my own consciousness. A shared, unspoken moment of consolation for those poor bastards being held against their will passed between us. Or, I imagined it so.

I thought about the tiny cell I'd lived in for all those years and the harsh conditions I'd endured. I quickly realized that what I had suffered was probably luxury compared to what the miserables in those trucks were facing. But what could I do about it? Sometimes you just have to accept that there's so much in life that's out of your control. I also realized that heading any further south was completely out of the question. Whatever fate had befallen anyone other than myself was clearly becoming far beyond my capacity to do anything about. Self-survival suddenly became priority. Now that I knew the coastal road was being used by Bounties, it was obvious we had to abandon it … as quickly as possible.

"Looks like we're heading back north, Hodges."

The added dilemma was, it was several miles back to the turnoff that would take us back to the interstate. And, if any more Bounties were heading south on the coast road, we'd run right into them. On the two-lane road, there would be no hiding in time. And, if we continued south, we'd be heading toward wherever it was they were taking the prisoners.

My thinking was becoming increasingly muddled. The sun was beating down on my head and I was getting dizzy. Like a bolt of lightning, a flash of heat exploded in the back of my neck and seemed to flood my brain. A sharp, throbbing ache stung through the base of my skull and spread like spider legs, reaching in all directions. My knees buckled and I fell to the ground. Inexplicably, the term 'aneurysm' came to mind. That's exactly what it felt like. An exploding blood vessel or something of the like. But, why now? Why here? Just when I needed all my faculties to deal with what was sure to come this way … and, there was absolutely no medical assistance to be had. There was nothing I could do but endure the pain and try to hold onto consciousness. It was a losing battle, I blacked out.

I came to with my face in the dirt and a lingering

headache. I didn't attempt to move at first, but just managed to open my eyes to see Hodges still sitting nearby. A faithful pet dutifully watching over his helpless master. Or, maybe he just didn't know what to do and had nowhere to go. What would happen to Hodges should I perish out here? What fate had befallen Valerie? What of everyone else? The mournful faces of the captive Muties and Moonkies played through my head like an old black and white newsreel. Back in school they showed us the films of the Holocaust victims being led away like sheep to the slaughter. Crammed into trains and lined up to enter showers that were their execution chambers. Rows and rows of dead bodies being bulldozed into giant piles. Man's inhumanity to man. How could so many stand by and allow it? How could so many be victimized without fighting back?

A hatred swelled within me for the callous injustice done to the meek by the ones in power. It seemed to renew my strength and I managed to prop myself up on an elbow.

"Hodges, could you get me some water from the truck?"

My faithful friend complied without hesitation. I drank and regained a degree of my senses. Not necessarily my 'good' ones. Hodges watched me drink and I offered him the bottle. He drank thirstily then just sat there looking at me.

"Well, what is it?" I asked. He didn't answer. Like I said, he never does.

"Oh, believe me, Hodges, I <u>KNOW</u> what you're thinking and it ain't gonna happen."

Again, the blank stare, then he went back to his drawing in the dirt with a stick.

"It's ridiculous to even consider what you're suggesting. I mean, sure, you're a raving lunatic, but with good reason and an excuse. But, me? Ha! I'm not that freakin' crazy. No way. Not yet, anyway."

We sat there for a time, me lost in my thoughts and Hodges just lost. All my life I had unfailingly chosen the absolute wrong decision every single time I'd come to a critical fork in the road where a choice was called for. It had led to disaster, pain, suffering, struggle, torment and strife. At this significant juncture, I saw no reason to ruin a perfect record.

"All right, Hodges, you win. Now tell me, do you happen to know where those trucks were headed?"

Hodges wiped his dirt canvas clean and began drawing with purpose. I leaned in for a closer look and saw that he was sketching a reasonably coherent map. One wavy line depicted the coastal highway, a straight line intersecting, what I interpreted to be a road a few miles south. A small 'x' showed our present location, and quite deliberately, Hodges traced the route the trucks traveled past the small 'x', turning off at the intersecting road. Only an inch or two after the turn, Hodges circled a spot and stabbed the stick into the ground. Then, for the first time I could recall, he looked up at me and made direct eye contact.

"Hee-re."

We waited until nightfall, then drove the few miles south to the turnoff in darkness – no headlights. I didn't have a plan, just a mission. The night air was refreshing and I felt much better than earlier in the day. I felt energized and alive as never before. Even in the near total darkness, I could see every turn in the road, every bush and tree. It was as if I was discovering untapped abilities for the first time. My contempt for the Bounties' brutality had awakened a sense of purpose and determination within that must have been dormant from nonuse. I felt strong, powerful, and vibrant.

A couple of miles after the turnoff, Hodges touched the steering wheel and I took this as a signal to pull over. We rolled the truck into the woods and proceeded on foot. We had the shotgun and a box of shells, my .38 pistol with four bullets, a Buck knife and a mini-crowbar. Hodges wrapped a small parcel of tools into a rag and stuffed it into his pocket. I didn't ask why, I believed that he had been to where we were going.

The trek through the woods got much easier when we came to a deer trail and followed it. I smelled a campfire, soon, and we neared an opening in the forest. Hodges halted mid-step, listened, crouched low, then moved slowly to the tree line.

Forty feet or so from our vantage point stood a one-story cabin with a covered porch. A lone Bounty sat smoking a cigarette and drinking from a cup. A fire flickered from a ten-gallon bucket, lighting his face as he leaned over it. He was unshaven and dirty. The firelight gave him an eerie, wraithlike appearance. He wore a gun belt with a sidearm, and a hunter's bow and arrows leaned against the cabin within easy reach.

To our right stood a chain link enclosure I estimated to be about fifty-by-fifty feet. Razor wire circled the top of the fence all around. Inside the corral were Muties and Moonkies of all sizes and variations. They stood shoulder-to-shoulder, stuffed in like sardines with no room to sit or lie down. Occasionally a growl or moan could be heard. Mostly, they stood motionless, obviously distraught and terrified.

Two SUV's were parked on the other side of the cabin, which meant that the van and larger transport vehicles had dropped off their cargo and moved on. I estimated that left five or six Bounties to deal with. With the arms I had, Hodges, and the element of surprise, I calculated the odds of a successful mission to be about 100 to 1, against. I needed to find out exactly how many Bounties were on hand and pinpoint their location. If I could get a jump on them all in one room – maybe. But getting to the cabin with a guard on the porch wouldn't be easy.

"Hodges, we need to get around to the back without being seen or heard."

The silent giant led me to a path that trailed just behind the tree line in a semicircle that brought us to within twenty feet of the rear of the building. Kerosene lamps flickered from inside. The slurred speech and intermittent laughter of drunken Bounties could be heard. There appeared to be only the one guard outside. Based on these circumstances, a plan quickly formulated.

"Hodges, I need you to stay here and keep a lookout. If you see anything unusual, give a signal … like this." I rustled some dry leaves from a bush. "And Hodges, if anything goes wrong, if any shooting starts … you get the hell out of here, you hear me?"

He nodded, I hoped he really <u>did</u> understand. There wasn't time for nerves or overthinking, this was going down and there would be no turning back. I knew if the Bounties caught us they'd have no qualms about executing us on the spot. Either that or take us prisoner. Given the choice, I <u>did</u> have a preference.

With one final deep breath I darted from the safety of the trees over open ground and slipped into the shadows between the two SUV's. There, I used the Buck knife to puncture tires on both vehicles. A light breeze that rustled through the trees created just enough noise to mask the sound of air seeping from the tires, I hoped. I hurried back to Hodges and laid out the rest of the plan.

"Hodges, you got any wire cutters in your tool pack?"

He pulled out the bundle and unrolled it. He had some heavy-gauge pliers that would be able to cut the fence wire. It was a pretty basic plan; one of us would take out the guard on the porch while the other one went to the far end of the corral and cut a hold big enough for the prisoners to slip through. If the Bounties caught on, I'd make a stand at the front door and do what was necessary to allow them time to get into the woods. From there, they were on their own, but at least they'd have a fighting chance in the trees.

I had the shotgun and pistol, but if the shooting

started I'd have to make the first ones count, then duck for cover to allow for reloading. I hoped I could overpower the porch guard without commotion, though ... that way the others could have time to get away undetected. I sent Hodges on his way and crept up to the back of the cabin to take a look inside and see what the Bounties were up to. What I saw inside turned my blood cold and made my pulse quicken ....

Five Bounties were drinking and laughing and tormenting a poor, naked Mutie girl. They had her pinned in a corner, she was snarling and clawing at them. There was little doubt as to what was meant to go down next, and the Mutie girl knew it too. She was putting up a fight though. Several fresh scratches showed on some of the Bounties' faces and the scene was turning serious before my eyes. I don't know if I completely lost what was left of my senses at that moment, but I did know two things for certain. One: I was going to do whatever I could to intercede on what was happening. And, two: I knew the Mutie girl. It was Valerie.

The plan to quietly overpower the porch guard went out the window with all the rest of any caution. As I rounded to the front of the cabin, there was just enough time to recognize fear and surprise in the Bounty's eyes as I clubbed him with the crowbar. In one motion I kicked in the door and raised the shotgun, blasting the nearest Bounty, then taking quick aim and clipping two others with the next shot. Mortal wounds weren't necessary, as long as they were disabled. I pulled the pistol and hit the next two dead center. I made sure none of them were moving, grabbed every weapon I could see and took ahold of Valerie by the wrist.

If I was expecting a warm hug and heartfelt 'thanks', I'd have been sorely disappointed. She let out a loud growl and bared her sharp teeth.

"Easy, Babe. I'm on your side."

I can't say the sentiment was mutual, Valerie didn't

recognize me. In the brief time since I'd seen her last, Val Fierno had become a different person. And, in fact, not really a 'person' at all. Her Mutie condition had advanced and she was now more animal than human.

The growling and defensive posture let up a little, and I was hoping that somewhere in there, a trace of the old Valerie remained. She allowed me to lead her out, like a lion tamer leading a wayward beast. I grabbed the porch guard's gun and checked to see if Hodges had released the captives. The last of them were exiting the corral at the far end and, apparently, Hodges had followed my orders and taken off when he heard the gunfire. I hoped he'd be all right.

"Come on, Valerie, let's get out of here." I tried to be soothing, even under the circumstances. "It's gonna be okay, Babe … it's okay." If only words could make it true.

Just before reaching the tree line, I paused and looked back to make sure we weren't being followed. I guess that's why they say, 'Don't look back, they might be gaining on you.' Sometimes it's true. The porch guard had regained consciousness and had raised his hunter's bow. The arrow was in the air before I could react, and crossed the distance in a flash. It penetrated my torso and was hopelessly lodged there. The pain and regret were instantaneous. If only ….

I took aim with the pistol and downed the Bounty with one hate-filled perfect shot to the head. I'd just killed or maimed a cabin full of Bounties and the only regret I had was that I hadn't made sure they were all dead. Val dropped down and examined the wound, looking up at my face in the process. I thought I saw a hint of recognition there.

We made it to the truck and I drove as well as I could with the arrow sticking out of my side. I knew it wouldn't take long before word got out about the escape of so many Muties and Moonkies. Bounties would be all over the place and out for blood. I wanted to get as far away as possible before I passed out, or worse. Val was keeping a close eye on me, leaning over and examining the bleeding hole in my side. At one point she yanked on the arrow and I let out a wail that rivaled the best mutant shriek. The thing was definitely wedged in there and I wasn't going to be able to get it out.

Where we'd go and what we'd do were unanswerable questions. How long I'd last in this condition was another one with the same mystery. Val patted at the wound with a rag, her feral eyes showing concern and empathy. In the dark of night, bleeding to death with a naked Mutant girl beside me, I did find the answer to one previously posed question that I had pondered earlier in the day. I believe I had finally found someone who cared if I lived or died.

*   *

CHAPTER 20: PHANTOM OF DOOM

"Oh Evil Phantom Reaper, turn 'way this poor soul's door;
For as you see, I'm not prepared to face thou Devil's roar."

(The Professor)

The period between sleep and awake is a twilight world. I suppose it's the place where one could go either way – back into the abyss of dreams and slumber, or rebirth into a new day with all its possibilities. It is also that place where it's not clear which the reality is. If given the choice, at times I'm not sure how I'd choose. Awaking with bourbon on my breath, still wearing yesterday's clothes and lying on the sofa in Richard's library was disorienting. What was actually distressing, however, was the typed note I discovered on the desk, addressed to me. It was from Richard and explained that he had taken Lannie, Andy, and Hawk, and left for Bakersfield early that morning. They had not wished to disturb me, but Richard felt it was paramount to get to the Bakersfield laboratories in order to work on the antidote at once. Andy and Hawk would provide security and Joe Rivera would assume that role here at the compound.

Carol entered carrying a tray of food and coffee. "Good morning. I thought I'd let you sleep, Jordan."

"Did you see this?" I held out Richard's note.

"Yes." Carol half-smiled, "I came in to check on you earlier and was also wondering where Richard and Lannie were. I noticed it on the desk. It's not like Richard to be so spontaneous, but, under the circumstances he must have decided the trip was necessary."

I was shaking my head rereading the note. "I can't believe he left without speaking with me first."

"Didn't you guys talk late into the night? I came in and cleaned up the evidence of a boy's night out … you finished off a quart of booze."

"Well, yeah … but he didn't say anything about taking off, at least, not so suddenly."

Carol raised her eyebrows and rolled those baby-blues as if to say, "What are you gonna do?" She laid down the tray and served. "You better get yourself together, Jordan, Joe Rivera told me that he's on his way over to the Gonzales' place to invite them to move in here. I'm gonna need help getting everyone situated. He also mentioned he might make it to the Gutierrez ranch as well. So, there's going to be a bunch of folks coming in pretty soon."

I rolled over to get up and cringed in pain. "Argh … dammit!" I had forgotten my injured leg.

"How are you feeling?"

"I've been better … but I've also been worse. It's nothing, I just need to loosen up a bit."

Carol raised the pant leg and examined the bruising that was visible outside of the bandaging. "This doesn't look like 'nothing', Jordan. This looks serious."

"It'll be fine. Do you happen to have a cane or crutches around here that I might borrow for a time?"

"I'll find something." Carol was looking at me critically. "I can't believe Richard would leave you in this condition. He didn't even wake me and let me look after you." She began picking up around the library and muttering. "I know it's the end of the world and all, but still, a little courtesy would be nice." She exited the library and I sipped my coffee. I was thinking that it was almost surreal how the day-to-day interaction and complexities of human relationships continue on, even in the face of the most extreme circumstances.

By the time I'd finished breakfast, Carol had returned with a wooden cane. I was stiff and my leg was still throbbing, but I could at least move around with the aid of the cane. I set up shop in the library and got out Richard's maps of the compound. By the time Joe returned with the first wave of the Gonzales and Gutierrez clans, I'd organized a tentative schedule of perimeter security. With the added manpower, we'd be able to double up on sentries for increased security. Joe decided, for the time being, he would relegate the Muties from the Gonzales and Gutierrez camps to his own cabin out near the quarry. This was actually in contradiction to Richard's wishes. He was firm about not allowing Muties on the grounds, however, Joe felt that at this time, he was doing what was best for the good of the compound. I agreed. Once Richard got back that might be a different story. Joe and I conferred and determined that should Richard remain adamant in his position, then it wouldn't be a major imposition to have the Muties merely retreat beyond the properly lines – even move into the Gutierrez ranch a few miles down the road – and still be accessible if they were needed. It would also allow them access to food and other needs, through diplomatic intermediaries.

Joe took time to check my leg and wrap new bandaging around the nastiest of the wounded areas. "That don't look too good, Professor."

"The cuts and scrapes will heal all right, I think I might have done something to the knee, though. It doesn't feel exactly kosher."

"I'm surprised Richard didn't take you with him to the

hospital in Bakersfield."

"I'll be able to get around okay, I think the swelling will go down in a day or two. As long as nothing's broken, I'll live."

As Joe finished up the bandaging, he spoke solemnly, "Just want you to know, Professor, I appreciate the way you treated my boys … and how you treat 'em all – Muties, I mean."

"I'm the last person that should be in judgment of any other, Joe. I don't know how much you know of my background, but …."

"I know you were in prison, don't know why … don't care much to know either, ain't none of my business."

"I was convicted of killing my wife."

Joe didn't respond to that. What could be said, anyway? I didn't mean to put it out there like that, but, sometimes, just confessing and getting it out helps ease the burden of carrying things around on your back.

"It was actually a terrible accident."

"It's not easy losing someone close."

"We'd grown apart over the years. Cora and I had a long history of, let's just say, opposing viewpoints. As it turned out, our contrary opinions became well documented testimonial evidence against me. Animated discussions became 'heated arguments', minor disagreements were characterized as 'episodes of unbridled rage'. Before the trial was over, I was doubting my own view of myself."

Joe graciously didn't respond.

"I was in complete shock and traumatized by her death, and it wasn't until months later, when I was locked in a cell and facing that life sentence, that I began to realize I'd let myself down by not playing a more active role in my defense."

"The legal system can be an overpowering opponent," Joe offered.

"I was vehemently portrayed as a calculating murderer,

and Cora the sweet, innocent victim. No one was surprised by the outcome, least of all me. It was the wrong time to give up … but by mid-trial, I was resigned to my fate."

"I'm sorry for your pain, Professor."

"It's a terrible thing, Joe, to look into the eyes of people who used to be your friends, and family, and see repulsion and hatred."

"Was no one on your side, Señor?"

"In the beginning, some stood by me. But eventually, they either switched sides or drifted away. That's the corroding effect of prison; pretty soon, one-by-one, people give up on you. Even if the jury gets it wrong, just being inside gives you a stench of the contemptible. It doesn't wash off and you can't ever recover from it."

"Like I said, Professor, none of my business."

It took the better part of the day to get everyone moved in. The men unloaded trucks of supplies and cargo that nearly filled the barn and storage sheds. The women organized food stocks and assigned sleeping quarters. Muties helped unload and carted provisions up to Joe's cabin where they established their own encampment.

We now had enough men that we'd be able to post twenty-four hour security – with two-man perimeter surveillance teams and front gate sentries. It wasn't so much that we expected trouble, but, after hearing Joe's account of how things were going in the south, it seemed prudent to be prepared. Times were uncertain, people (and others) were desperate. It was bound to get worse before it got better.

Dinner that night turned out to be a grand, upbeat event. It reminded me of what a first Thanksgiving might have been like. Even the Muties came and went freely and mingled easily as they transported huge basketfuls of food up to the quarry. Everyone was lively and animated, there was an air of optimism that belied the tragic times we were all living through. I wished Richard and Lannie could have been there. For the evening, no one spoke of mass casualties, devastation, or foreboding doom. Mike Gutierrez had two young children of his own who played happily with Roberto and Angela Quinones in the back yard ... chasing one another and laughing and squealing.

As twilight descended announcing the coming of night, Donna Quinones called them inside, and the next shift of sentries and perimeter guards geared up for their rounds. They checked their rifles and kissed their women before heading out. It brought me back to the harsh reality of the nature of our existence. Whatever was out there that might do us harm at least would face a formidable resistance. Like a lone cavalry outpost, our compound stood as a symbolic oasis of civilization in an ever-increasingly hostile, jungle-like world. I wondered how many other similar communities there were out there. A fleeting thought passed over me and I chased it away immediately ... refusing to allow it to take root in my psyche. I couldn't allow that, not now. By proxy I'd inherited the temporary position of compound leader, and doubt or trepidation were inconsistent with the thoughts and qualities I needed to entertain and exemplify.

The old, lonely malaise of self-defeating pondering would be left for those darkest moments right before dawn, when monsters and creepy crawling thoughts roamed through the vapor and whistled through the crevasses of my brain ... whispering their solemn doubts and nibbling at my spirit in their muted Judas breath, urging me to abandon hope and allow the vultures and phantoms of doom to nest in the discarded remains of foolish optimism. There to feast on the bones of what was left of any chance or expectation of a favorable future.

No, I wouldn't allow the morbid thought, or the despairing possibility that we, and only we, were what remained of civilization. At least for the night we could sleep safe and sound, secure in knowing that no one could get in and do us harm, not without warning ....

Just before dawn I was awakened by a dream, or

premonition … or sound. I sat up in my bed, surrounded by darkness and listened, trying to discern if I was alone. I detected an eerie presence in the room, but was frozen in place. The only light was a single, tiny moonbeam that tore through a fold in the window curtain and painted a stroke of illumination on the far wall about halfway up. It lit some irregular object there, and I racked my brain trying to recall what picture or wall hanging hung in that particular spot.

I sat there, absolutely motionless for the better part of an hour; too fearful to move, not wanting to know if what I believed to be was real or imagined. Every few seconds a fresh wave of chills and terror rushed through me. The faint rasp of my own breath echoed in my head and my aged muscles were cramping. I feared I'd erupt in tearful sobs of resignation, giving up my own ghost to an unseen phantom that was likely my own tortured imagination playing a demented trick … taunting me while laughing at a grown man yielding to a schoolgirl's fears.

Then, whether it be imagination, illusion, or predator, the spot of moon on the wall came to life. A single blink revealed the image there to be very much alive. The phantasm slowly stepped forward, my heart pounded ceaselessly and my breath caught in my throat as the shadowy image stood at my bed. I squeezed my eyes tightly shut, willing it to disappear. It would not.

The Phantom of Doom leaned over me and grasped my hand insistently, pulling me upward. I felt it wanted me to rise and follow.

My terror turned to shock when I realized that Death had a face and a name … "Valerie!"

* *

CHAPTER 21: ONE BULLET

(Frankie V.)

Pain is a debilitating experience. Extreme pain can be crippling; especially when it exposes your limitations and frailty. It can get so bad that all you want is for it to end – no matter how that's to be accomplished. I eyed the revolver in my hand, one bullet left … just enough to do the job.

We'd made it back to Richard's compound, somehow. I don't remember the drive or how long it took. I guess seeing me in that weakened state sort of shook Valerie back to her pre-advanced mutation stage. I think she even remembered who I was. I knew I couldn't just drive right up to the gate; no telling how they'd receive Val. So, we plowed into the trees on the north side of the road (before we got too close to the compound) and drove as close as we could get. I didn't know what I was planning on doing after that, I guess I didn't have any plan at all. I had a faint recollection of Valerie leaning over me, then she just took off. I figured she went for help, but she'd been gone for a while and I wasn't in any condition to be waiting around to see how much worse the gut-wrenching pain in my lower right side was gonna get. That revolver was looking better and better.

"Hold it right there, Mister."

Great. Unexpected visitors. One armed with a shotgun, the other with some sort of club or axe. I wondered if they'd do me the favor of clubbing me to death or shooting me. Whatever it was going to be, could we please get on with it. The diplomat and peacekeeper in me took over ….

"Fuck you!" I aimed the revolver with full intent to miss my target, I just wanted them to finish me off quick and easy. I held the pose as long as I could. I was quickly getting dizzy again and my vision was clouded. However, it wasn't difficult to understand that my new companions were, what else, Muties! Why the hell they didn't just shoot and get it over with I couldn't understand. I must have been some kind of sight, bleeding all over the truck cab, arrow sticking out of my side, sweating and dirty. The gun became heavy in my hand and I dropped it. When I tried to bend down to retrieve it I leaned forward a bit too far and the shaft of the arrow pressed against the seat.

"Motherfu …!"

That was it, body and mind shut down and the lights went out. No lofty dreams with angels and bells, just black.

I came back pretty quickly, I think. I was on the floor of the forest and Valerie was leaning over me applying a damp rag to my head and pouring small amounts of water into my mouth. The other two Muties were standing by, not threateningly, more like … concerned. The pain was there but I wasn't as aware of it as before. Someone else came into view, a familiar face ….

"Professor!"

"Yes, Frankie. I'm here, you're going to be all right, just hang on." He examined my wound and I could tell he didn't like what he saw. "You're going to need medical attention, Frankie … more than what's available here. But we'll take care of you, my friend." He turned to one of the Muties …

"Topo, hand me that first aid kit." He pulled out a couple of capsules and fed them to me. Val poured another swig of water into my mouth.

"That will help with the pain, Frankie, I need to disinfect the wound. This might sting a little." I didn't even feel it. "What in the world happened, Frankie? Well, never mind, you can tell me later … you need to save your strength. Just lie here a few minutes and rest. I see you found Valerie, though. Her condition seems to have advanced."

"Easy, Professor. You don't want to get on her bad side, you know how sensitive she is." We both took a brief glance Valerie's way. Even in her progressive stage of mutation, she was still an alluring creature. Somehow her face had increased in beauty over the past days. The look in her eyes was a bit more distant though, her focus, at times, faraway. "You know I like my women like I like my coffee – wild and hairy."

"Well, I'm just glad you're here, Frankie … that you're both here."

"Who're your friends, Professor?"

"Topo and Nieto, they patrol the outside grounds."

"Richard allows that? That's a new twist."

"Richard isn't here right now. He went to Bakersfield to work on an antidote."

"A cure? Is that even possible, Professor?"

"I don't know, Frankie. It's too soon to tell, but … we'll talk more about it later, please, rest now. We'll get you to the house …."

"Professor!" Topo exclaimed, "There's a bunch of guns here." He was calling from the rear of the truck.

"Oh yeah, I managed to confiscate a few items from the Bounties …."

"I'm sure there's a story behind that, Frankie, but like

I told you, just be still for a few minutes. We'll get you inside and patched up."

The sound of motors and tires on the entrance road made us all freeze in place and look through the dense trees. A line of trucks and SUV's rumbled past, stirring up dust and creating quite a disturbance. They pulled up to the front entrance of the compound and stopped at the closed gate. The sentries came forward, armed and menacing. They gave no indication that they would be willing to open the gate. A group of armed men got out of the lead truck and approached the sentries. The line of vehicles reached beyond our view, there must have been at least twenty or thirty.

"What the hell," the Professor gasped, "I'd better go out there …."

"I wouldn't do that, Professor," I warned, "Let's listen and see what they have to say before you do anything you might regret."

"What are you talking about, Frankie?"

"Just wait."

We crouched down in the brush and listened. The group of men who'd driven in the lead vehicles gave hand signals to the line of trucks. Men began exiting their trucks and stood at some semblance of attention, guns at the ready. They appeared to be Bounty types; some in beginning Mutie form, others, still Munies. All of them seemed aggressive and prepared for action. The leader took another step toward the gate and spoke ….

"We're all sworn Bounties with the sanction of the Mierdamonte regime. We're here to search the premises!"

The sentry shouted back, "You got a warrant?"

Luckily, one of the sentries on duty, at least, wasn't any pushover. He stood his ground staunchly.

"We don't need no warrant. There's been Bounties killed down Farmersville way, and before that, two other brother Bounties got murdered toward the west side district. We aim to find whoever done it and bring 'em in."

"What makes you think they're here?"

"I didn't say that, all I said was we want to search the place."

"Well, until Richard Adams returns, ain't nobody comin' in to do no searchin'."

"When's Adams due?"

"No telling. He's down in Bakersfield meeting with Mierdamonte. I suggest you get in touch with your boss and make sure you know what you're doing."

The Bounties conferred, then the lead one stepped forward. "You see any strange Munies comin' around this way? Might be travelling with a Mutie girl."

"I ain't seen nothin'."

The Professor and I exchanged looks.

The Bounties conferred again, the leader spoke, "All right, this is your final warning. I've got over a hundred men here, all of them armed. Either you let us in or we'll force our way. You've got two minutes to decide."

"Frankie, I've got to go out there. Richard left me in charge, it's my duty."

"Professor, you heard what he said. You know who they're looking for. You and I are both new faces around here. You step out there and they'll take you in for certain."

"He's right, Professor," Topo spoke up. "Best thing for you to do is get the hell out of here for the time being. There doesn't need to be any bloodshed, they could let them search and maybe they'll go on their way."

As we spoke other compound members were coming down from the main house and joining the sentries. A man I later learned to be Joe Rivera took charge ….

"I'm head of security of the Adams' compound. There's not going to be any searching or vigilante mobs allowed on these grounds. We're just as armed as you are, and I'd wager to say, just as prepared to defend our property as you are to exert your authority." With that said, the men from the compound spread out in a defensive posture and raised their guns.

The lead Bounty took a step backward. "You got one minute."

"Professor," Topo whispered, "We're gonna need your friend's guns." Without waiting, he and Nieto began unloading the firearms from the truck and checked each one for readiness. "We'll make a stand from here. Once the firing starts, you can take the truck and get to the road. Head north, the Gutierrez ranch is about two miles up, on the right."

"I'm not going to leave you here to fight alone. You see how many men and guns they've got. You're going to need every hand. We're outnumbered five to one."

"Not exactly," Topo stated.

Out of the woods shadowy figures emerged moving toward the road. Muties of every size and shape appeared ready to attack with sticks and stones or bare-handed, if necessary.

"You take your friend, Professor, and get as far away from here as you can. He'll need you to take care of him. Leave the girl, take the truck and go."

Valerie wasn't without opinion. She crouched forward leaning over me and hissing, "No!" She grabbed me by the shirt and picked me up effortlessly, putting me into the cab of the truck. She looked back at the others with fire in her eyes.

Topo relented, "Take them and go, Professor. You can't do anything here."

The minute was up and the Bounty leader hollered toward the gate, "Well, what's it going to be?"

Joe Rivera stepped forward and loudly cocked his rifle – the rest of the compound men did the same. The line of Bounties began to edge closer. Although they seemed to have the numbers, they couldn't be certain of how many men were still in the compound and they certainly didn't know about the flank attack from the Muties they faced.

The leader held up his hand.

"You see how many men I've got. You know this will be a massacre."

Joe raised his rifle, "You're going to be the first to go."

The Bounty turned and spoke with some of the others then turned back to Joe.

"As of this minute, your compound is locked down. No one goes in, no one comes out. We're gonna send a runner to get orders from Mierdamonte before we force our way in. But the whole place is locked down!"

Despite the threatening manner in which the edict was pronounced we all let out a mutual sigh of relief. Even the Bounties seemed less agitated, they broke up into small groups and smoked, leaning against their trucks.

For the moment it appeared a bloody disaster had been averted. It would take several hours for a message to travel to Bakersfield and back. In the meantime, our little band of tattered miscreants was in a potentially vulnerable position.

"It won't be long before they figure out they should surveil the perimeter looking for weak spots – they might even surround the compound," Topo stated.

"My thoughts as well," admitted the Professor.

"You need to take your friend and the girl and get out of here, Professor, before it's too late."

The Bounties, for the most part, were gathered into two main groups. One large bunch was way down the road; a closer pack was clustered around one particular truck that had country music blasting from a tape player. Shotguns, trucks, country music, and mutating, redneck Bounties with bad attitudes was a scene from some hillbilly nightmare hell that I didn't want to be any part of. As Toby Keith got louder and more vocal in his support and pride of a nation that, for all intents and purposes, had ceased to exist – and before anybody got the idea to don sheets and start burning crosses – Topo and Nieto helped push the pickup backward and out of earshot of the

Bounties.

Goodbyes were brief and the Professor started the truck and pulled into the brush, away from the road. We followed the same path that we'd left coming in, and soon enough found ourselves near the main highway. I was in pretty bad shape and couldn't be of much help, merely clinging to life was my main objective. Valerie held me protectively, concern showing in her large, feral eyes.

"What now, Professor?" I asked.

"I'll go take a look, if the coast is clear maybe we can get on the highway and put some distance between us and that army … give us some time to figure out what to do next."

He jumped out of the truck; it was more like a slow limp, the Professor was using a cane now and favoring his right leg. I hadn't noticed that before.

We must have made for a comedic-looking trio of fugitives. An old man with a bad limp and a cane, a sorry-looking greasy, grimy dude with an arrow sticking out of his side, bleeding all over everything, and an intoxicating, naked, wild mutant girl that looked like she could kill you or eat you or fuck you to death at the drop of a hat. It crossed my mind that nobody had bothered to clothe Valerie, then I realized there would have been no purpose in doing that. As the Professor hobbled up to the road and looked both ways, I happened to glance up at Valerie's eyes and recognized a familiar look there.

"Easy, girl. I'm definitely not up to it … Valerie. Good girl … down …." I patted her head and she arched her back like some kind of overheated feline in season. How bizarre and unreal everything seemed. How unlikely and ridiculous to find myself in these circumstances. The distance from the truck to the road was not more than forty feet, I'd estimate. In the Professor's condition it would likely take him about five to eight minutes to get back to the truck. I sensed that Valerie, even in her mutated state, could make that calculation as well. She was sort of purring and cozying up to me; I knew I didn't have the strength to resist her (physically, mentally, or emotionally). So when she began scratching her nails (more like talons) up my leg, I just rolled my head over to the side and decided to let her have her way. That's when things got even weirder.

Valerie was amazingly gentle and dexterous when she needed to be; at the same time, she was both animalistic and carnal in her desires. Even though I hadn't completely forgotten my pain or my closeness to possible death, I never felt as alive as I did when I was this close to Valerie. She had a way of rolling her eyes back when she was in the heat of passion; all that was visible were the whites of her corneas … it gave her already otherworldly appearance, an eroticism that was undeniable and irresistible. My whole body felt tense and stretched and taut, everything about this scene was bigger than life. I opened my eyes and the surrealism got even more fantastic when I was shocked to see a huge, wet-with-blood head, staring straight at me within inches of my face. The bulbous one-eyed beast swayed unsteadily and leaned toward me. Familiarity, queasiness and recognition merged in a culmination of frenzied realization ….

It was Andy. Andy, from the compound … the nice one. I pushed Valerie away, well, I tried.

"Valerie. Dammit. Get off." Luckily she came out of her mating trance and eased up long enough for me to unlatch the door and half fall out. Andy had dropped to the ground. It appeared that his head had been bashed in. One eye was so swollen shut that it looked like he'd gone fifteen rounds with Ali, in his prime. The skull on one side was dented and gashed, he was barely hanging on. I leaned in.

"Andy. It's Frankie … what … what happened?" Inappropriate question. Andy wasn't in any condition to be answering anything. He was breathing, his good eye flickered open and he raised his bloody hand to my shoulder … he pulled me close. I could barely make out his hoarse whisper. Within another thirty seconds he was gone.

The Professor limped up, aghast at the scene he came upon. "Is that Andy?"

"Yes, well, it was. He's gone, Professor."

"What in the world happened?"

"He said, that Hawk took Richard and Lannie. That he tried to stop him, but …."

"Took them? Took them where?"

"All he said was, 'Daly City'. Does that mean anything to you, Professor?"

"Daly City? What in the world?" The Professor stopped in midsentence, he raised his eyes upward as if thinking deeply. "Seth Edelstein. Hawk must have heard us talking; he must be taking them to Seth's."

"Why? What's so important that he would kidnap and murder?"

"Seth Edelstein developed the Paracelsus virus, he may have also created an antidote, or at least the formula for one. He lived in Daly City."

"Paracelsus virus? What's that?"

"I'll explain on the way. We've got to get to Daly City. We've got to save them."

"Save them? Professor, I don't know if you've noticed, but we can't even save ourselves. What the hell do you expect us to do once we get there? Do you even know where in Daly City that Seth lives? Do you know how far it is to Daly City? There's Bounties and Muties and Moonkies and who knows what else out there. Look at us; we're pitiful. You're half-lame, I'm more gone than not, and Valerie … well, Valerie is …."

I looked at her. I looked at the Professor, and Andy – dead on the ground. There was an army of Bounties behind us, and a mountain of obstacles standing in our way, should we pursue the Professor's course, ahead of us.

"Professor," I began weakly, "It's impossible."

He gave me that stare up into the sky look, leaning on his cane and came back down with a slight grin on his face that seemed oddly, uncharacteristic ….

"Impossible, Frankie, is surviving the last lockdown that we endured."

*

The drive, luckily, proved uneventful for the most part. Twice, we had to stop and pilfer stranded vehicles for their gas. It seemed there weren't as many cars and trucks that hadn't been previously drained up this way. There weren't any Bounties either. There wasn't anybody, except us. Just south of San Francisco, the truck gave out.

"Out of gas, Professor?"

"The gauge says there's still a bit left, but it is awfully low."

We checked under the hood but couldn't discern anything out of the ordinary. Neither one of us was really mechanically inclined. It was getting near sunset.

"The city is just over that hill, Frankie. There ought to be plenty of cars near town. I'll take the can and see if I can find some."

"It's almost dark, Professor. Be careful … don't be gone too long."

I laid on a grassy knoll with Valerie sitting over me. I'd eaten every aspirin in the first aid kit, but the pain from that damn wound wasn't letting up. The bleeding had stopped but the arrow was deeply embedded in my gut. I'd never be able to withstand the kind of pain required in order to extract it. I read the look on Valerie's face as she examined it. I'd seen that look before – I knew what it meant. A few weeks ago I didn't even know her or the Professor. Now they were closer to me than anyone I'd ever known. There was much that needed to be said, but not much time to say it.

"Valerie, there's something I need to tell you …

something you need to know."

Her face clouded over and she turned away. She didn't want to listen and didn't want to hear it.

"Valerie, I …."

She shook her head violently, turning so I couldn't see her face. The Professor's return interrupted the uncomfortable moment. He was limping badly and exhausted from the trek. His face was ashen and the look in his eyes revealed that the news was not good.

"Well, Professor? Did you find any gas?" I asked hopefully.

Seconds elapsed before he spoke. "It's gone. It's all gone."

"What's gone? What do you mean?"

The look on his face was difficult to describe … distress, confusion, fear, and worse, hopelessness.

"The city, the whole damn city … San Francisco is gone!"

What had begun as a hellish nightmare, had deteriorated into a catastrophe. It appeared that our arduous journey had ended abruptly, leaving us in limbo. Where were we to go? What was left to be done? And how long would we survive out here? Worst of all … should the Professor and I fail to endure our injuries, what would happen to Valerie? Was it fair to allow her to continue alone? And, did I have the courage to do what I knew needed to be done? I felt for the familiar weight of the revolver in my waistband … only one bullet left. I had been saving it for myself, but now, maybe it would have to be used for a more humane purpose.

*   *

CHAPTER 22: BLOOD IN THE AIR

(The Professor)

The stark reality of what I had just observed couldn't adequately be conveyed in mere words. Over the last hill (that would normally afford one a glorious view of San Francisco), was a devastating and shocking scene. Somehow, the entire city: concrete, wood, cars, roads, bridges ... and people, were gone. Where a magnificent city had stood, the Pacific Ocean had claimed. It was simply gone. At first I thought that I had miscalculated my bearings. Then, I noticed the signs ... the highway signs that told a much more ominous truth. 'San Francisco – Next Five Exits'; except, the exits led straight into the ocean. Disoriented and still in shock, I returned to my companions to share the dreadful news. Valerie wasn't too impressed, I believe she may have not understood the implications. Frankie seemed distraught. After all we'd been through, and now this.

When circumstances are so incredibly dire, sometimes the best you can do is simply carry on ... tend to the mundane, as it were. I hadn't found any gasoline but suspected the old truck wasn't stalled as a result of lack of petrol. It was nearing nightfall and I certainly didn't want to be caught in complete darkness out here, with no cover or shelter.

"Frankie, let's give it another go and see if we can get this thing running, shall we?"

My friend was in terrible condition. His arrow wound appeared to be in a disadvantageous location and was wearing on him mightily. However, he labored over to the truck and we began the routine of checking every connection and possible problem.

"Why don't you get in and try and crank it, Professor? I'll fiddle around here."

It may have been beneficial for us to be so concentrated on our immediate task. It distracted us from the bigger problem, or, problems. Valerie opened up the passenger door and jumped in, as if anticipating us to pack up and go at any moment; just another excursion to Disneyland on a warm summer night. As I repeatedly cranked the old clunker I eyed the surroundings. Nothing in the rearview mirror, just ribbons of road. Nothing to the right or left, just overgrown grass and trees … it was potentially what might be in the trees that gave me the greatest discomfort. Once it got dark, who, or what, might appear from out of the cover of the bush?

Just when my imagination began its descent into complete paranoia, a miraculous event … the engine turned over! Frankie was just as excited as I was and he slammed the hood down and hobbled to the cab before it could stall out again. The creaking old heap sputtered a few times then caught its second breath as I pulled onto the road. I didn't want to revisit what I had witnessed over the hill so I pulled a three-point turn and headed south.

"Where are we going, Professor?" Frankie asked.

"We're going to have to backtrack. A few miles south there should be an east-west connecter road, near Los Bañas. I believe we'll be able to cross over to Highway

One, then head back north to Daly City. With any luck, the roads are still intact, and, if we make it to the coast, at least we'll be near the ocean."

We stopped and checked every vehicle we came across for gas and finally found one the scavengers had overlooked. We siphoned and poured the precious liquid into the truck tank, all the while watching for any signs of movement in the trees. It seemed our luck was holding out for the moment. It took about an hour and a half to get to the coastal highway; we decided to go ahead and try to make it to Daly City before stopping.

"You know exactly where we're going, Professor?"

"Richard showed me Seth Edelstein's address on an envelope, let me see …." Oh feeble brain don't fail me now. For the life of me I couldn't think of the address. The initial panic subsided and I took deep breaths, willing myself to calm down and think. I ran through the alphabet in my head. The letter 'h' seemed to trigger a remembrance.

"Let's see, I believe it begins with 'h' … something heavenly … like, Heaven's Gate? Heavenly Scent?"

"We're gonna need help from some of your angels on this one," Frankie muttered.

"That's it. Heaven's Angel Lane!" I exclaimed, "Or something like that."

"There's a gas station, Professor, pull in."

I turned in and Frankie disappeared inside. I checked the pumps, they weren't working. Frankie reappeared with a map of Daly City. We searched the index.

"Here's a Heaven's Angel Way. That's got to be it."

Daly City is a mostly residential community of modest two-story homes, built closely together. It didn't take us long to locate the sixteen-hundred block of Heaven's Angel Way. I stopped at the corner, then pulled the truck over and parked. If Hawk had indeed kidnapped Richard and Lannie and taken them to Seth Edelstein's, then we'd have to approach on foot. We sat in quiet darkness, listening and watching. There was no movement anywhere … just a normal neighborhood street – except everyone was dead or gone. Well, almost everyone.

"What kind of weapons have we got Frankie?"

"I've got this," Frankie showed me a stainless steel revolver, "but only one bullet." We both turned and looked into the truck bed, remembering that Topo had unloaded all the guns to defend the compound. "Wait!" Frankie pulled a Buck knife from his pocket and opened it. He grimaced in pain as he carved, then cut through the arrow shaft that was protruding from his mid-section, leaving only about an inch of the wooden shaft remaining. "I should have done that a long time ago." He handed me the knife.

"We're going to have to rely on the element of surprise, I guess, Professor."

"Well, we've been lucky so far," I observed.

Even in the darkness I thought I could detect a look of incredulity coming from both Frankie and Valerie. "Well, relatively, of course."

We moved stealthily down the row of houses until locating 1664, the next one would be Seth's. We crouched behind a hedge and observed. A dirty, tattered truck that we recognized from the compound was parked in the driveway. Like all the other houses, this one was dark and there was no indication that anyone was inside – except for the presence of that truck. We crept up to the side of the house, then began a slow, deliberate window-to-window search of the first floor. It was stone-cold dead silent inside. As we rounded the corner to the back yard a telltale flicker of light from the basement window revealed the presence of life within. Who and how many remained a mystery.

As a college professor my idea of adventure revolved around a glass of vintage wine, a roaring fire, and a good book. As my heart pounded in my chest I was well aware that neither Poe nor Shelly had ever gotten my pulse as elevated as this real life drama. The mere thought of taking those few required steps, bending low, and peering into that basement window had lodged an immovable dry lump in my throat. Thankfully, Frankie touched my arm and held up a hand to indicate 'stay here' as he slid silently around. He then dropped to his hands and knees and, ever so slowly, moved into position to look inside. He held that position for what seemed like a very long time, then motioned for me to join him. Valerie followed behind.

I mimicked his movements and he pulled back, allowing me a peek inside. The ground-level window was covered by a curtain inside, but there was just enough space from a dislodged eyelet to allow a pretty good view of a large portion of the basement. A few feet away, and directly opposite the window, was a long work bench, lit by two kerosene lanterns. There was a man in a white lab coat hunched over the table. I could only see his back, he had longish hair and seemed intent on whatever he was working on. To the left, against the wall, there were what appeared to be cages – about the size and dimension of phone booths. The implication seemed clear ... these were human, one-man cages. I was suddenly startled when someone came into view from the right. He was wearing a red checkered hunter's shirt, jeans, and a gun belt. I immediately recognized him to be Jude Haakenson, better known as 'Hawk'.

Hawk looked over the lab coat man's shoulder and placed his hands on the work table, leaning in – as if to get a better look. I was torn between fear of discovery and curiosity ... curiosity won out and I remained glued to the window. Hawk finally disappeared from view and lab coat man turned his head to watch him go. The basement was divided into rooms and apparently, Hawk had left this one.

I could see the shadowy features of lab coat man's face. He had a prominent brow and cheekbones. His nose was flat and rounded, his mouth was slightly distended, as if swollen. He turned and faced the window and stared directly at me. I froze in fright, too paralyzed with fear to move so I remained in my awkward position like a deer in the headlights. Not only was I panic-stricken with the thought of possible discovery, but shocked to see that the lab coat man was Seth Edelstein! But not just Seth Edelstein as I'd known him around the Bay Area academic community … Seth Edelstein in advanced mutant stages. Quite advanced. Seth was a Mutie!

He turned back to the table and I was released from my fear-induced trance. Apparently, hopefully, Seth was merely starting into space and didn't see me. I decided it was highly unlikely I could be seen in the darkness; Seth certainly didn't react. Frankie and I retreated to the corner of the house. I spoke excitedly …

"I saw Hawk. And the man in the lab coat, that's Seth Edelstein. He's a Mutie!"

"A Mutie? Are you sure?"

"There's no doubt, I got a good look at his face."

"Did you notice all those cages, Professor?"

"Yes, but it was too dark ….. I couldn't tell if anyone was in them."

"You saw Hawk?"

"Yes. He's wearing a sidearm."

"We have to assume Richard and Lannie are in there, maybe in those cages. I wonder how many rooms there are in the basement."

"I don't know, what are you thinking?"

"Well, off the top of my head, I see two options. We could try and get into the house through the upper floors then make our way down to the basement. Or, maybe I can get a clean shot at Hawk through one of the windows."

"How many bullets do you have?"

"Just one."

"It would have to be a perfect shot. If you only wounded him, or missed … it could turn into a terrible tragedy. Especially since we don't know where Richard and Lannie are."

"What do you think Seth's story is?"

"I can't say with any certainty but I feel confident in guessing that he's not a willing accomplice to Hawk."

"I guess we better check the other basement windows, see what we can see."

"Or you can go nighty-night."

Out of the darkness and a mere foot or two away, Hawk had crept up and caught us off guard. "THUMP!" With the butt end of what appeared to be a shotgun, he hammered Frankie in the head. He went down like a sack of potatoes. Hawk retrieved Frankie's pistol; our one-bullet defense was down to none. I didn't have time to panic, it all happened so fast.

"Hello, Professor," Hawk growled, "If you can carry your friend I'll let him live, for now. If not …." Hawk let the shotgun barrel drop to Frankie's head.

"I've got him."

"One second." Hawk patted me down quickly. He missed the Buck knife in my front pocket. At least, that seemed fortuitous. Another bit of luck – in the darkness Valerie had disappeared. Apparently, Hawk wasn't aware of her.

He held the shotgun on me as I tried to lift Frankie. That was futile so I resorted to dragging him, careful not to scrape or disturb his wound. Hawk led me to the rear doorway, which had a small flight of concrete steps descending to the basement. I held Frankie by the shoulders and dragged him down. Seth held the door open, wide-eyed and obedient to Hawk.

"Over there," Hawk ordered, pointing to the wall of cages. With great difficultly I managed to get Frankie into an open cage. Hawk followed and secured the mesh door with a padlock. Next to Frankie was another prisoner … Richard! He was slumped on the floor of his cage and not moving. Beyond Richard there were at least four more cages, some of them occupied. I looked for Lannie, but couldn't see him.

Although the inhabitants of the other cages were slumped similarly to Richard, I could make out distorted facial features. It was obvious from my vantage point, that they were all obviously drugged or otherwise physically incapacitated … it was also apparent, they were all Muties, or even Moonkies. A distinct animal-like odor was prevalent and the creatures groaned and snored in labored breaths.

"Bruno," Seth Edelstein exclaimed.

"Seth. What the hell have you done here, Edelstein?"

"I'm working to find a cure."

"To undo what you've done?"

"Yes."

"You're experimenting on live subjects?"

"It's for the greater good, Bruno."

"Just serving mankind, then?"

"To achieve a greater good, sometimes it's necessary to endure a great evil."

"You don't appear to be the one suffering."

"You don't know what I've gone through, Jordan."

I looked toward Hawk. "Are you certain it's mankind you're serving, Seth?"

"You girls can bicker later," Hawk spoke. "Come with me, Professor, I think you might appreciate this." To Seth he ordered, "Get back to work!"

Hawk led me into the next room. In the center there stood a gurney with Lannie bound, gagged and secured to it. He was conscious and his eyes widened when he recognized me.

"Lannie," I exclaimed. "What the hell are you doing, Hawk? Why in the world would you do this?"

"Well, Professor," he began as he cuffed one of my hands, then the other to a water pipe that extended from the floor to the ceiling. "It's really quite simple. I overheard you and Richard's little conversation about an antidote. I got to thinking … an antidote for a virus that's capable of wiping out most, or all, of the human race has got to be the most valuable commodity on the planet."

"You're doing this for greed?"

"Not just for greed, Professor." Seth entered and approached Lannie. I now noticed that Lannie had both arms extended outwards and tubes had been inserted intravenously, attached to blood bags hanging on either side. It appeared they were draining Lannie's blood."

"It's also a matter of principle," Hawk stated simply.

"Principle? What are you talking about?"

"I've heard the rumors and overhearing your discussion with Richard confirmed what a lot of us suspected."

"What?"

"That Lannie's a clone. All you scientists got together and started making a bunch of genetically altered super-humans designed to take over the planet. Except you didn't account for the end of the world scenario, as it happened. At least not this soon. What you also failed to consider was that there's still a very large faction of good old red-blooded boys around that ain't takin' kindly to being overrun by a hoard of aliens."

"Lannie's hardly an alien, Hawk. And I didn't have anything to do with the development of genetically enhanced anything. However, you must realize, any experimentation or development is in the interest of science and meant as a contribution to mankind … not as a threat."

"Whatever. With the boy dead and gone and me in possession of the only wonder blood, I can kind of write my own ticket."

"Dead and gone?" Seth spoke up, "You never said anything about killing the boy!"

"Shut up, lab rat. You don't have a say in this," Hawk continued his diatribe. "In order for man to live on, there's got to be a worthy sacrifice. Who could be more worthy?"

"You're completely insane."

"Am I, Professor?" Isn't the definition of insanity to keep repeating the same mistake over and over and expecting a different result? Your kind has had their turn. Science keeps coming up with more and more 'advanced developments', like the atom bomb and particle accelerators and genetic research … you see where all that got us. How about we hand things over to some guys with some common sense for a while? Just some regular folks. Let us run things for a while and maybe it'll get back to how it's supposed to be."

"I really doubt killing a boy is how it's supposed to be, Hawk."

"For the good of mankind, Professor."

"I'm not going along with this, Hawk," Seth said.

"Well that's not entirely up to you, is it? Of course, you've only really got two choices here. My way, you stay alive and work on your antidote, or, your way … and you die right now." Hawk smiled and pointed the shotgun at Seth.

"The boy's blood does contain extraordinary natural antigens that might lead to a significant breakthrough toward the development of an antidote. Of course I want to continue working to find a cure. That doesn't mean I agree with murder."

"Ain't you the one who invented the virus?" Hawk said pointedly.

Seth hesitated, but answered honestly, "Yes, that's true."

"Well how many folks you figure died or are mutated 'cause of it?"

"It was developed in order to prevent war, at least, that's what I was led to believe. It was specifically produced in a manner that prohibits a cure; however, with the introduction of Lannie's remarkable blood into the antidote process … there may be a possibility …. It's a fortuitous coincidence to find him in time."

"A coincidence?"

"Yes."

"A very big coincidence."

"There are no big coincidences, or small coincidences … just, coincidences."

"Oh, I think this is a big one. You might also call it miraculous."

"I'd call it quite fortunate. And if you sacrifice him, Hawk, as you call it … you may be sentencing us all to extinction."

"That's what the blood supply is for. With the wonder child out of the way, I'm the only one with the miracle blood. I can get anything I want from Mierdamonte. Maybe even become Governor myself … or, who knows."

"That's quite a delusion of grandeur, Hawk," I observed.

"Not to mention, nobody said Lannie was the only one with natural antibodies in his blood. There might be several out there, we just haven't come across them yet," Seth added.

"Then why did you say, if I kill the boy I might be sentencing us all to extinction?" Hawk questioned.

"I was only suggesting that as a scenario, in that Lannie is the only subject I've come across in my limited research that's had this ability built in to his genetic code. With time, I'm sure we might find others …."

"But right now, Lannie is the only one. And, now is what's important to me and the rest of those still living. I'm sure the boy doesn't mind sacrificing himself for the cause. To really live you've got to find something worth dying for, right Professor? It is the noble thing to do."

"What do you know of nobility, Hawk? You're trading what could be the future of the human race for a handful of silver and egotistical vainglory."

Some of the confined Muties had awakened and were

beginning to get restless in the tiny cages. Groans and shrieks soon echoed throughout the basement.

"Tend to that, lab rat. Quiet them heathens down!"

"It's feeding time, I'll have to go upstairs and see what food is left."

"No, I've got a better idea." The evil look on Hawk's face revealed a thought that surely had to be diabolical. "Bring me the fallen hero."

Seth scratched his wooly head. "Huh?"

"Bring in the Professor's friend." Hawk tossed the padlock key to Seth. "A double sacrifice. Twice as much fun, eh, Professor?" He then positioned himself over Lannie, terror showed in the boy's eyes and I was feeling the same. Seth was helping a stumbling and groggy Frankie in as Hawk drew his large hunting knife from its sheath. Frankie fell in a heap to the floor at Hawk's feet. He grabbed the semi-conscious Frankie by the hair and pulled his head back, exposing his neck. He positioned the knife blade at an angle on the right side.

"By the power vested in me by … hell, I don't know the rest of it. But them monsters gotta eat and ain't nothing like a little fresh meat to satisfy the appetite."

How any man could be so evil and despicable is hard to fathom. Hawk was actually smiling as he tormented us all before pulling the knife across Frankie's throat.

"Tell you what, Professor. I'll give you the choice. I was going to cut your friend's throat and feed him, piece by piece, to them monsters. But I'm feeling generous. One time offer … I'll let you take his place. You can give up your own life to save your friend's."

"Deal."

"Aw come on, Professor. Just like that? You ain't gonna haggle or nothing?"

"All right, my life for Frankie and Lannie's."

Hawk laughed derisively, "That's the spirit. Except that ain't gonna happen."

"All right, how about this … I'll let you live if you let

us all go," I stated defiantly.

Now Hawk was really enjoying himself. A broad smile spread across his large face. It didn't last, however. His demeanor and words turned vitriolic, "Now why in the hell would I even listen to that bullshit?"

"Because if you don't you'll regret it."

"What? Like a guilty conscience or something like that?" Hawk derided.

"Something like that."

"Professor, I'm tired of playin' with you. That was your last chance. I'm gonna do what I'm gonna do and there ain't nobody gonna stop me." He reached for Frankie again positioning the knife in a lethal pose.

"I wouldn't say, 'Nobody', Hawk."

"Who then? Who's gonna save you, Professor? You got a guardian angel?"

"Yes."

Hawk followed my gaze to the little window three-quarters of the way up the basement wall. It was probably only about two feet wide by approximately ten inches tall, barely large enough for a good sized animal to slip through, if the glass wasn't there. All that was visible there were two large eyes staring intently inward. By the time Hawk even processed what he was looking at, it was too late. The glass shattered in an explosion of sharp shards, spitting scattered debris across the basement floor. A wild yelp echoed in all of our ears, followed by a demonic hiss. Valerie had seen Hawk raise the knife to Frankie's throat and that had been the spark that ignited hell's fury on the unlucky villain. A man, even an armed man, is little or no resistance to a woman impassioned with rage and fury ... especially a Mutie woman ... especially Valerie Fierno. Claws and fangs dug into skin and muscle, exposing the true delicate nature of a man's life.

Frankie was able to pull Valerie off before it got any worse. When he embraced her it was no longer a man holding a woman, and she him .... What once would have been a welcoming kiss and tender hug, now looked more like a beautiful, but wild beast licking the hand of her master. We all stood transfixed by the scene before us, blood and gore everywhere, monsters in cages and mankind's destiny in limbo. Relieved to be alive, for now, and uncertain of the future.

The hungry Muties howled and the cages rattled, the scent of blood in the air did not go unnoticed.

* *

CHAPTER 23: THE STRANGEST THING

(Frankie V.)

Seth Edelstein and Professor Bruno were standing over me on one side, Richard and Lannie leaned in from the other. Lannie held a lamp near my midsection while Seth and Richard opened up the wound in my abdomen, trying to make enough room to extract the arrow. Val was directly over me, watching every move.

"This might hurt a little, Frankie," Seth warned.

"Mmmm," I suppressed a shriek. "You're a liar, Seth. That hurts more than a little."

"Grrrr …." Valerie let out a threatening growl.

"It's alright, Babe. They're trying to help."

"You might want to bite down on something," Seth advised.

"Tell you what, how about you bite down on something ... and make it a big one. Yeeowww!!!" I felt a meat-tearing rip as they wrestled the tip out. It was one of those jagged, cross-serrated jobs with prongs facing backwards, probably for bear hunting. Seth held it up to the light, a glistening red sheen covered it from tip to broken shaft.

The Muties in the cages were going ape shit … jumping up and down and howling.

"Will somebody shut those damn beasts up," Richard pleaded.

"They're hungry, it's past their feeding time and all the blood's got them worked up."

"What do you feed them?" asked the Professor.

"I was on my way out to try and find something when you all showed up. There's not much left for them I'm afraid, unless …." Seth looked over at Hawk's remains lying near the staircase.

"You're not suggesting?" the Professor halted mid-sentence.

"There's some spoiled hamburger meat in the upstairs cooler. That might hold them."

"Why are they even here, Seth?" Richard inquired. "Why are they caged?"

Seth scoffed, "If they weren't, you'd wish they were. Those aren't Muties, they're full on Moonkies. They'd kill you and eat you, or vice-versa, just as soon as look at you."

"How'd they get that way?" the Professor spoke accusingly.

"I'm trying to find a cure, Bruno."

"Using live guinea pigs for your experiments?"

"Hey, we have our hands full right here," Richard scolded. "Can we concentrate on the task at hand, please?"

It felt like he was trying to sew my insides together with rusty nails. It also felt like sandpaper scraping nerve endings in my gut.

"He's going to need blood," Richard stated.

"Use mine," Lannie offered. "It's already bagged."

The Professor spoke, "How do we know it will match?"

The sounds in the room faded and the ceiling began to spin. I was either going to die or throw up. If, given the choice, I preferred the former. I was going in and out, it was an odd scene. Three distinguished Stanford professors attending my wounds while debating the clinical and ethical dilemmas of medical experimentation … to me, looked like Moe, Larry, and Curly. I was completely at their mercy and had given up hope that this would end any way but badly. Lannie, himself a living paradox to Seth – in that, Seth knew all the scientific amalgams contributing to the mutation virus but couldn't prevent even himself from falling victim to it – while Lannie's own innocence seemed to contribute to his invulnerability.

Seth's physical mutation didn't appear to be affecting his mental processes, a point which the Professor noticed.

"How far has your own mutation progressed, Seth?"

"I've managed to retard the cognitive degeneration through a concoction produced from a variety of homogeneously prepared antibodies. Unfortunately, I've sampled so many compounds that I'm not certain which ones are effective. With the infusion of Lannie's remarkable blood, however, it's possible I might be able to develop something revolutionary."

I was fading again. I felt like I was back in school in biology class and Mrs. Blue was droning on and on about genetics and alleles and blood types. I used to sit next to Mary Bozello – Mary B. with the dark skin, sad eyes and huge bozellos. It didn't take long to learn she didn't mind being distracted from the boring lectures by my own scientific experimentation. My research centered on how far I could get with Mary while sitting in a crowded classroom without being noticed. A major breakthrough came when Mrs. Blue decided to make every Friday 'science movie day'. Lights out, projector on, Mary's blouse open, and teenage angst soothed by a renewed interest in anatomy. New heights to be mounted and conquered. Two months in, and at the climax of my exploration, a sudden 'lights on' exposed both Mary's peaked interest, and my own growing pinnacle of our most vigorous research, Mary stubbornly refused to be distracted from her hands-on probing and completed her task with a determined stroke of inspiration. The event would heretofore be known as: 'The Eruption of the Class of 1994'. Mrs. Blue was aghast as she stood by wide-eyed and mouth agape. Mary's sadistic nature was exposed as she took aim and scarred Mrs. Blue's psyche for life with the memory of her favorite blue dress, stained from stem to stern with the fruit of our scientific discovery.

Seth's lecture droned on … "That's because most genetic information is awash in uncertainty. Not all mutations are caused by a single, readily identifiable viral effect. Most result from the interplay of affected genes and a host of other factors, from amount of exposure to environment. That's why there are so many variations in how mutations are affecting the populace. From one person to the next, you can see variations. We're nowhere near where we need to be for a thorough understanding of all the why's and how's. In such revolutionary biology, we must compare the variations found in afflicted patients with those of healthy people. A variation that occurs repeatedly in Muties and Moonkies, but not in Munies, may either cause mutation, or live in the same neighborhood as the mutation-causing genes."

"What's the key?" the Professor asked.

"Answers to these questions lie in the deepest recesses of each person's 100 trillion cells – coiled in each cell are the bundles of DNA, 23 from each parent. Each bundle of DNA is made up of four chemicals – adenosine, thymine, cytosine and guanine – paired two-by-two in a twisted ladder called a double helix."

I guess Richard and the Professor could follow this, I was straining just to remain conscious. Seth continued …

"The precise sequence of these base pairs is basically 99.5% identical in the entire planet's population, and vary by just one pair of bases for every 5,000 found along an individual's genome. A person's genome is made up of 3 billion base pairs. I believe that patterns of base-pair variations can guide us to genes that are susceptible to the virus."

"How long would it take to analyze a person's base pairs?" asked Richard.

"With the equipment I have? Years for each individual."

"We don't have that kind of time," said the Professor, stating the obvious.

"Even if I locate a specific gene that's commonly affected in a number of mutants, I'd still have to develop a drug, try it on test subjects, then on healthy subjects to insure safety and effectiveness."

"You were able to stop, or at least slow the mutation process within yourself, might you be able to repeat the same experiments on others and achieve similar results?" asked Professor Bruno.

"Thus far I've only been able to suspend the cognitive effects. As you see, I'm still mutating physically. And, there can be side effects to this kind of radical experimentation." Seth looked at the mutants in the cages.

"What kind of side effects?"

"There could be accelerated mutation, or, even death," Seth answered grimly.

"What about with the infusion of Lannie's blood?" Richard asked.

"Lannie's blood is the purest I've ever encountered. He doesn't appear to be susceptible to the virus, in any manner. All others I've tested are at least prone to dormant cohabitation of the infection. It's possible that a compound of Lannie's blood and the right anti-viral drugs could produce an antidote."

"I don't see any reason not to at least try," Richard said.

"Normally," Seth said, "We'd conduct tests on lab animals for months, even years. The alternative is to utilize live subjects …."

I felt like they were all looking at me, so I spoke, "You're already pumping me with Lannie's blood, might as well throw whatever else you've got in there."

"Are you certain you want to do this, Frankie?" the Professor asked.

"Professor, I've never been more uncertain of anything in my life."

I was forced to lie still while Lannie's blood drained into me – replacing what I had lost and allowing the stitches of my arrow wound to settle. I allowed myself the temporary luxury of relaxing, physically anyway. Seth busied himself at his work bench, viewing samples under a microscope, mixing various concoctions and analyzing data. Val and Lannie retrieved the meager food supplies that remained in the house and fed the Moonkies. The group decided that someone would have to go on a scavenger hunt for supplies at daylight. Seth had already hit most of the houses in the neighborhood so he suggested they begin at least a block away. Richard and the Professor wrapped Hawk's body in a floor rug and secured it.

We decided to discard his remains by locking his body in one of the many abandoned vehicles on the street. Not the most optimum solution, but it would serve the purpose. No one was in any condition to be expending energy by digging a grave. The Professor filled Richard in on the situation back at the compound. We all tried to convince Richard that his presence there likely wouldn't prevent whatever was going to occur from happening, but it was obvious he felt compelled to return as quickly as possible. Of course, Seth needed as much time as he could get in order to work on an antidote. It didn't seem as though anyone saw fit for us to split up. Under the circumstances, safety in numbers appeared to be the only logical course.

"I'm going to need a specimen sample from your girlfriend," Seth announced.

"Why you telling me?" I asked.

"You seem to have some degree of influence with her," Seth answered.

"Why don't you just ask her yourself?"

Seth didn't move from his bench. "She doesn't seem … receptive."

"Are you scared of her, Seth?" No answer. "Is that because she's a Mutie, or because she's a girl?" I teased.

Seth's brow wrinkled, "Yes."

With some subtle coaxing, Valerie gave in and a blood sample was retrieved. Seth's hand was shaking the entire time and Val didn't disguise her displeasure at being poked. She appeared to be growing more feral by the hour and I readily agreed when Seth suggested we try one of his antidote prototypes that he'd mixed with Lannie's blood, on her.

At dawn, Richard, the Professor, and Lannie went in search of food. I suggested they take Val for protection, but Seth wanted her to remain so he could observe her reaction to the antibodies. They took Hawk's guns just in case.

Seth put sedatives in the Moonkie's food, so they were calm. He worked steadily while Val and I laid down and got some rest. Seth said he couldn't afford to sleep just yet, and he was amped up on homemade amphetamines. The others got back pretty quickly with a couple of pillowcases full of canned and bagged food items. We ate cereal, canned peaches and corn, stale bread and grape jelly. It was one of the best meals I've ever had.

While everyone migrated upstairs to catch a nap, Seth worked on and Valerie stayed close to me. I was feeling much better, even energetic. My wound wasn't bothering me anymore. I think the fresh blood from the transfusion and antibiotic cocktail might have actually helped. I joined Seth at his work bench; he was peering into the microscope. He furrowed his brow and did a double-take.

"What is it, Seth?"

"The accelerated cell transmutation apparent in Valerie's first samples, prior to the infusion of antibiotics, and following the serum … it's probably way too early to draw any conclusion, but …"

"But what?"

"Well, according to what I'm seeing, it appears that the advanced transmutation … has halted."

What do you mean, halted?"

"I can't be absolutely sure, but, I believe, after the antidote – the one with Lannie's blood – she quit mutating."

"You mean, you've found a cure?"

"Whoa, whoa … it's way too early to jump to that conclusion. It merely appears that the mutation has slowed, or even stopped … for now. We have no idea if that will remain the case, this is just a preliminary observation."

"But, it is a sign of improvement!"

"Yes. I would definitely say that is true."

"So, you might be on track to finding a cure?"

"I'm merely saying that her initial response to the antidote appears positive. Any prolonged effects have yet to be determined. It could be temporary, there might even be adverse effects that could show up later. It's really way too early to state anything conclusive."

"Regardless, Seth, her mutation has stopped for now. That's incredible!"

"There is one other … development …" Seth began, but trailed of as he continued to view his microscope.

"What's that?"

"Well, Frankie, it seems that … and I'm not an actual M.D., I mean, I didn't specialize in that field in the least, and I'm certainly no expert. I have a molecular physics degree and a Master's in microbiology. My minors were actually unrelated and …"

"Seth, for God's sakes, just shut up and say it. You're all amped up on that juice. What is it? What's wrong with

Valerie?"

"Well, it's not that there's anything wrong with her ... I mean, besides the whole mutating thing. It's just that, well ... what's 'wrong' with her, as you put it is ... it's just the strangest thing."

"Spit it out, Seth!"

"Well, Frankie ... she's pregnant. Valerie is pregnant."

* *

CHAPTER 24: DREAMS OF THE DAMNED

(The Professor)

Even while enduring the arduous turmoil of surviving such a devastatingly cataclysmic circumstance as the apocalypse, one must attend to the seemingly mundane. Munies, Muties, even Moonkies must sleep … it is then when the past has a chance to catch up and nightmares come to life. My ex-wife, Cora, apparently deemed it her responsibility to fill my few hours of respite with her ghostly presence. Whether I was in the confined space of a prison cell or in the unfamiliar sleeping quarters of some mad scientist, Cora found her way into my dreams. Refusing to allow me even one night's repose; supplanting guilt and remorse for peaceful rest.

"Well, Jordan, I see you've managed to get yourself into another fine mess."

"Are you blaming me for this as well?"

"Oh, no. Not YOU, Jordan Bruno. Nothing's ever your fault, is it?"

"Can't you give me some peace, Cora? Can't you

allow me a moment's rest?"

"Did you? Did you allow me any?"

"It was not any of my doing, you know that."

"A coat hanger doesn't wrap itself around a neck, Jordan."

"Cora!"

"And tighten itself, turn by turn."

"Cora!"

"Cutting off oxygen and blood, life and future, leaving nothing but a body. Well, you can bury my body, but I'll never let you lay the painful remembrance of your sin to rest."

"Cora!"

"No, Jordan, I won't let you rest … not until you finally join me. Then you may rest."

"Should I dress for a warm climate?"

"Droll, Jordan. I doubt you'll find it so funny when it's you who is begging for one drop of water to wet your parched tongue … willing to bargain away your miserable soul for relief."

"You're really such a drama queen, Cora. At least you're with your family."

"You'll pay for that, Jordan."

"I already am. Why won't you leave me alone?"

"You haven't earned that, Jordan."

"What must I do?"

"You might try looking out for your Godson a little better."

"Lannie? I'd lay down my life for that boy."

"Then why are you lounging in bed while he's in danger?"

"What do you mean, Cora?"

"While you slumber and sleep, the innocent shall wander and weep."

Giving up on sleep, I wandered downstairs to look in on the others. I could hear Richard's heavy snoring from behind the bedroom door next to mine. At least someone was getting rest. As I descended the stairs into Seth's dungeon of doom, the first thing I noticed was Hawk's blood still adorning the concrete floor in a carpet of crimson. Frankie and Val lay together on the ragged sofa, breathing and dreaming as one. I didn't see Lannie, he must have taken one of the upstairs rooms. Passing into the lab, or work bench area, something seemed unusual … what was it?

Oh my God! The Moonkie cages … they're gone! No sign of the Moonkies, Seth, or Lannie.

My head was spinning as I rushed to wake up Frankie and Valerie. They were slow to come to life and seemed out of sorts, as if they'd been drugged.

"The Moonkie cages are gone! And Seth … and Lannie," I cried in panic. Before getting a response, I bolted up the stairs to awaken Richard and check the other rooms for any sign of Lannie. He was nowhere in the house. I ran back downstairs where the others had gathered.

"He must have drugged us when he administered that last dose of antidote," Frankie surmised.

The sound of a car engine cranking over came from the backyard. We all rushed out.

A small garage, separate from the house, stood a few feet from the back door. The wooden door was open and in clear view was an old model Range Rover, packed and loaded to the gills. In the back of the Rover, two Moonkie cages had been loaded, on their sides. A heavy-duty moving dolly stood to the side, the kind used for heavy appliances and furniture. Seth was in the driver's seat and pumping the gas while trying to start the engine. Lannie sat passively in the passenger's side. Richard rushed to Seth's door while I yanked Lannie's door open and pulled him out.

"What the hell do you think you're doing?" Richard yelled at Seth.

Seth quit cranking the motor and his mouth moved

rapidly, but no words came out.

"Lannie, are you alright?" I asked.

He responded quite calmly, "Yes, why wouldn't I be?"

I looked from Lannie to Seth and back again. I couldn't even verbalize my contempt for Seth at the moment.

"We were just going to let the Moonkies go," Lannie explained innocently.

Richard asked Seth pointedly, "Is that right, Seth? Is that what you were doing?"

"Where else would we be going?" Seth tried to appear calm. He was failing.

"All this gear, Seth? Looks like you're loaded up for quite a long haul."

"We have to let them go a safe distance from here …. Otherwise they'll just come back and hunt us down."

No one was buying the flimsy explanation. "Then why not let it be known to the rest of us, Seth? And why drug Frankie and Val?"

"You were all sleeping. I didn't want to wake you. It looked like you needed the rest. And, maybe they just had a reaction to the serum."

"You needed Lannie's help?" I said accusingly.

"He was the only one awake. I couldn't have managed those cages without his assistance. He wanted to come along, isn't that right, Lannie?"

"I don't mind," Lannie replied. "What's the big fuss?"

"The big fuss is, Seth here is a liar and a kidnapper," Richard said as he pulled a loaded travel bag from behind Seth's seat. He unzipped the bag and retrieved several bags of Lannie's blood and packets of chemical dry ice. Also in the bag was Seth's laboratory equipment, including test tubes, beakers and the microscope.

"Quite a lunch bag you packed there, Seth. Care to try and explain that?"

Seth didn't answer, he was clearly caught red-handed and without recourse. Amazingly, he continued to try and weasel his way out.

"Of course I was going to obtain samples from the Moonkies before releasing them, and I couldn't just leave the equipment behind. I didn't want anyone in the house messing with it. If you all want to accuse me of … whatever it is you're accusing me of, that's up to you, but …."

Seth didn't get a chance to finish that sentence. Frankie had rounded the Range Rover and grabbed him by the shirt collar. He had him suspended over his head at arm's length by a single hand and was choking him viciously.

No one made a move to come to Seth's aid. He gasped and gurgled while flailing his arms and legs. Frankie calmly went about the business of strangling him as if it was almost expected.

Finally, Richard interceded, which was probably a very good thing for Seth. I've never seen Frankie that vicious. "Frankie, that's enough."

Frankie seemed to come out of some kind of animalistic trance and realizing what he was doing, dropped Seth to the floor with a thud. "Sorry, I don't know what came over me."

"Nothing's going to be accomplished by violence," Richard said. "If we resort to that type of behavior then we've lost whatever humanity we've managed to hang onto."

"But, taking Lannie …" I interjected. "Seth, what in the world were you thinking? Where were you going?"

Seth still wasn't talking.

"Maybe where you come from, Richard, violence is not the answer … but, where I've been, it's a way of life," Frankie said calmly. I knew what he was talking about, the brutality one witnesses in prison changes a man … if he allows it. Sometimes, however, it's the threat of violence that achieves the desired result.

Frankie turned to Valerie; she seemed to understand

without a word being exchanged between them. She slowly stepped toward Seth, her eyes wide and dangerous. Her steps were silent and her claws seemed to elongate even as she stepped toward him. Nostrils flared and teeth exposed, Valerie's presence was startling and ominous. She stood over Seth, ready to pounce. The tension in the little garage was palpable and I was afraid once she began there would be nothing to prevent her from tearing poor Seth into bloody shreds.

Frankie spoke. His voice had an eerie, hypnotic quality to it, calm, but ever so threatening ....

"Seth. Last chance. Where were you going?"

Seth's eyes were big as he closely watched Valerie. He was a good hundred pounds heavier than the girl-beast, but, even though he was a Mutie himself, she was far further advanced and closer to a wild, dangerous animal than he.

"Professor," Frankie began, "Take Lannie out of here. He doesn't need to see this." I made a show of gathering up the boy and beginning to exit the garage.

"Goodbye, Seth," Frankie said with finality.

"Wait! All right. I'll tell you," Seth blurted out. "It's not going to do you all any good, but I'll tell you."

Frankie put a hand on Valerie's shoulder; she didn't release her stare from Seth right away, but stood tense and rigid. Frankie took her by the arm and pulled her to him. She breathed a heavy sigh that sounded like a cat's purr and wrapped herself into Frankie's side. Seth let out a long sigh of relief and resignedly, began his explanation.

"Where I was going, where WE were going, is a place that will never let you all in. There's a good chance they wouldn't have let me in, not without Lannie, anyway."

"What place is this, Seth?" Richard asked.

"When I was working at the government's military genetics research facility in Colorado, I was briefed on the existence of a 'Safe Zone' that had been established in the event of some cataclysmic catastrophe. Since I was one of the few scientists privy to the classified research we were conducting there, I was given clearance that allowed me to become aware of this safety zone."

"There's a safety zone?" Frankie asked.

"That makes sense," Richard spoke. "Of course the government is going to have places to retreat to in case of nuclear war, or other events."

"Is it near here?" I asked.

"No, not at all," Seth replied.

"Where, Seth?" asked Richard.

He inhaled a deep breath before answering, "South Dakota."

"South Dakota!" I exclaimed. "That's a good fifteen-hundred miles from here. You were going to try and cover half the country? And take Lannie?"

"It's the only way I could be sure they'd allow me in," Seth implored.

"But, as you said, you were given clearance. If you're allowed to even know of the location, and since you're one of the developers … THE developer, really, of the virus, wouldn't they welcome you in with open arms?"

Seth answered flatly, "No. I wouldn't be allowed to get anywhere near the place … not like this."

"Because you're a Mutie," Frankie stated.

Seth looked up resignedly, "That's right, because I'm a Mutie."

"But, you're so close to an antidote, surely that would hold weight," Richard said.

"Maybe, but I'd have to get close enough to convey that information. And the fact is, they likely wouldn't let that happen. The place is secure. I mean REALLY secure. Not your basic mall cop type security, either. I'm talking about nuclear facility type security. Not only that, it's hidden. You'd never even know you were near the place unless you knew what you were looking for."

"Underground?" We asked.

"In a way. It's in the side of a mountain."

"There are no mountains in South Dakota," I said.

"There are hills, plenty of hills," Seth said knowingly.

"The black hills of South Dakota!" Richard said.

"That's right. And they might let me in with Lannie. I'd be able to show them that with his blood, there might be a cure. I'd be able to work in peace in a real laboratory. But if I showed up with all of you, we wouldn't get anywhere near the place."

"Why? We're all still human." Frankie and Val gave me a look. "Well, most of us."

Seth shook his head. "Lannie's the only one that hasn't been affected. You all have been exposed, the virus is still dormant within you. Besides, once word gets out … everybody's going to be flocking there. They'd just shut it down and none of us would get in."

"Who do they let in?" I asked.

"Who do you think? The politicians, the military, the rich and powerful. The greatest minds in science, or friends and associates of those who can buy their way in."

"Did you really think you could make it all that way without help?" I asked. "And did you believe taking Lannie was worth it? Don't you see how harmful that would be, Seth? To his family, to all of us?"

"In so many ways, Jordan, it's the only way. I'd be able to get in to the safe zone, utilize their facilities and come up with a reliable antidote, save humanity … and Lannie would be safe himself. As for the harm I'd do, you have to understand, I've been working on an antidote since this all began. I've been under enormous stress; and look at me. I'm mutating, physically anyway, as we speak. You really can't expect the absolute best out of me, considering. Not to mention, I've gone, I don't remember how long, without sleep. I'm sorry for my actions, of course I am … but, there are considerations. I believe you should think about the bigger picture. If there's going to be any possibility for a cure, I should be allowed the opportunity to work in facilities that offer the best chance for success.

And, Lannie should be given the chance to be in a safe place."

"You're surely not suggesting that we allow you to just go, are you? To take Lannie and embark on that surely treacherous journey," I asked incredulously.

"I believe you should consider it," Seth stated.

"We'll all go," Richard said.

All heads turned in unison toward Richard. I asked, "All of us?"

"Yes. We'll return to the compound and find out what the status is there, but then, we'll all go to the safe zone."

Seth was shaking his head again. "You see, that's why I didn't want to say anything. You're talking about that whole compound of yours, aren't you? Do you realize the logistics of carting a whole caravan of people across the mountains and over the prairie? Not to mention, we're going to have to travel north – give the radiation zone a wide berth. It could take months. Finding food and gas for a large group would be impossible."

"First, we'll find out what's going on at the compound. Then we'll decide who's coming and how difficult it'll be. I understand the concerns, but obstacles are meant to be overcome. Frankie, give me a hand and let's gather whatever we can that's useful and load it onto the compound truck. Professor, keep an eye on Seth, will you?"

Richard put a protective arm around Lannie as they disappeared into the house. Valerie followed Frankie, leaving Seth and I alone in the garage. Seth rubbed his eyes with his palms and slowly got up.

"I'm sorry about my actions, Jordan, really I am. I truly believed I was doing the right thing. Maybe the mutation has affected my cognitive abilities more than I thought."

Seth shuffled over to the back of the Range Rover and lifted the back gate to look in on the Moonkies.

"Seth, why in the world would you bother to haul those Moonkies, cages and all? You would have made a clean getaway without doing that. Were you really going to release them?"

Seth looked at me with a meaningful grimace on his face. The Moonkies had crawled to the close end of their cages and had their noses pressed against the metal, sniffing and whimpering. Seth leaned in and pressed his face on the cage of the smaller Moonkie. He seemed utterly fatigued and deflated.

The smaller Moonkie began a low, guttural moan that sounded like a wounded animal in distress. The moan formulated into word-like sounds. "Ahhh ... daaa ... da-dee."

"Oh my God, Seth. No, not that. Your child?"

"My wife and daughter, Jordan. They caught the virus early, before I could do anything about it. Now, it's too late."

The sight before me tore through my heart with pain, empathy and irony. The man most responsible for the virus had been affected the most intimately. We all were being affected, some more than others, though. I'd hated Seth a few moments ago, for what he had tried to do. Now, I understood the reasons for his actions and the hatred melted away. It was replaced with sorrow, not just for Seth and his family and not just for the rest of us here ... but for all of humanity. That included those of us who were no longer completely human, but still knew of sorrow and suffering and dreams destined for doom.

*   *

CHAPTER 25: CRUEL REVELATION

(Frankie V.)

The revelation that the Moonkies in the cages were Seth's own wife and daughter spread through our little group quickly. The fact that he would have taken Lannie and left the rest of us behind somehow was forgiven. With so much at stake and so much to do, none of us had the time or energy to dwell on wrongs done, or meant to be done. Seth probably thought in some sense that he was doing the right thing. It's only human to strive for virtue; it's also human to fall short. We each have the potential for success or failure at any moment. I knew I had fallen short myself on more occasions than I cared to relive. Not one of us could claim an unblemished life. It seemed to me that the more difficult it was to do the right thing, the more obvious the choice. And it was obvious to us all that we had to return to the compound as soon as possible. Regardless of what we faced, at the moment this was our destiny.

Val and I rode with Seth driving the Range Rover, his wife and daughter uncomfortably secured in the cages lying prone in the back. Richard, Lannie and Professor

Bruno followed in the compound truck. We'd loaded up anything we thought might be useful and headed out. The drive was quiet and I fiddled with the arrowhead that Richard had extracted from my abdomen. I found a loose strand of leather and fashioned a necklace out of the trinket and presented it to Valerie as a gift. She accepted it like a child receiving a valued treasure on Christmas morning. She still couldn't talk, but Seth's antidote had apparently halted the mutation, for now. She didn't seem to be getting any worse. Those huge, feral eyes took in every movement of each of us in the vehicle. I sensed that Valerie, despite her advanced Mutie condition, was alert and aware beyond normal capacity. I didn't have to communicate with her in words to understand that behind those animalistic eyes was a caring empathetic soul.

About an hour into the drive Seth pulled over and cut the engine.

"Frankie, would you mind giving me a hand?"

He got out and walked to the back of the vehicle and popped the door. The others had pulled in behind us and Seth went back and talked to Richard for a moment, then returned. Richard backed the compound truck up several feet and waited. I helped Seth drag the Moonkie cages out onto the road's shoulder.

He shut the truck hatch and spoke solemnly, "Go on back inside the truck, Frankie. Lock the doors, and whatever happens, don't come out."

"Seth, are you sure about this?"

"I know I can't bring them with us, Frankie. I also can't keep them caged up any longer."

"You tried the last antidote? The one with Lannie's blood?"

"They're too far gone. I've known that for a while. I've been holding them for all the wrong reasons."

"You think they'll be all right? I mean, out there, on their own?"

"Man or animal, Munie or Moonkie … if it were you,

would you choose to live safely in a cage, or take your chances in the wild?"

Some questions don't need the answer spoken aloud, I got back in the truck and locked the doors. Val looked at me questioningly. I turned sideways in the seat and watched. Seth leaned down and popped the cage locks and took a couple of steps back. It didn't take long, the Moonkies flung the doors open with a loud crash and suspiciously sniffed the air of freedom. The larger one, which we now knew to be Seth's wife, stepped from the metal cubicle and approached Seth, halting within an inch of him. The smaller one, the daughter, crouched behind her cage and observed intently.

I could read fear in the expression on Seth's face, and, although mutated himself, compared to his wife, his features were distinctly more human. She could quite easily rip him apart instantly. A coat of thick, matted fur had grown over her entire body. Her shoulders were muscular and hunched. Her arms, hands and fingers had grown long and dangerous looking, razor-sharp talons had replaced the nails. Her face was leathery and the brow thick and bony, shadowing bright, yellowish eyes. The nose had flattened, and now the nostrils flared large and wide. Her mouth was wide and her lips pulled tight over large fangs. I couldn't discern whether Seth's wife even recognized him anymore, nor whether what happened next was a result of that knowing, or not ....

In a motion so quick that I couldn't follow it with my eyes, the she-beast reached out with one claw-like hand and throttled Seth, pinning him to the ground. Val screeched loudly. The smaller Moonkie jumped up and down, howling plaintively. Seth's wife let out a blood-curdling wail that surely could be heard for miles; it was Pandemonium.

I don't remember how it happened, but I suddenly found myself outside of the truck, standing near the mayhem. Seth's monster-wife, or, I suppose under circumstances she could be referred to as 'ex-wife', was atop the helpless mutant-scientist, choking the life out of him quite convincingly. Although intent on her task at hand, she suddenly became aware of my presence and looked at me with those huge eyes and I quickly wondered what exactly it was that I was doing there. In the time it took for her to emit one intimidating, snarling hiss, I instinctively pulled the pistol out of my waistband, pulled back the hammer and took aim. Even in the moment, I was acutely aware that I only had one bullet left and I reasoned that this had better be one hell of a perfect shot, because a wounded Moonkie wasn't going to do anybody any good, least of all – me. BLAM!

The look on Seth's wife's face was electric and her reaction, instantaneous. She leapt sideways, grabbed the smaller Moonkie by the scruff of the neck and sprang into the wooded area near the roadside in a split second. All of a sudden I was standing alone, behind the Range Rover with a dumb look on my face, I'm sure. Richard and the Professor scrambled out of their truck and ran toward me, Seth was gasping and coughing, trying to gulp air back into his lungs and Val ran to my side, wide-eyed, still very naked and still drop-dead gorgeous.

Seth's first words were, "Did you hurt her?"

"Naw, I shot in the air just close enough for her to feel the bullet go by her head. I was hoping the gunshot would be loud enough to scare her off."

The Professor spoke, "But, you only had one bullet!" What were you going to do if that hadn't worked?"

"I didn't want to overcomplicate things with a complex plan."

"She could have ripped your head off," Seth said.

"Yours too. Why do you think she chose choking instead?" I asked.

Seth thought, "Takes longer that way … maybe she was enjoying it."

A pool of blood was gathering beneath Seth's head. I

leaned in and took a look.

"Don't move, Seth. I think you've been cut."

Richard examined the laceration on the back of Seth's neck. "Frankie, apply pressure here. Jordan, grab the first-aid kit!" There were three clean gashes where Seth's wife had dug talons into skin.

It appeared Seth's eyes were dilating, even in the bright sunlight. He was going out.

"We should get him to the compound, and quickly," Richard said. "She missed the artery, but he's going to need stitches."

"I don't know, Richard," the Professor began, "the Bounties were threatening a siege when we left there … we don't know what we're going to be heading into."

Richard thought for a moment, "All right. Jordan, pull the truck up and we'll load him into the back. We'll find a secluded spot and I'll stitch him up as well as I can. We'll be safer getting off of this road, though. We'll approach the compound after nightfall." He rummaged through the first-aid kit and made sure there were sutures, antiseptic and nylon thread.

After carefully loading Seth into the truck bed, Val and I shoved the empty cages back into the Range Rover and we all headed for the next exit. We followed the turnoff to the west, and found a deserted motel about a half-mile down. We parked in the back, out of sight, and I retrieved a couple of room keys from the office. We set up a sort of operating room in a corner suite, where Richard, the Professor, and Lannie tended to Seth. Valerie and I did some exploring to see if we could find anything of use. Other than plenty of linens and towels, there wasn't much. We did find some soap, toothpaste and shampoo, a room with a tub full of relatively clean water, and oddly enough, an old Polaroid camera that was still in working order. I used an ice bucket and cleaned up in the sink while Val submerged herself in the tub. I helped her soap up from head to toe and it was all I could do to keep her from pulling me into the bath with her. She was strong as a wildcat, but giggled like a schoolgirl. I was taken aback by the lilting sound of her laughter. I tried to remember if I'd ever heard her laugh like that.

I wiped the grime from the bathroom mirror and earnestly set out to try and erase some of the filth of the past days from my face. It had been a rough stretch, but it was still difficult to comprehend the harsh toll it had exacted on my appearance. My skin wouldn't seem to come all the way clean, no matter how hard I scrubbed. I'd given up on shaving, it didn't seem to be doing any good; the beard kept growing back thicker. I'd never noticed all the lines in my face before. I guess all the years living in a cell must've aged me.

Conversely, Valerie had never looked better. As she stepped from the bath and dried her hair, she practically glowed with natural beauty. Somehow, the lines on her face had softened and even her eyes appeared more normal. She laid down on the motel bed to rest and I couldn't help but be drawn to her. I found myself making excuses in order to be near her. I checked the incision areas of Seth's serum testing and took the opportunity to examine the rest of her body. She appeared, in a word, flawless. Her skin radiated a healthy sheen, her hair was thick and lustrous. Even after the harsh conditions we'd been subjected to, Valerie seemed unblemished. Her strength and intensity were also intact, she grasped my arm forcefully and pulled me nearer.

After a short nap, I rose to splash water on my face and checked on my own condition in the bathroom mirror. Deep grooves ran down the length of my cheeks, and burrows trenched my forehead. My eyebrows had become overgrown, and I guess one too many prison yard fights had left my nose enlarged. But, it was the eyes that revealed the most. Hard, cold, shining orbs of the deepest black stared back at me. The reflection was cruel in its inability to deceive, console, or sugarcoat the revelation it held.

How long I had been mutating, I didn't know for certain. How long I had before I'd be a full on Mutie … or, Moonkie, was also a frightening mystery.

* *

CHAPTER 26: THE LAST LOCKDOWN

(The Professor)

Richard carefully sutured Seth's neck wounds and we all leaned in to admire the handiwork.

"Well," Richard spoke, "That's the best I can do. He'll live."

Frankie asked, "Do you think he could use some fresh blood? Lannie's transfusion really helped me out, maybe it could do the same for Seth."

"I'm about bled out, I think," remarked Lannie.

"There's still a couple of bags of your blood stored on chemical ice in the Range Rover."

"Seth's mixed most of that with his antidote concoctions," I observed, "and we don't know which is which. We might do more harm than good."

We all looked upon the prone Seth; he wasn't looking too good at the moment. Frankie spoke, "A person's got to want to get better in order to heal, I'm not sure Seth believes there's much to live for."

"There's a pretty good chance that Seth is the only

human … or, well, only one alive who can develop a working antidote. If saving the human race isn't reason or purpose, I don't know what is," Richard stated firmly.

"He just lost his entire family, and his wife tried to kill him," Frankie said.

"That wasn't his wife anymore."

"Will you all just shut the hell up and quit talking about me as if I wasn't here, or as if I'm already dead?" Seth complained, as he came back to consciousness. "Lannie, get me my travel bag from the glove compartment, will you?" Lannie darted out to the Range Rover. "You all make everything seem so tragic and crucial … as if the world won't go on without us. Believe me, somehow, it will. And even if it doesn't, what's it all mean? Regardless of what happens, our existence or extinction, after we're gone we're not going to know the difference anyway."

"That's quite fatalistic, Seth," I observed.

"I worked my whole life trying to accomplish something of use and benefit to mankind, including building a family with hope for the future; where did it lead to? I've destroyed the world and my wife tried to kill me. The virus I developed to prevent war and destruction, caused nothing but destruction."

"A lot of wives try to kill their husbands, Seth," I said, "Maybe she just wasn't the 'one'."

"So what are you implying? That perhaps there may still be someone out there for me? Maybe I'll meet someone?" Seth remarked scornfully.

Lannie returned with a small leather toiletry kit bag and handed it to Seth. He leaned up on the bed and winced noticeably as he dug through the pouch and retrieved a plastic film canister. He popped the lid off and shook a small pile of powdery granules out onto the nightstand. With a portion of a cut-off drinking straw he snorted the substance into both nostrils, then lay back.

Noticing us all watching, Seth spoke. "Ginseng,

ephedrine and freeze-dried energy drink. My own recipe.
If I'm going to save the entire human race, I'm going to
need to be awake to do it."

Frankie and Valerie loaded up the Range Rover, then
helped Richard, Lannie and I get Seth secured in the back
of the compound pickup. We stood in a circle in the
motel parking lot and came up with a tentative plan. We
decided to drive to the Gutierrez place first, and leave the
Range Rover there. Richard's compound was less than
two miles from there, and there was a dried creek bed that
wound through the woods, leading to the front entrance.
We'd approach under the cover of darkness and ascertain
whether the Bounties were still on site. Hopefully, they
hadn't raided the property yet, or, even better, had left.
Either way, we would be able to surveil the scene before
we approached. It was about two hours until sunset, just
enough time for us to reach the compound at, or near,
twilight.

As we drove, twice we saw roving bands of Moonkies
swarmed around vehicles on the highway. Richard
observed that they were scavenging, and since they had
resorted to doing so out in the open, it meant they were
probably desperate, which meant their food was getting
scarce. In the rearview mirror we could see them watching
us with keen interest, as if waiting to see if our vehicles
would break down. I refused to consider how that
misfortune might play out. Overwhelmed and eaten alive
isn't anything anyone wants to think about.

On schedule, we arrived at the Gutierrez ranch as
darkness began to fall. We unloaded all the gear from the
pickup and secured it inside. They had generators that still
had gasoline, so we decided to put the bags of Lannie's
blood (infused with Seth's antidote prototypes) into the
refrigerator for safekeeping. With the gear unloaded, we
could all fit into the pickup and drive as near to the
compound, along the creek bed, as we could get. When
we got to within half a mile, Frankie and Valerie took the

lead with Richard and I following. We left Lannie with Seth in the pickup, as the four of us carefully trod through the woods. Lannie had Hawk's shotgun, with instructions to either shoot to kill, or signal if he needed us.

A few hundred feet into the forest, we stopped and knelt down.

Frankie spoke in a whisper, "Professor, you and Richard wait here, Val and I will get as close as we can and take a look."

It was the appropriate plan, as it allowed Richard and me to remain in eyesight of the truck, about halfway between the compound road and Lannie and Seth. As Frankie and Valerie disappeared into the darkness, we settled in.

"How you holding up, Jordan?"

"I'm all right, considering …. What are your thoughts?"

"It depends on what Frankie finds out. If the Bounties are still there, and I'm hoping that if they didn't give up and leave, that they still are – because that means we're not too late and the compound is still secure – then we slip in and attempt to get the others out."

"Get them out? How in the world would we manage that?" I asked.

"When we built the compound, of course I considered security issues. Under the main house there is a tunnel that leads south, just around the quarry. There is another entrance on the north side, through those thistle bushes." Richard pointed to an overgrown thicket that engulfed the fence and perimeter area, on the far end of the compound boundary.

"We might be able to negotiate an entry. This is your property, Richard."

"Under the circumstances, that's likely to be irrelevant. The fact that a militia of armed men have threatened the sanctity of the compound indicates that their intention isn't to negotiate. Otherwise, a diplomatic contingent would have been the initial approach. No, it wouldn't be prudent to take a chance, not with the lives of the others at risk."

"What then, Richard? Even if we manage to get the others out, where do we go and what do we use for transport? Are you seriously considering making the trek to the safe zone? That's half a continent away ...."

"I don't know, Jordan. At least there's some hope of safe harbor out there. I don't think the situation here is secure any longer. Mierdamonte is obviously expanding his reach, and I don't want to have to face a situation where force and violence is the only solution. It's better we go now ...."

"We might not be welcome there."

"Then we'll find our own place, make our own way ... someplace where we can live free, like men should. A fresh start for us all."

The sound of rustling leaves alerted us that Frankie and Val were returning. They appeared out of the dark and crouched between Richard and me, breathing heavily ....

"What did it look like, Frankie?" Richard asked in a whisper.

"In a word, locked down. The place is surrounded. I'm surprised there aren't any Bounties along this stretch of the perimeter. There are at least fifty trucks parked on the entrance road and they're armed and definitely dangerous."

"We may have gotten here just in time, then," Richard said. "It appears as though they're preparing to mount a raid. The only thing that's likely prevented it thus far is that they don't know the size of the force they'll be encountering. I think our best plan is ... since they don't know we're here, is to ...."

BLAM!!

From the direction of the pickup, Lannie had fired a shotgun round.

"They're gonna know we're here now," Frankie said what we were all thinking.

He was right. From the direction of the compound road a wave of foliage bent and crushed under the weight of a surge of humanity as Bounties responded in the direction of the gunshot.

"Let's go!" Richard ordered, although he need not have. We were all already running back to the pickup. My imagination spun wildly with possibilities. Why had Lannie fired? Was he alright? Whatever we were to find I couldn't reason that it would be good. Adrenaline surged through my bloodstream, terror arose in my mind – spreading its constricting tentacles from the base of my skull to the uppermost reaches of my brain. Overwhelming numbers of armed Bounties were closing in from the rear, and what lay ahead was an unknown. In the darkness, the image of the pickup through the trees was hazy and indistinct, just shadows.

As we neared, the frightening sight before us slowed our steps to a hesitant stagger. A swarming mob of vicious-looking Moonkies had surrounded the truck and Lannie was atop the cab brandishing the shotgun defensively. Seth was huddled in a corner of the truck bed, terror-stricken.

With our hearts in our throats and frozen in our tracks, Richard, Frankie, Valerie and I looked at one another wide-eyed – knowing that to wade into that blood-thirsty crowd and attempt a rescue via hand-to-hand combat – would be suicidal. Yet, no other option seemed to be forthcoming. We were four helpless souls against overwhelming odds, and time was also the enemy. Any moment now, Bounties would emerge from the forest and we would be trapped. Whatever was to be done had to be immediate.

Above the din of growling and heavy breathing of the Moonkies, Lannie's clear voice rang out from his perch above the angry mob ….

"Wait, all of you! Remember who you once were, who you still are. You are not animals!"

Large eyes, sharp teeth, and ravenous appetites hesitated momentarily, as if to listen to Lannie's plaintive cry. Whatever humanity that remained in the beasts, perhaps, might be receptive to reason.

"Within each of you remains the essence from which you came ... if you'll only listen and feel the quiet spirit in your heart. There's still a peacefulness dwelling there ... a connectedness to each other and all of mankind. Mutation doesn't alter that."

The mob seemed to hesitate, as if transfixed and hypnotized by Lannie's words, mesmerized by his logic. Maybe, we could somehow capitalize on the momentary respite to usher Lannie and Seth out of harm's way. Lannie glanced over at Richard and I and we made eye contact. We made subtle gestures, imploring him to try and extract himself from the center of the Moonkie crowd. It would have to be quick, the Bounties were closing in fast.

Inspired by his own brief success, Lannie took a deep breath, ready to continue his oration ... before he could speak, Seth crawled up onto the cab and stood up shakily. He raised his hand above his head and proclaimed ...

"I have the cure!" He held a small glass vial of prototype antidote in his hand. "I can cure the virus," he yelled.

The Moonkies crowded in closer and gasped in unison. Lannie took advantage of the distraction and crawled down from the truck, joining us at the periphery of the mass of Moonkies.

Seth continued, "I can cure you all! This is a temporary antidote, and the only dose left that's fully prepared, but with blood from the boy and my own formula, a cure is available." We knew this to be a stretch of the truth but under the circumstances, half-truths and false hopes might save lives and buy us time.

The five of us edged around the crowd. Richard

whispered, "We need to get to that cave entrance without being followed ... if we can just slip away ...."

"What about Seth?" I asked.

"Not all of us are going to make it, Jordan."

The click-clack of rifle rounds being chambered announced the arrival of the Bounties. In the darkness, our group was mostly indistinguishable from the mass of Moonkies. If gunfire erupted, we would likely be mowed down in the slaughter.

Then a Bounty yelled, "Nobody move!" An army of Bounties appeared behind him, all armed, guns drawn and at the ready. We all froze, even the Moonkies.

"What's that you got there, Partner?" the head Bounty spoke to Seth.

Seth stared, mouth agape. He finally spoke, "The antidote, I've got the antidote."

"Where'd you get that?"

"I developed it, I'm a scientist."

The Bounty seemed incredulous. "You don't look like no scientist."

Some of the Bounties chuckled. "What the hell are you doin' out here? You alone?"

Seth hesitated, in my mind I implored ... "No Seth, don't do it ..."

Too late. Seth's eyes involuntarily darted in our direction, "I'm with them."

In perfect Judas form, Seth pointed to our little group of fugitives, standing near a stand of trees, inches from a getaway.

Seth wasn't done. "The boy's blood. It's a nearly pure antidote. I can produce all the serum we need with his blood."

We all thought in unison, "Damn it, Seth."

Frankie was standing right next to me and Bounty eyes were now transfixed on our location. He whispered quietly, but forcefully ...

"Professor, when I say go, take Lannie and Richard

and haul ass!"

"What?"

"When I say so, take them and go …."

"When?"

The lead Bounty spoke, "What boy?"

Frankie nudged me and whispered, "Now!" He then stepped in front of Lannie, Richard and I and shouted: "Me! I've got the miracle blood!" Frankie was loud and animated, distracting the Bounties' attention. "But he's lying," he pointed to Seth. "He's got a whole shipment of antidote. It's in the truck. Enough for everyone!"

It was like yelling 'FIRE!' in a crowded theater. The reaction was frenzied and automatic. Moonkies, Muties, Bounties all converged on the pickup and began tearing at one another and anything they could get their hands on, trying to get at the antidote. It was like bees on a hive.

Richard grabbed Lannie and Frankie pushed me in their direction, we began running through the woods in a mad dash. I looked back and saw Frankie and Valerie fighting Moonkies and Bounties, keeping them from following us … giving us time to at least get a good lead. Frankie was wrestling with two or three attackers and Valerie was ripping flesh and biting and clawing in desperation. I hesitated, thinking of going back, thinking of my friends and all we had been through together, thinking I'd never known anyone who would lay down their life for me before. Richard grabbed my arm and pulled me along. The sounds of jungle warfare receded as we disappeared into the forest. I knew I would never see Frankie nor Valerie again.

Through an especially thick growth of brambles, Richard led us to the entrance of the hidden tunnel that passed directly underneath the main house of the compound. Joe Rivera had already organized a mass exodus that began when sentries noticed the commotion outside the gates. We arrived in time to see the last of them scurrying down a ladder with bags and knapsacks of personal items and supplies.

The tunnel ended on the south side of the compound, near the quarry. The woods there were dense and there were no roads, just worn paths. We had a fairly large group of refugees; including several from the Gonzales and Gutierrez clans, Carol, Donna Quinones and her two children, Joe Rivera and his sons, Hawk and Andy's now widowed wives, Lannie, Richard and myself. Although we had no vehicles, we moved steadily east toward the mountains, then north along the foothills. We scavenged as we went and stayed off the roads. We reasoned accurately that whoever had survived the melee back at the compound would likely not come in search of us. They would have their own set of troubles and priorities to be concerned with.

Weeks, then months passed as we traveled north. We crossed the mountains through a pass in Idaho just before winter. As the snows began, several of the group splintered off and headed toward Canada. In Montana we found discarded vehicles we were able to get running. We crammed what remained of our caravan into two old cars and continued east. We had to avoid most of the mountain states toward the south, due to heavy radiation. We'd seen nothing but death and devastation since crossing the mountains. We hoped Seth's revelation of a safe zone would prove to be true. As time went on, however, it became less and less of a goal. We were beginning to live day-to-day, from one food or clean water source to the next. Gasoline was hard to come by and at some point we realized we would soon be back on foot.

To pass the time and keep everyone's mind off the desolate conditions, I would recite what I remembered from the Philosophy class I sometimes taught back at Stanford. Advising that: "There is only room in our minds for a single thought at a time. Might as well tend the garden of our minds and plant positive ones."

I reasoned that out of the suffering any of us

encounters, the development of values and character emerges. However, this growth is only possible if we each recognize what the message of the situation means for us.

There was plenty of time to consider the lessons as we drove. The land desolate, our thoughts, scattered. The shadow of a massive murder of crows washed across the sky as we left Montana. I thought about Frankie. I realized that when he had freed me from that locked prison cell and we headed out into a strange world that we hadn't expected nor could have possibly been prepared for, it was a rebirth. It was an opportunity to leave the past behind and let go of long lingering hatreds and prejudices ... right wrongs, improve distorted ways of thinking, and live life as it was meant to be lived. I discovered that it's not necessarily what one achieves or accumulates that is truly important, but rather, the quality of day-to-day experiences. A person's relationships in the world and his attitude toward those he meets reflect the quality of his life.

I witnessed Frankie exorcise his demons by caring more about a desperate mutant girl than he did for himself. The friendship we shared and the loyalty he possessed, compelled him to sacrifice his own life in order for the rest of us to postpone our journey to the afterlife. That, and the other things I'd seen, would affect me all the rest of my days: the sorrow seen in Seth's eyes when confronted with the family he'd lost and what he'd exposed the world to; the depth of intellectual and spiritual understanding of a simple boy, in my godson, Lannie; the leadership of Richard; the brutality of Hawk; a treasure of experiences compacted into the mere blink of an eye in the grander scheme.

It's said that the experiences which a man finds most adverse are those which force him to seek out their cause and unwittingly begin the search for life's meaning. The disappointments in his emotional life, the physical suffering, and the misfortunes he encounters ought to teach us all to discriminate more carefully, to examine more deeply, and to feel more sympathy with the sorrowing.

The end of the world, for me, was a new beginning. What lay before me was uncertain – a path surely filled with strife and hardship – embarked upon with hope and the memories of friends found and enemies encountered. None of us can avoid the road we must travel, nor avoid the perils we shall face ... after all, we are human.

The loss of everything left behind had been the key to unlock my own mind, which finally freed me from my self-imposed imprisonment. The last lockdown of my body, mind, and spirit ... was only a distant memory now; fading like shadows of raven's wings on the horizon.

* * * * *

EPILOGUE

(Valerie)

<u>Journal entry date:</u> I don't know the date. When I began mutating I lost track of things like dates, names, places …. When I met Frankie and the Professor, I began communicating again and it sort of came back to me, for a while. I've decided to begin keeping this journal for one reason … my son. I'll be giving birth soon, I can feel the gestation period coming to its inevitable climax. It isn't the most optimum time to be bringing a child into this world. However, we must all accept the circumstances as they are presented to us.

My physical state seems to be improving. My mind has never been so alert. I believe the progressive transformation began the day of the battle at Richard's compound. Frankie and I fought hard and determinedly in order for the Professor, Lannie and Richard to escape. I suppose it is correct that one can't help another without helping oneself. Somehow, in the extreme disorder, Frankie and I managed to slip away. The Bounties and Moonkies were engaged in such a struggle for life that they soon forgot about us. The Bounties appeared, at first, to have the upper hand. They had superior weaponry that held the Moonkies at bay for a time, but when the ammunition ran out, things turned quickly. We could still hear the screaming and yelling and crying all the way from the Gutierrez place. We grabbed everything we could manage, including the blood supply, and escaped in the Range Rover.

I believe we decided to return to the ocean near our first meeting place, because it held fond memories. It's where I first fell in love with Frankie. It's relatively safe here. No Moonkies come near the water and the Bounties don't come this far west anymore.

We sustained many injuries in the fighting and decided that we would use up the blood supply that contained Seth's prototype antidotes. It wouldn't have kept for long anyway. Frankie drained one bag into me and the other into himself. It turned out to be true that the antidote has different effects on each individual.

I began to improve almost immediately. Within days my speech began to return, then the physical characteristics of mutation began to recede. Even more astounding, I believe my intellectual capacity has improved markedly since the transformation.

How that is even possible, I'm not sure. But I can understand and even 'sense' things more lucidly since I began improving. That's how I know my baby is a boy. Maybe it's just wishful thinking though. I believe a boy would be better suited for the world he will face.

Last week, while rummaging through the glove compartment, I came upon an eyeglass case buried in the back corner. Secreted in the bottom of the case was a single piece of neatly folded notebook paper with a series of complex equations and chemical compound formulas. I recognize the handwriting as Seth Edelstein's and I believe this to be the most recent antidote formula. What I'll do with it, I'm not certain. Attempt a trek to the safe zone with a newborn baby? For what purpose and to what end?

To save the human race? Is a thinking, reasoning being more worthy of dominion if he uses his gifts inhumanely? I've experienced life from both sides and am well aware of the potential for cruelty and violence from either. I've found that not all humans are humane and not all beasts are beastly. Perhaps there is good and bad and the potential for both in all creatures. And, maybe a new beginning is necessary.

I haven't seen any Bounties since the battle at the compound, and the few Moonkies that have come around don't bother us. I believe we're safe here. We've been able to catch fish in the ocean and forage for fruit in the orchards in the forest, and the abandoned farm fields still yield crops. There's a fresh water spring less than a mile inland.

In spite of all the struggle and turmoil, we've been happy here. The happiest I've ever been. If I could, I'd keep everything as it is … stop the sun in the sky and make time stand still. Every sunrise is a blessing and each sunset a reminder of the harsh realities life brings.… But, nothing stays the same. Frankie began changing soon after the last transfusion. At first, it was incremental, then accelerated. I thought we would be able to deal with it more easily, since I'm so intimate with the mutation experience. By mutual agreement we began caging Frankie up during the night. The Moonkie cages in the Range Rover have been useful. He had to be locked down at night because that's the time when he forgets who I am sometimes. I'm not certain when the day will come when I can no longer allow him out. That's the time I dread most, the night of that last lockdown.

THE END

THE L.A. DREAMZ SERIES

The original story of Icicle Bill led to a series of noir style detective novels featuring Fallon Dawn Hunter as the neophyte Hollywood investigator and Joanie Kwan, her incomparably alluring crime-fighting partner. Set in and around L.A., characters and locales are often inspired by actual people and places. All of the novels are loosely tied together and strive to be fast-paced entertainment and quality literary fiction.

Icicle Bill
Goodbye Natalie
Cherry Moon
Last Lockdown
Outcast
Terminal Alibi - 2017
Where the Woods Won't End – 2018

OTHER BOOKS BY THE AUTHOR

American Prisoner
Babb's Writer's Workshop
Savages (w/Ron Gregg)

D. Razor Babb is a former network affiliate news reporter and announcer, and winner of three national PEN awards.

His books and additional information about the L.A. Dreamz Series are available at SeriesWriters.com or from Amazon.com.